The Armada Boy

Also by Kate Ellis

The Merchant's House

The
Armada Boy

Kate Ellis

THOMAS DUNNE BOOKS
St. Martin's Minotaur
New York

THOMAS DUNNE BOOKS.
An imprint of St. Martin's Press.

www.minotaurbooks.com

ISBN 0-312-25198-X

First published in Great Britain by Judy Piatkus (Publishers) Ltd.

First U.S. Edition: July 2000

10 9 8 7 6 5 4 3 2 1

With thanks to Michael Thomas
and Elenore Lawson

Prologue

Norman Openheim lit a forbidden cigarette and inhaled deeply. It was good. He put the silver lighter carefully back in the pocket of his baseball jacket and blew out a stream of warm, savoured smoke into the chilly night air.

He stood there in the middle of the ruined chapel. It was good to know that some things hadn't changed in fifty years. He had smoked back then . . . everyone had. Cigarettes had been simpler currency than sterling. He had smoked on this very spot, his girl in his arms. But then he had had no worries about the health risks of nicotine and tar. He had lived for the moment, not knowing whether he would be killed by a German shell or bullet the next day or if he would soon be drowned in the icy sea off Normandy. Everyone had smoked back then.

The unaccustomed nicotine made Norman feel a little light-headed. Dorinda, his wife, had put her dainty, pedicured foot down ten years ago. No more cigarettes; they were bad for your health. This one was the first he had tasted in all that time . . . the first act of rebellion. It felt so good that he could almost imagine he was seventeen again, the age he had been when he had last stood on this spot.

A high-pitched whining in his ear reminded him that his hearing aid was playing up again, returning him bitterly to the realities of his ageing body . . . malfunctioning, flabby and balding. Seventeen was a long time ago.

He pushed back his baseball cap and sucked hungrily on the cigarette. Birdsong . . . there used to be nightingales. He remembered hearing their sweet song as he had made love to Marion in

1

the shelter of the crumbling chapel walls. He touched his hearing aid and winced as it emitted a vicious electronic crunch. He banged it a few times before it gave up the ghost altogether. Maybe it needed new batteries. But it didn't matter . . . not here, not now . . . not while he contemplated that youthful coupling with his pretty local girl: the pleasure, the excitement, heightened by the hovering imminence of death at the hands of the enemy.

As his hearing aid was broken, Norman did not hear his killer approaching slowly behind him . . . and he was unprepared for the blade that pierced his ribs and penetrated his beating, aching heart.

MONDAY – 10.30 AM

Dorinda Openheim tapped her tiny patent leather shoe impatiently. The colonel, a large, square man with grizzled hair, strode towards her frowning with concern.

'Sorry, Dorinda . . . we can't wait much longer. You're sure he said nothing?'

Dorinda shrugged. 'I took one of my pills last night. I was asleep when he came to bed and he was gone when I woke this morning.'

Colonel Willard G. Sharpe raised his bushy grey eyebrows. Soldiers he could figure, but women . . . If Norman was avoiding his pocket-sized harridan of a wife, Colonel Sharpe regarded that as a wise strategy.

'We'll have to begin without him. The vicar from St John's church is taking the service . . . we can't keep the good padre waiting: got to keep friendly relations between old allies, especially when you remember the sacrifices these folk round here made back in '44.'

Dorinda pursed her lips. The hardships of a few English villagers fifty years ago didn't concern her: her husband's unexplained absence did.

'Look, Dorinda, Norman's all grown up now . . . he can take care of himself. We should be at the memorial by a quarter to.'

Dorinda looked round at the group waiting by the hotel door; the subdued veterans and their smartly dressed, chattering wives. She would go without Norman. The colonel was right. Norman was grown up . . . he could do what the hell he liked.

She caught the eye of a tall, white-haired man who was

hovering at the edge of the waiting group. She thought, not for the first time, how distinguished Todd Weringer looked in his smart navy blue blazer and slacks . . . not like Norman who never had that darned baseball jacket off his back. She smiled sweetly; Todd Weringer smiled back and winked.

'Shall we go without him, then, Dorinda?' said Colonel Sharpe impatiently. 'He's probably out reliving a few old memories. He knows the lie of the land round here . . . he won't get himself lost. He'll probably make his own way to the service.'

'Sure. Let's go.' Dorinda turned and marched towards the door, her hand brushing Todd Weringer's as she passed.

MONDAY – 11.00 AM

The chantry chapel of St Dennis, founded by Sir Roger de Carere in 1263, had stood ruined and overgrown at the edge of the village of Bereton since its closure by Henry VIII in 1545. It slumbered amid its weeds like Sleeping Beauty's castle – being of use only to courting couples – while the village's spiritual needs were taken care of by the ancient parish church of St John a few hundred yards away.

Neil Watson of the County Archaeological Unit was planning to awaken the ruins from their sleep. He parked his rusty Mini in a wide part of the lane leading out of Bereton and walked back the few yards to the overgrown footpath that led to the chapel. Neil liked to be early; to have a chance to look round the site of an excavation before his colleagues and their equipment arrived. He liked to take in the atmosphere of the location; to imagine the events, the people, the emotions that had shaped the place before he started dissecting the evidence of its past.

He was relieved to see that the path to the chapel was passable, kept that way by curious walkers and young lovers from the village.

He passed through a crumbling archway into the body of the roofless nave, its floor covered by patchy grass, its walls shoulder height to the left but much taller to the right. The windows at the chapel's east end, though empty of their tracery and jewelled glass, were remarkably intact. A half-crumbling tower still stood proudly at the west end. The chapel must have been quite a place in its day.

3

Neil strolled towards the east end, kicking an empty plastic bottle. Here and there the ground was littered with cans, cigarette packets and the occasional used condom: how the youth of the village would miss this place while the site was fenced off for the excavations. They would have to use their ingenuity to find somewhere else or spend the next few months pursuing chastity and useful hobbies. Neil knew which option he would have chosen at their age.

At first he thought the dark shape in the south-east corner of the chancel was a pile of old clothes, dumped there by an environmentally unaware villager. But as he drew nearer he saw the pile had a human shape.

'Shit,' he mouthed, looking down at the elderly man who lay before him on the ground. A baseball cap was stuck firmly on the head and the jacket that proclaimed the name of some American sports team looked bizarrely inappropriate for someone of the dead man's advanced years. He stood over the body and stared at it, willing it to go away or wake up and transform itself into a drunken vagrant ... anything that wouldn't disrupt his well-planned dig.

Neil delved into the pocket of his shabby waxed jacket and took out a mobile phone. He pressed the buttons, still looking warily at the dead man and the startled expression that was frozen in the staring eyes. 'I need to speak to Detective Sergeant Peterson,' he said, the tension audible in his voice. 'It's urgent.'

Chapter One

Although the most recent 'invasion' of our beautiful village came in 1944, when the area was evacuated by the US forces for the D-day landing rehearsals, we must bear in mind that history has a habit of repeating itself.

It was back in the reign of the first Queen Elizabeth, in 1588, that Bereton was invaded by sailors from the Spanish ship *San Miguel*, which was wrecked after being separated from the great Armada approaching up the English Channel.

From *A History of Bereton and Its People*
by June Mallindale

Detective Sergeant Wesley Peterson put the phone down. He could see the inspector through the glass office partition. He was slumped in his chair surrounded by files; jacket off and badly ironed shirtsleeves rolled up to reveal a large tattoo on his forearm in the shape of an anchor. Detective Inspector Heffernan had the harassed look of a man trying desperately to keep one step ahead of Tradmouth's criminal fraternity. He had just received a report of another burglary. What he didn't need, Wesley thought, was a possible suspicious death.

Wesley took a deep breath, gave a token knock and went in. 'Sorry, sir, I've just had a call from . . .'

'Don't tell me any bad news, Wes, I don't want to know. These burglaries from weekend cottages . . . it's got to be the same lot: same mode of entry, same sort of things nicked. Is Steve back yet?'

Wesley, London-born and -bred, sometimes had difficulty catching the subtleties of Heffernan's Liverpool accent. He leaned forward, hoping to get a word in.

Heffernan continued. 'Have you finished that report on the stolen yacht?'

'Yes, it's all done . . . and there's been a call from Morbay to say that it's turned up in the marina there. Sir . . .'

Something in the sergeant's voice made Heffernan raise his tousled head. 'What is it? I'll tell you, Wes, the only news I want to hear right now is that all the local villains have repented of their evil ways and are forming an orderly queue downstairs to turn themselves in.'

'Sorry, sir, I've just had a call. Suspicious death at Bereton. There's a patrol car on the way and I've called Dr Bowman and SOCO.'

Gerry Heffernan buried his face in his large, callused hands. He was a church-going man, not given to swearing, but on this occasion he allowed himself the luxury of a colourful sentence in keeping with his merchant navy background.

Wesley tried hard not to grin. 'There's another thing, sir.'

'Come on, Wes, spit it out . . . things can't get worse.'

'Do you remember Neil Watson from the County Archaeological Unit? He found the body. It's bang in the middle of a dig he's about to start and he's in a bit of a state about it. You know what it's like nowadays if something's delayed and goes over budget. . . .'

Heffernan stood up and glowered at Wesley. He remembered Neil Watson all right . . . a friend of Wesley's from his student days who had been studying archaeology with him at Exeter until their paths diverged and Wesley joined the police force to undertake investigations of a less academic nature. 'Your mate's not the only one who could do without this. Here we are with our pet villains trying for a productivity bonus and your mates start digging up bodies.'

'He didn't dig it up, sir. It was just lying there, apparently.'

The inspector ignored Wesley's last remark and reached for his jacket. 'We'd better get down there.' He sighed. 'It could be natural causes . . . we can but hope, eh?'

Wesley nodded. He'd worked for Gerry Heffernan for six months now, long enough to know that behind the bluster lurked an amiable, even gentle, man.

6

The swing-doors crashed shut behind them as they passed the station's front desk.

'Morning, gentlemen, lovely morning.' Bob Naseby, the desk sergeant, held up a huge hand in greeting.

'Morning, Bob. Can't stop . . .' Heffernan hurried through the foyer, Wesley in his wake.

'Sergeant . . . I know you're in a hurry but can I have a word . . . about you know what?'

Wesley turned. 'We're in a bit of a rush now, Bob. Later on, eh?'

Bob Naseby nodded knowingly and reached beneath his counter for his steaming cup of tea as the station doors swung shut.

'Couldn't see the queue of waiting villains. Maybe they'll be in later . . . they'll be having a nice lie-in seeing as it's Monday. What was that all about?'

'What, sir?'

'You and Bob Naseby . . . the "you know what"?'

'Oh, that? I made the mistake of telling Bob that my great-uncle played cricket for the West Indies. Now he's convinced that I'm going to be the division's answer to Brian Lara.'

'That was a big mistake, Wes.'

'I hadn't the heart to tell him that it's not in the genes . . . he was only my uncle by marriage. I didn't even make the cricket team at school.'

Heffernan laughed wickedly. 'No escape now. Once Bob gets your name down for that cricket team there's no trial by jury, no plea-bargaining and no appeal.'

Bob Naseby was notorious for his obsession with the game of cricket. Wives and girlfriends seethed as he took their menfolk off to spend their off-duty hours on the cricket field in the summer months. 'I'll just have to come clean . . . tell the truth,' said Wesley with finality.

'My mam used to say honesty is the best policy. We should have that plastered up on every cell wall, don't you think?'

They drove on for a while in amicable silence. They were on the coastal road to Bereton which meandered above sandy, tree-lined coves. The spring sunshine filtered through the branches throwing golden sparks out on to the clear blue sea.

'This view, Wes,' said Heffernan. 'I bet it's as good as anything you'd find in the Med.'

7

'You don't find anything like this in the Met, sir.' Wesley, transferred from the Metropolitan Police six months back, smiled, enjoying his private joke.

The road to Bereton wound off to the right, leaving the coastal road with its sweep of pebbled beach behind. The wall-like Devon hedges obscured the view into the fields until, half a mile inland, they came to a village of pastel-painted cottages, clustered round a handsome medieval church and a squat thatched pub. A hand-painted sign showed the way to a rival hostelry and another sign, ancient but more official, pointed the way to the chantry.

'It's the chantry we want,' said Wesley.

'What's a chantry when it's at home?'

'It's a chapel ... usually built by someone wealthy, so that prayers and Masses could be said for their souls when they died. Priests were employed to staff them. They were quite the rage till old Henry VIII put a stop to them.'

'You seem to know a lot about it.'

'I'm a mine of useless information, sir.'

'That's what comes of an expensive education.'

'This particular chantry was quite substantial,' Wesley continued. 'It was referred to as a college. There were four priests employed ... one as the normal parish priest and the other three just to serve the chantry. That's what Neil's excavating. Only the chapel shell remains but there must have been more buildings. He's trying to find out what's there.'

'Fascinating,' said Heffernan unconvincingly. 'So you've seen Neil recently, then?'

'We went for a drink last week.'

'What did your Pam think to that?'

'She came with us.'

'In her condition?'

'Making the most of our freedom, sir ... before we need to worry about baby-sitters.'

'You'll not have much freedom if this turns out to be murder, Wes. Mystic Gerry predicts lots of overtime ... unpaid and all if the super has his way.'

Wesley parked behind Neil's Mini. He would have recognised the rusting vehicle anywhere – it was unchanged since their student days. A pair of police patrol cars were parked in front of Neil's, their occupants absent. They walked back towards the chantry and saw that the area had been cordoned off with blue-and-white tape. Heffernan made a mental note to praise this piece of efficiency . . . credit where credit's due, he always thought.

The first person they encountered was Neil, leaning disconsolately against the chapel's rough stone wall by the half-demolished west door.

Heffernan spoke first. 'I've got one thing to say to you.' Neil looked mildly alarmed. 'Next time you want to go finding bodies will you wait till all our villains have announced a strike . . . or a work-to-rule at least. As if we've not got enough to do. I just hope it's natural causes.'

'So do I,' said Neil with feeling. 'Every day we delay this dig we're going over budget. And we're co-ordinating it with a project out in the bay. It's bloody inconvenient.'

'Bloody inconvenient for the poor bugger in there and all . . .' Heffernan stormed past into the shell of the chapel where something in the far corner was attracting quite a crowd. SOCO had arrived.

Wesley hung back to talk to Neil. 'What time did you find him?'

'Just when I rang you. I've got my mobile.' He produced a tiny mobile phone from his pocket and displayed it proudly.

'Very nice,' said Wesley admiringly. He had never associated Neil with high technology. 'Were you on your own?'

'Yeah. Just came to see the lie of the land. I've sent the others away for now. I'm meeting them in the Bereton Arms at opening time if you want to join us . . .'

Wesley shook his head. 'I won't have the time . . . unless it's natural causes.'

'Let's hope it is, then. Pam okay? How long till the baby's due?'

'Ten weeks and she's fine . . . blooming. Bit tired at school.' Wesley's wife had been supply teaching since their move to Devon. She had found a long-term contract in a school that she liked and was reluctant to give it up until nature dictated that she had to.

'Won't be long now till you're having all those sleepless nights.'

'I get them already working for Gerry Heffernan. I'd better get in there . . . see what's going on. I'd find your mates, if I were you.

There's no point hanging round here. We may need a statement later but I know where to find you. You didn't touch the body or anything like that, did you?'

'Come on, Wes. . . .'

'Sorry. Stupid question,' Wesley said apologetically. Neil was a trained archaeologist who knew how to deal with evidence as well as any policeman.

Wesley found the inspector talking to a tall, genial man who greeted him with a casual affability that made him expect to be offered a drink and canapés at any moment.

'Good to see you again, Sergeant. How's that wife of yours? I hear a happy event is imminent.'

'Fine, thanks, Dr Bowman. And yourself?' He knew that Colin Bowman couldn't be hurried: the social niceties had to be observed.

'I was just telling the inspector here, I cut my hand rather badly gardening . . . not as bad as this poor chap, though.'

He stood aside and Wesley saw the body, the object of all the attention, for the first time.

'How did he die?'

'Stabbed, poor chap. Straight through the back and into the heart . . . single wound. If it had been an inch either side it would have hit a rib.'

'So it was someone who knew what they were doing?'

'Either that or they were lucky. Must have come up on him from behind. He's got a hearing aid: I've checked and it doesn't seem to be working. That means he might not have heard his killer. Look at his face . . . he looks a bit startled, doesn't he?'

'Well, you would if you'd just had a knife stuck in your ribs,' said Heffernan, not too helpfully. 'What was he doing in a place like this anyway?' He pointed to a grey object next to the body. 'Is that what I think it is?'

'Yes . . . a rat,' said Colin Bowman with distaste. 'Not the most salubrious of companions even in death.'

'Have you examined it?'

The doctor looked disdainful. 'Why should I do that? I'm a forensic pathologist, not a vet.'

'It's just that . . .' Heffernan touched the rat gingerly with his shoe. 'Have you noticed it's been wounded?'

Colin Bowman bent down with fresh interest. 'Might have been killed by a dog or something.'

'Too neat.' Heffernan pointed, not wanting to touch the thing that lay with its tail stiff, just touching the dead man's arm. Wesley bent over to see. 'I reckon,' said Heffernan with a confidence he didn't feel, 'that looks like a knife wound.'

Colin Bowman was wearing rubber gloves. He touched the creature. After a few seconds he stood up and nodded. 'I think you could be right, Gerry. Why stab a rat, eh? Strange . . . bizarre. I'll take it back to the lab . . . have a better look.'

'And the post-mortem?'

'I'll have our friend here on the slab either later today or first thing tomorrow. As to the time of death I can't be too accurate at the moment but I'd say between 9 and 11 last night. Can't speak for our furry friend.' He looked again at the man's corpse. 'Any idea who he was? The clothes are a little, shall we say, flamboyant for a gentleman of that age.'

'Doesn't fit in with any of our missing persons . . . have to look further afield.' Heffernan shrugged.

'Well, I'll leave you to it, then, Gerry . . . Sergeant. Happy hunting.'

'Why is he always so flaming cheerful?' asked Heffernan rhetorically as the doctor disappeared through the chapel archway.

Wesley bent down to look more closely at the body. A man in his late sixties; baseball cap, baseball jacket over a shocking-pink shirt. His clothes and shoes didn't look cheap, neither did they look particularly expensive: but there was something about them that rang bells in Wesley's head. He looked up at his boss. 'Do you know, sir, I reckon he could be an American.'

Heffernan sighed, contemplating diplomatic repercussions and severe blows to the 'special relationship'. 'That's all we bloody need,' he said.

Dorinda Openheim did her best to look dignified as the white-gloved bugler sounded the last post. She shivered as a gust of fresh March wind penetrated the thick pink cloth of her best suit.

Most of the wives wore black. Maybe she should have worn black – it might have been more appropriate. But it was too late now.

The vicar with the plummy English accent was talking again. Vicar? He looked little more than a kid. A couple of the veterans were laying a wreath at the war memorial. How much longer would they have to stand outside in the cold?

And where was Norman? She fidgeted as she remembered the previous night, then she glanced across at Todd Weringer, his handsome face a study of appropriate solemnity as he remembered his fallen comrades.

'Let us pray,' the vicar intoned.

Dorinda shut her eyes tight and prayed that nobody would discover her secret.

Even police officers need to eat. They opted for the Bereton Arms, a little thatched inn near the church which, although shabby, served an adequate ploughman's lunch and, Heffernan confirmed, not a bad pint. Wesley, driving, made do with orange juice.

They were taking the last bite of home-made granary bread when Neil arrived. Wesley knew the couple he was with: Matt and Jane had worked with Neil on the excavation of a Tudor merchant's house when Wesley had first arrived in Tradmouth. They greeted him like an old friend. Heffernan, feeling left out, finished off his pint and left, telling Wesley not to linger too long over his orange juice.

Jane spoke first. 'You know I was off to Jamaica?' she gushed in well-bred tones. 'Well, I've decided to stay round here for a while. Same thing . . . underwater archaeology. I'll get a bit of experience here before I go further afield.'

'Underwater?' Wesley hadn't envisaged anything quite so exotic. Jane, who managed to look up-market in her torn jeans and mud-caked sweatshirt, was about to enlighten him when Matt took over. Wesley wondered if this incongruous pair still had a thing going . . . and whether Matt was the reason for Jane's decision about Jamaica.

'An Armada wreck . . . in Bereton Bay . . . only recently discovered. There's quite a story behind it,' said Matt. He looked at Wesley accusingly. 'Is it you who's holding up our dig at the chantry?'

'Not me personally. A dead elderly gentleman . . . possibly American by the look of his gear.'

'If it's one of that lot at the Clearview Hotel, it'll ruin their reunion, poor things,' said Jane earnestly.

'Whose reunion?' At last a clue to the corpse's identity.

'A party of American veterans. They were here in the war and they've come on a reunion trip . . . some are with their wives. We were talking with some of them yesterday . . . telling them about the Armada wreck.'

Matt nodded. 'They're having some kind of service at the memorial by the beach this morning. Some of their comrades were killed practising for the D-day landings on Bereton Sands. It was interesting talking to them . . . hearing first hand about what went on.'

'Did any of them ask about the chantry?'

'Yes. They saw us with our diving gear and asked us what we were doing. We told them all about the wreck and the dig at the chantry.'

'So one of them might have decided to go up there and have a look.'

'It's possible. But if they were here in the war they'd have known about it anyway.'

Neil, who had been listening quietly as he savoured his beer, asked the next question. 'You didn't notice any of these Americans wearing a baseball cap, did you?'

Jane emitted a tinkling laugh. 'Neil . . . they all had baseball caps. I joked with them about it. I said that I noticed they were still in uniform. I don't think they saw the funny side, do you, Matt?'

'And a baseball jacket with a name on . . .'

'The Buffalo Bisons?' said Wesley helpfully.

'No, I don't remember that. Do you, Matt?'

Matt shook his head obediently.

Wesley raised his glass to the double act. 'Cheers. Thank you for helping the police with their enquiries. There's just one more thing. Why are some of you working on the old chantry and some of you on an Armada wreck?'

'There's a connection,' said Neil. 'Apparently some sailors, we don't know how many, got off the *San Miguel* alive and staged a sort of invasion of the village. There's a local legend that they were killed by the villagers and buried at the chantry which wasn't being used by then. The villagers refused to have them in the churchyard with all their nearest and dearest . . . very charitable.'

'You can see their point,' said Jane. 'If you were being terrorised by a gang of hairy Spanish sailors . . .'

'So you're looking for their graves?' Wesley was becoming so interested that he was almost forgetting the time.

'Yeah . . . and any artefacts that might be in them. And we'll be taking the opportunity to have a look at the chantry buildings too . . . killing two birds with one stone while the funding's available. Any idea when your lot'll be finished so that we can get going on the dig?'

This brought Wesley back to reality. 'Probably a couple of days . . . I'll see what I can do.' He stood up to go.

'Love to Pam,' said Neil softly. Wesley nodded and strolled out of the pub into the spring sunshine.

Wesley told Heffernan the news. The inspector grinned broadly. 'Those mates of yours aren't as useless as they look. Come on . . . Rachel and Steve'll be along soon to do a house-to-house. Let's go down and have a look at these Bereton Sands. Got your bucket and spade?'

The name Bereton Sands was cruelly misleading to the unsuspecting holidaymaker. There wasn't a grain of sand in sight. The flat, wide sweep of beach round the shallow bay was entirely made up of pebbles on what seemed like a gravel base. Okay for skimming stones, if you liked that sort of thing.

The sea glistened, calm and benign, on this fine March day. A road ran above the beach. On one side of it was a carpark, practically empty this time of year. In front of the carpark was a carefully tended area topped by a tall granite pillar. The war memorial. It bore the words 'To the memory of those members of the US forces killed during the preparations for the D-day landings in April and May 1944 . . . we shall not forget.' Another small white marble stone stood to one side. 'To the people of Bereton and the surrounding countryside who gave up their homes so that the D-day operations could be rehearsed in this green and pleasant land. Their sacrifice was not in vain. With grateful thanks from the armed forces of the United States of America.'

The small group of elderly people who had been clustering round the memorial began to disperse, shaking hands with the young clergyman in the crisp white surplice who had presided over the proceedings. The group drifted back towards a white hotel that stood beside the road at the far end of the beach.

Wesley Peterson and Gerry Heffernan stood by the car,

contemplating their next move. The clergyman hurried past them, his surplice draped over his arm. He was in his early thirties; too young for the war to be even a distant childhood memory.

'Excuse me, sir. Police. Can we have a word?'

The clergyman immediately looked guilty; a natural reaction, Heffernan had noticed, of many members of the public whose lives were beyond reproach.

The fair-haired, bespectacled young vicar of Bereton made the conventional polite noises of regret but could tell them nothing apart from the name of the veterans' former commanding officer who had made the arrangements for the memorial service at which he had just officiated. They released the vicar to go about his business and strolled after the slow-moving gaggle of Americans. 'No hurry,' said Heffernan casually. 'Let 'em get settled back, have a piss, rest the arthritic joints. Wonder why they haven't reported one of their group missing? You considered that, Wes?'

'Maybe they don't know he's missing yet.'

'Let's find out, shall we.' They began to approach the hotel's double-glazed porch.

'Got the price of a cup of tea, mister?'

Wesley and his boss turned to see a young man standing behind them. He was in his late teens; thin with blotchy, pallid skin. A dirty woolly hat covered his hair. He wore a tattered army overcoat; filthy but warm-looking. He stared at them with defiant grey eyes. 'Just a cup of tea . . . I'm homeless . . . haven't got nowhere to live.' He spoke with a cockney twang that Wesley found familiar. East End . . . south of the Thames.

'You're a long way from home,' said Wesley; he spoke quietly, trying not to inject any aggression into the situation.

The lad's eyes widened as he heard Wesley's well-spoken voice. 'I thought you were with them Yanks.'

'Only beg from Yanks, do you?'

'They got money. You haven't got a quid, have you?' The youth added hopefully.

The two policemen exchanged glances and each one delved into his pocket. But their surge of generosity was interrupted by a smartly dressed middle-aged woman who sprang through the glass swing-doors of the hotel like an angry lioness.

'Get away. I've told you before, this is private property. I'll call the police if I see you here again . . . go away.'

The beggar raised two fingers to the woman and held his hand out. Wesley found a pound coin; the beggar took it with a grin.

'I mean it,' the woman shrieked. 'If you don't clear off I'm calling the police.'

'We are the police, madam,' said Heffernan. The woman looked him up and down with disbelief. His unkempt hair, crumpled shirt and dirty old anorak, coupled with his strong Liverpool accent, clearly didn't inspire confidence. He extracted his warrant card from an inside pocket and the beggar, realising his luck was about to run out, ran off towards the beach.

The Clearview Hotel was described in the brochures as 'family-run, comfortable, convenient for the beach, with delightful views over the bay; all rooms *en suite* with tea-making facilities'. The angry woman introduced herself as Mrs Dorothy Slater, the owner of this desirable paradise. She led them into a deserted lounge where the red patterned carpet clashed alarmingly with the green flock wallpaper.

'How can I help you, gentlemen?'

'Your American guests . . . are they all staying here?'

'Yes. They've come in a party.'

'When did they arrive?'

'The day before yesterday . . . Saturday. They're here till Wednesday, then they're off to London to see the sights.'

'Would you know if any of them are missing?'

Mrs Slater looked surprised. 'Nobody's mentioned anything to me. Is that why you're here?'

'It could be, Mrs Slater. Nothing's certain yet,' said Wesley reassuringly. 'Would it be possible to speak to your American guests? Just routine . . .'

'I don't see why not. Most of them are in the bar but some have gone to their rooms.' She looked the policemen up and down. The young black one seemed respectable enough . . . very well spoken. But the other one . . . she was afraid he might lower the tone of her establishment. She hoped they wouldn't stay long.

It wasn't long before they had a name . . . Norman Openheim. Nobody had seen him since last night.

Wesley took Dorinda Openheim to one side. 'Mrs Openheim,' he said gently. 'I'm sorry to have to ask you this but we'd be grateful if you'd come down to Tradmouth Hospital. A body's been found and we're very much afraid it may be your husband. I'm very sorry but it is necessary . . . we wouldn't ask you if it wasn't.'

Wesley always felt awkward with grieving relatives, but Dorinda Openheim, small, compact and immaculately coiffeured, sat there impassively. There was no anxiety, no tears, just an uninterested nod.

'I'll do it. Just tell me when.'

'As soon as possible, if that's all right. I'll ask a woman officer to go with you if you prefer.'

She looked at Wesley. She liked him. He was thoughtful . . . very English manners. She liked a thoughtful man; Norman could never have been described as thoughtful.

The next question had to be asked. Wesley braced himself. 'Could you tell me where you were last night . . . between nine and eleven?'

There was no show of indignation. 'I was here . . . in my room . . . reading.'

'What time did your husband go out?'

'I've no idea. He was downstairs.'

'Did he say where he was going?'

'No.'

'And you didn't think to report him missing when he didn't come back?'

'I took one of my pills . . . nothing wakes me when I take one of those little beauties. I thought he'd come back last night when I was asleep and gone out again this morning before I woke up. I was a bit worried when he didn't turn up at the service. It was the highlight of the trip for the old soldiers . . . apparently.' She looked bored. Wesley caught a note of irony in her voice.

'Is there anyone who can sit with you, Mrs Openheim? I don't like to think of you being on your own at a time like this.'

'I can manage. Don't you worry about me, honey. I'll be just fine.' Her chin jutted out determinedly.

Wesley had no cause to doubt her last statement. He muttered his condolences again then left her alone in the small room off the main bar while he reported back to the inspector. It occurred to him that she hadn't asked the obvious question . . . how did her husband die? But grief did strange things to people. They didn't necessarily act in the way you'd expect.

* * *

17

Wesley had gone, leaving Dorinda alone. She studied her shiny, manicured nails carefully. She felt numb. She should have felt something for her husband of thirty-five years. She should have felt something . . . but she didn't.

The door opened and Todd Weringer poked his distinguished grey head into the room. 'You on your own, Dorry?'

'Sure . . . come in. They think it's Norman. They want me to go and see him at some hospital.'

'You want me to go with you?'

'That sergeant guy said something about a woman officer . . . I don't know, Todd. I can't think straight.'

Todd Weringer put a large, comforting arm about her shoulders. 'Just keep cool, honey. Everything's going to be fine.'

She stood up. He took her in his arms.

'It's okay, honey, it's okay.' Todd Weringer bent and kissed Dorinda Openheim. She responded, putting her arms about his waist and writhing gently under the pressure of his lips. If they kept cool it would be okay . . . everything was going to be okay.

Chapter Two

Who knows what would have become of England if the Spanish Armada of 1588 had succeeded in its aims; or, for that matter, if the D-day landings, so courageously rehearsed on our beach and in our countryside here at Bereton in 1944, had failed. The whole history of our island rests on the outcome of events such as these.

Back in 1588, Sir Francis Drake, a local man who knew the Devon coast well, sailed out of Plymouth to engage Spain's mighty Armada. Drake captured the crippled flagship the *Nuestra Señora del Rosario*, sending his prize back to the port of Tradmouth. As the rest of the ships continued eastwards along the Channel, the *San Miguel* became separated from the main Armada: her foremast had been damaged during the engagement with Drake's ships, making navigation difficult. She ended up on the rocks of Bereton Bay. Many of her crew drowned in the chill waters of the English Channel but a number escaped, swimming to the shore and crawling exhausted, up Bereton Sands.

From *A History of Bereton and Its People* by June Mallindale

Detective Constable Rachel Tracey held on to the gatepost and stood on one leg. The new shoes were killing her . . . especially the left one. It wasn't the wisest decision to wear them for a house-to-house. Steve Carstairs, wearing his expensive leather jacket, inspired by his favourite TV cop shows, looked at Rachel unsympathetically. He longed for car chases, drugs raids and armed stake-outs. The realities of day-to-day policing in rural Devon had never quite matched up to his fantasies.

'Come on, Steve . . . just one more.' Rachel, methodical and down-to-earth, didn't mind routine in the least.

'They're all blind and deaf round here . . . nobody's seen anything.'

'Somebody might have.'

'They'll all have been tucked up in front of the telly with their cocoa. Not much night life round here.'

'There's a pub.'

'Wow . . . the village that never sleeps.'

Rachel ignored her colleague's last remark and marched up the neat garden path to the flaking front door of Apple Cottage. 'These trees'll yield a good crop come autumn.' Rachel, the farmer's daughter, surveyed the apple trees that lined the path like a guard of honour approvingly.

Steve, thinking himself above such bucolic talk, said nothing and rang the white plastic doorbell.

A woman of indeterminate age opened the door wide and studied her visitors. She was overweight with straight, greasy, shoulder-length hair. Her clothes were cheap, market-bought, and did nothing to flatter her appearance.

'Mother's asleep,' she announced unexpectedly, her accent pure Devon.

Rachel held up her warrant card. 'We're police officers. We'd like to ask you a few questions . . . nothing to worry about. Did you see anything unusual between nine o'clock and eleven o'clock last night?'

The woman suddenly looked wary; her eyes narrowed. 'How do you mean . . . unusual?'

'A man was found dead up at the old chantry this morning. His clothes were quite distinctive: a baseball cap and a jacket with the name "Buffalo Bisons" on the back. You didn't see him yesterday evening by any chance? He was an elderly man.'

Rachel was confident that she wasn't mistaken. The woman looked worried as she shook her head.

A door opened inside the cottage and a teenage boy came into view. Rachel guessed that he was about eighteen; he had cropped hair and a vacant expression on his pasty face. Overweight like his mother, his jeans displayed an unfashionable expanse of backside and his overstretched T-shirt strained across his chest. 'Who is it, Mum?'

20

'Nobody, Wayne. Just go back in.'

'May we speak to your son, Mrs . . . er . . .?'

'Restorick. No point in speaking to him . . . he didn't see nothing. He was here with me all night.' Defensively.

'Mum . . .' Wayne's voice wafted from inside the cottage, an importuning whine. 'Gran's wet herself again.'

'I'll have to go. I didn't see nothing.' The door was closed firmly.

'Believe her?' asked Steve.

'No.' Rachel smiled at her colleague, hoping he wouldn't take it as a come-on. Steve Carstairs considered himself irresistible to women, but he was too obvious for Rachel's taste. And Steve's attitude to Wesley – the racist wisecracks he'd made when the sergeant first arrived – had hardly endeared him to her.

'I think we should ask around in the pub this evening. There might be some regulars we haven't spoken to in the house-to-house . . . ones that live further afield.'

Rachel had never rated Steve's deductive abilities very highly, sometimes asking herself how he had ever made it into CID. But she realised this suggestion was a good one . . . as long as she wasn't going to be the one forced to spend an evening in his company. She had other things planned . . . a quiet evening in Dave's flat with a takeaway and a bottle of wine would be the preferred option. But police work had the habit of ruining the most carefully laid plans.

'I'll suggest to the boss that we go for a drink tonight, then . . . chat up a few locals. How about it, Rach?' He winked at her knowingly. Rachel turned and marched off down the path, trying hard not to limp.

It was going to be a long day. There were statements to take from all the veterans and their wives: someone might be able to throw some light on Norman Openheim's movements.

Wesley had just taken Dorinda Openheim back to the hotel. She had identified her husband's neatly laid out body without a hint of emotion. Wesley had never seen a newly bereaved widow so coolly self-possessed.

Heffernan told him to take a break and get something to eat. He drove the six miles back to Tradmouth and home. He would check on Pam . . . see if she was all right. With the baby due in ten weeks

– their much-longed-for, much-tried-for first-born – he felt the impulse to ensure that no disaster had occurred in his absence.

It was a quarter to five. Pam's VW was parked in the drive. As Wesley opened the front door he heard voices, one distressed, the other comforting. He felt a stab of irritation. He had come home for a respite from the pressure of the day. What he didn't need was aggravation.

Wesley opened the living-room door. Pam was sitting on the settee, her arm placed comfortingly round the shoulders of a sobbing young woman. A baby, about a year old, crawled dangerously near the dried flower arrangement in the fireplace; they would have to do something about rearranging the room when their own was born.

Sue, their next-door neighbour, looked up when she heard Wesley come in and tugged a tissue out of her sleeve to dry her eyes.

'What's up?' asked Wesley.

'Those bastards at the building society,' Pam pronounced angrily.

Wesley knew that the small engineering works owned by his neighbour, Jim, had gone into liquidation some months back. Jim had looked for work but to no avail. Now Sue and Jim had come to the end of the road . . . they were to lose their heavily mort-gaged home. There were no words that Wesley could find. 'Sorry' seemed inadequate.

Sue gathered her baby up as it began to investigate the dried flowers and it screamed loudly. She took her leave bravely. She would have to feed the baby . . . life went on.

When Sue had gone Wesley took Pam in his arms and kissed the top of her head.

'I feel so useless,' she said bitterly.

'They can't just evict them, surely. Where will they go?'

'Bed and breakfast in Morbay . . . go on the waiting list for a council house.'

'Shit. First the works and now this . . .'

'It's time they had some good luck. Poor Sue . . . Short of winning the lottery and paying off their mortgage arrears there's nothing we can do to help them.'

Wesley felt as bad as Pam did about their neighbours' plight, but he had a job to do if they were to keep a roof over their heads.

'Sorry, love, I've only got an hour to grab myself something to eat. I've got to go back to Bereton. There's been an American tourist found murdered . . . war veteran over here for a reunion.'

'Bereton? Was he over here in the war for the D-day landing practices?'

'Yeah . . . How do you . . . ?'

She got up and walked over to a pile of school books on the dining table. 'Here.' She threw one over to Wesley and he opened it. The handwriting was good . . . a credit to the teacher. 'It's a project my year sixes are doing. Local history. The whole of the area round Bereton was evacuated late in 1943 and 1944 . . . people were thrown out of their homes, pets put to sleep, livestock moved to farms in different parts of the county. It was quite an operation. Just like poor Sue really . . . you're told to get out of your home and you have no choice.'

'But it was only temporary, wasn't it?'

'Some didn't come back and those that did found their houses and farms had been damaged by shelling and overrun with rats. The Bishop of Exeter left a notice on the church gate at Bereton asking the Americans not to damage the church . . . it received a direct hit which blew out one of the walls. They all got compensation but imagine leaving your house and coming back to find it's been shelled to bits.'

'You know a lot about it.'

'I asked the kids to talk to their grandparents. It's surprising how many remembered the evacuation and were keen to talk about it. There were some stories . . . locals creeping back to poach rabbits, girls being taken to the deserted villages for a bit of courting with the Yanks. There was even a murder.'

'I'll have to read that stuff when I've got time. You've not got anything there on the Spanish Armada, have you?'

Pam looked at him with the envy teachers feel for those unfamiliar with the National Curriculum. 'Tudors are next term . . . hopefully I won't be there.' She blew him a kiss and went into the kitchen to make an omelette.

He followed her. 'I met Neil this morning. He discovered the body.'

'Not like Neil to do anything so dramatic.'

'It was on the site of a dig he's doing . . . something to do with the Spanish Armada.'

Pam knew the danger signals. She had met Wesley at university where she had been studying English and he archaeology. She knew by now that once he became interested in a dig, especially with Neil Watson fuelling his enthusiasm, he wouldn't rest until every question was answered, every mystery solved. She had often wondered why he had chosen the police as a career: his parents were both doctors, so it must have been his grandfather who put the idea in his head – he had been a senior detective back in Trinidad. She supposed archaeology and detection had something in common: both involved painstaking sifting of evidence, back-breaking routine until a clear picture emerged. For all her complaints about unpredictable hours, Pam was resigned to being a policeman's wife.

'So you'll be lending Neil a hand, will you . . . when Gerry Heffernan lets you off the lead?'

'I might drop in from time to time if we're going to be in Bereton. Might be interesting.' He saw a look of reproach in his wife's eyes. 'But I won't spend a lot of time there . . . promise. After all, you need looking after.' He patted her swollen belly. 'And this one too.'

'I'll give you a special dispensation to have a drink with Neil tomorrow night. I've got a parents' evening. But you'll have to be back by ten.'

'Can't you make that half past?'

'Shut up and eat your omelette.'

Wesley obeyed. He knew it was best to quit while he was ahead.

Litton Boratski – former Sergeant Litton Boratski – lowered himself carefully into the venerable chintz-covered armchair, explaining apologetically that his arthritis was playing up. Wesley and Heffernan made sympathetic noises and waited while the tall, thin man arranged his limbs.

He looked at them with ice-blue eyes. 'Sorry about old Norman. I heard he was murdered . . . is that right?'

'I'm afraid it looks that way, sir.'

'Who shot him? Do you know?'

Wesley looked at his boss. 'He wasn't shot. He was stabbed.'

Boratski raised his bushy grey eyebrows. 'Now who the heck would want to do a thing like that?' His slow American drawl made it sound as if he were asking who had taken the last piece of apple pie on the plate.

'That's what we're trying to find out, sir. Can you tell me about this reunion . . . who arranged it, that sort of thing?'

'Haven't the others told you?'

'Yes, but we'd like to hear things from your point of view.' Wesley tried a bit of flattery. 'After all, you were the sergeant, I believe.' Boratski nodded proudly. 'You must have got to know your men pretty well.'

'You ever been in the army, boy?'

Wesley shook his head: the army, encouraging physical rather than intellectual activities, was hardly Wesley's cup of tea. His basic police training had been a little too hearty for his taste and he had made every effort to join the CID at the first available opportunity.

'Everyone should join the army, son. You're a cop, right? If all these kids today had to do their bit for their country, I reckon you'd be out of work.'

Heffernan couldn't resist the challenge. 'And we'd end up with villains who could run faster and shoot straight . . . we wouldn't stand a chance.'

This wasn't what Boratski wanted to hear. He gave the disreputable-looking inspector a contemptuous look and concentrated his attention on his smarter-looking subordinate. Wesley could see the mischief in his boss's eyes . . . Heffernan relished the role of devil's advocate.

'Mr Boratski.' Wesley made a determined effort to steer the interview back on course. 'What can you tell me about Norman Openheim?'

'Norman? Norman was John Doe.'

'Sorry?'

'John Doe . . . an ordinary, regular guy. He owned a garage up in Buffalo; that's where we all live, up near the Canadian border. We're the Buffalo Normandy Veterans Association.'

'Did you see him often?'

'We all meet up for a reunion once a year . . . it's quite an event. The wives come too.'

'And his marriage? Was it happy as far as you could tell?'

'You can't judge what goes on in other folk's bedrooms, Sergeant.' Boratski looked thoughtful. He was hiding something.

'You think there was something wrong? Did Mrs Openheim confide in anyone? Your wife, for instance? Maybe the women confided in each other.'

'I'm a widower, Sergeant, and I wouldn't say Dorinda was one for girly talk.'

'But there was someone she was confiding in?' said Heffernan, leaning forward.

'I don't want to talk out of turn.'

'This is a murder inquiry, Mr Boratski.' The jovial expression had disappeared from Heffernan's face. It was time for the truth. 'Hitler didn't get Norman Openheim all those years ago but now someone else has . . . and I'm going to find out who it was. Now what do you know about Dorinda Openheim? Whatever you tell us will go no further if it's not relevant.'

'I can't say anything for certain. It's just . . . Dorinda's a very discreet woman, you understand.'

'Are you trying to tell me she's having a bit on the side?' Heffernan was never one to call a spade a digging implement.

'A bit on the . . . ?' Boratski looked genuinely puzzled.

'An affair,' Wesley translated helpfully.

Litton Boratski sighed. 'If you must know, she's been mighty friendly with Todd Weringer since his wife passed away.'

'Did Norman know about this?'

Boratski shrugged. 'Didn't say anything if he did.' He leaned forward confidentially. 'I guess he was glad someone was taking Dorinda off his hands for a while, if you know what I mean. She can be a touch . . .' He searched for the word. 'Overpowering. My late wife always used to call her the Mighty Atom.'

Wesley smiled. The Mighty Atom was a good description of the diminutive Mrs Openheim. 'So you don't think there was any antagonism between Mr Weringer and Mr Openheim . . . no jealousy?

'Not that I saw . . . they seemed to get on pretty good.'

Intrigued as he was by this senior citizens' ménage à trois, Gerry Heffernan decided to turn back the clock. 'During the war, did you have much to do with the locals round here?'

'Sure . . . we used to give them things they couldn't get over here. Chocolate, nylons, gum . . . that sort of thing.'

'And have any of you met up with old acquaintances since you've arrived in Devon?'

Litton Boratski looked mildly embarrassed. 'Most of the men round here were away fighting in '44.'

Heffernan nodded knowingly. 'So you had to make do with the women . . . what a shame.'

Boratski looked at him, uncertain how to take his last remark.

'Did Norman Openheim do any fraternising with the natives?'

'Gee . . . Norm was just a kid, youngest in the company. He'd lied about his age to get in the army. What was he? Sixteen . . . seventeen? If he kissed a few pretty English girls who would have blamed him?'

'Was the old chapel used for courting in those days?'

'Yeah . . . yeah, I believe it was.' Litton Boratski sounded uneasy. Maybe the chapel held a few erotic memories for him, Wesley thought.

'Did Norman use it?'

'Gee . . . I can't say. But I'll tell you one thing, Inspector . . . back in '44 we didn't know if we'd still be alive the next week or the next day. That sort of thing can make a man want to get the most from every moment. Sure, lots of us had women over here. We lived for the moment. Folk today don't understand how it was. We were out in that bay on open landing craft. It was winter and the sea spray got into our uniforms and made our skin freeze and we were scared shitless. On one exercise a craft near to us was sunk by German E-boats . . . everyone on it was killed, and that was just a practice run for what we were going to have to go through in Normandy. Then if we made it, we crawled up that beach, our knees bleeding on those darned pebbles, soaking wet, freezing . . . shaking with fear, with the tanks rumbling a couple of feet away and the bullets whining over our heads. They used live ammo. . . .'

'Bloody Nora . . . Why?' Heffernan asked.

'To see how the men would fare under real battle conditions. I guess it wasn't just the Nazis who killed our men on that operation. Ours not to reason why . . . I guess some four-star general thought it was a great idea at the time. So you see why we lived for the moment.'

'*Carpe diem*,' Wesley muttered thoughtfully.

'You what, Sergeant?' Heffernan said, puzzled.

'*Carpe diem*, sir. It means seize the day.'

'You got it, son. We seized the day.' Boratski nodded.

'And were there any local lasses in particular that Norman Openheim seized?'

'That I can't remember, Inspector. It was a long time ago and I was their sergeant, not their mom.'

Somehow Heffernan suspected that Litton Boratski's memory was selective. There was something he was hiding. He stood up and held out his hand. 'You've been very helpful, Mr Boratski. Thank you for your time.'

Boratski stayed put. 'Don't you want to know who killed him?'

Heffernan sat down again. 'Who?' At this stage any suggestions would be gratefully received.

'Those bums who've been hanging out round here. It'll be one of them. I know one of them threatened Norman. He was a bit shaken. We might have liberated France but we sure ain't as young as we were.'

'Bums? Who do you mean?'

'They ask for money . . . young, dirty. One of them's got a pesky dog.'

'We've only seen one of them . . . are there more?' Wesley asked, interested.

'Sure are . . . about three. Don't know which rock they crawled out from under but . . .'

'And they actually threatened Norman Openheim? What happened?'

'They asked for money and he said no. One of them turned nasty.'

'Which one?'

'Vicious-looking varmint with a shaved head.'

'Did anyone see what happened?'

'No . . . no one. Norman told us about it afterwards.'

'So most people knew?'

'I guess so. I suggest you get those varmints behind bars . . . and fast.'

'We'll certainly be having a word with them.'

'A word, Inspector? There's only one language that sort understand.'

'As I said, sir, we'll be having a word. Thank you very much for your help. We might want to talk to you again.'

'We're off to London on Wednesday, don't forget.'

'We'll have to see how our enquiries progress. Good evening, sir.' Heffernan stood, his face impassive.

Boratski pushed himself painfully to his feet. 'But we've got tickets for *Cats* on Wednesday night . . .' he muttered pathetically.

As Heffernan said to his sergeant when the old soldier had left the room, the moggies might have to wait.

Nine thirty . . . too late to interview any more of the veterans' party. Those that were still in the bar looked to be ready for bed. They had got through half of them. The rest could wait until tomorrow.

'Let's get out of here, Wes. Pam expecting you back?'

'She knows I'll be late.'

'Time for a drink, then?'

Wesley looked at his watch. His conscience was telling him that he should be getting back. 'Just a quick one.'

'Rach and Steve are making enquiries in the village pub . . . nice work if you can get it. Why didn't we think of that line of enquiry? Let's see how they're getting on.'

They drove to the Bereton Arms and parked in the small, half-empty carpark behind the pub. Wesley recognised Neil's Mini in the corner.

'Isn't that your mate's car? No spending the night talking about artefacts . . .'

Wesley grinned. 'Not the whole night, sir. I can't be too long.'

Rachel and Steve were at the bar talking to an elderly man who had the weather-beaten look of one who had spent a lifetime on the land. They introduced him to Heffernan as Walter Ambrose, a farmer who trudged the mile from his farm to Bereton each evening, rain or shine, down the narrow lanes to partake of several pints of best bitter and keep abreast of the local gossip.

'I hear there's been a murder . . . one of them Yanks what turfed us out in the war,' he said to Heffernan, his eyes glowing with interest and alcohol. This was probably the most exciting event to hit Bereton since 1944. 'I passed the old chantry on the way home.'

'Did you see anything unusual?'

'I was telling these youngsters here . . .' He indicated Rachel and Steve. 'I saw someone running out of the chantry path and off towards the church.'

The inspector looked round for Wesley. This could be important. But his sergeant had met up with Neil Watson and his mates and was deep in conversation; he could catch up on this later.

29

'Would you recognise who it was? Could you give a description?'

The farmer looked at Heffernan as if he were a prize Jersey short of a herd. 'It were about ten o'clock. I always leave about ten . . . I got milking in the morning. It were pitch dark . . . we ain't got no street lights in Bereton, you know. I just saw a figure . . . in the shadows. It were only a half-moon.'

'Could you tell if it was a man or a woman? Tall or short?'

Ambrose banged down his empty glass. 'Buy us another pint and I'll have a think about it.' Here, Heffernan thought, was an astute man.

Ambrose took two sips of his new pint before pronouncing authoritatively, 'It were a young fellow . . . I'm sure of that. Don't know if he was tall or small . . . that's your job to find out. I'll only do your detective work for you if you come and help me out with my milking.' He chuckled.

'Did you know any of the Yanks who came over here in the war?'

'Oh, aye . . . very generous they were. I were too young for the army . . . just a lad. Those Yanks used to hand out chocolate and that . . . us kids loved 'em. There's folk round here who had different ideas, mind.'

'How do you mean?'

'Whole year's harvest we lost here. Would you forget if you were turfed out of your home and had to have your herds destroyed?'

There was no answer to that. Heffernan decided he would do Pam Peterson a favour and drag her husband away from his cronies. On the way back to Tradmouth, he asked Wesley for an update on Neil's latest exploits.

'He's diving in the bay tomorrow. They've located the wreck of the *San Miguel*. There's a lot of stuff down in the bay from the war, landing craft and tanks sunk, but the wreck's well away from that lot, thank goodness. They've used sonar to locate it and there've been a few good finds already. Lovely cannon . . . virtually intact. It all gets rushed off to Exeter for conservation so there's not much to see here.'

For once Gerry Heffernan, an ex-merchant navy officer and lover of all things nautical, listened with interest. 'They're not getting you down there, are they, Wes?'

'I'll stick to dry land. Talking of which, Neil wants to know when he can start in the chapel.'

'I'll see what SOCO have to say . . . shouldn't be that long.'

'So what have we got?' asked Heffernan after a few minutes of amicable silence. They had reached the outskirts of Tradmouth. Wesley would have to drive into the cramped centre of the medieval port to drop his boss off at his small whitewashed house on the cobbled quayside.

'We know Norman Openheim had a run-in with one of the beggars and that Farmer Ambrose saw a young man running away from the chantry at the relevant time last night.'

'We'll have to invite them to the station for tea and biscuits . . . if we can catch them. Then there's Norman's missus indulging in a bit of hanky-panky with one of his old comrades.'

'Do you suspect her?'

'I don't know, Wes. It's early days . . . anything could happen.'

Dorinda Openheim stood naked in front of the long mirror in her bedroom (spacious and *en suite* with tea-making facilities and trouser press). Time and that plastic surgeon at the Aphrodite Clinic had been kind to her. Her breasts, silicon-filled, stood out proudly and any excess fat had been liposuctioned away six months ago when she had rid herself of her second chin. It had been worth every penny. Now that she was a widow, she would devote her considerable energies to ensnaring somebody who would appreciate her efforts.

She slipped her diaphanous nightdress over her head. She wondered if Todd would knock discreetly at her door. Probably not . . . he would consider it inappropriate. Todd had a wonderful sense of what was appropriate.

She walked round the bed to where the electric kettle stood on a spotless melamine tray on a small polished oak table. She fancied a coffee.

She let out a cry as she stubbed her naked toe on something hard. She bent down to see what that something was. Norman's case . . . she should have known. Even in death he was causing her inconvenience. Those cops would probably want to see it. They were welcome to sift through his dirty socks and underpants: if she had her way she'd chuck it straight into the sea.

On a sudden impulse she opened the shabby leather case. She

31

was right: nothing but underwear. Then she spotted a corner of paper. She moved a pair of purple boxer shorts aside and took out an envelope: pale blue airmail with an English postmark addressed to Norman in a neat, almost childlike hand.

She opened it. Inside was a letter which she read with growing disbelief. When she had finished she squeezed the thin paper in her fist. 'Who the hell is Marion?' she asked out loud as she threw the crumpled letter on to the bed.

Chapter Three

There are local records in existence that tell of what happened on that fateful day in August 1588. Reading them, it is easy to imagine the emotions of those surviving Spanish sailors, dedicated to their holy enterprise of returning England to the Roman Catholic faith, as they swam ashore from their ship, the *San Miguel*, run aground on the treacherous rocks of our bay. Many of their comrades had drowned and those who survived crawled, exhausted and bleeding, across the hard pebbles of the beach. Beacons were lit on the headland as a warning and the good folk of Bereton, armed with whatever weapons they could lay their hands on, made for the shore, hoping for pickings from the wreck.

We can only guess at the manner of reception those Spanish sailors received. And of course those other men who came from the sea – our American allies in 1944 – would have been received with the same mixed feelings, as the people of Bereton were ordered to leave the homes their ancestors had occupied for centuries.

From *A History of Bereton and Its People* by June Mallindale

Wesley Peterson watched as Colin Bowman, smiling pleasantly and chatting away, made the long incision down the front of the body and removed the vital organs in an alarmingly casual fashion. Wesley looked away, feeling slightly sick.

Gerry Heffernan, however, was oblivious to the gruesome procedure and chatted away, asking questions which the pathologist answered in a jolly, conversational way. It was a pity,

Heffernan had often thought, that Dr Bowman's patients were never in a position to appreciate his cheery bedside manner.

'Well ...' Colin Bowman stood back and watched absent-mindedly while his technician sewed the body of Norman Openheim back up. 'I can't tell you much that you don't know already, Gerry.'

When Colin had changed and they were sitting in his office sipping a cup of Earl Grey, the pathologist decided to enlighten them further.

'I'll put it all in my report, Gerry, but I can tell you that my initial diagnosis has proved to be correct. He was killed by a single stab wound to the heart with a long thin blade. Either an extremely lucky strike or someone who knew what they were doing.'

'And the weapon?'

'Long thin knife of some kind ... anything been found?'

'Not yet ... still looking.'

'He died pretty well instantly. He wouldn't have known much about it. As for the time of death, we're lucky to know exactly when he ate his last meal. From the state of the stomach contents I'd say ten o'clock or thereabouts.'

'Anything else?' asked Wesley.

'He was a healthy man for his age ... bit overweight but generally in good shape apart from the hearing problem we know about. As to the fatal wound ... I had a bit of a prod about and from the angle of entry I should say you're looking for someone a bit smaller than the victim.'

'Could a woman have done it?'

Bowman thought for a second. 'As it missed the ribs it wouldn't have needed that much force. A fit woman – or an angry one – could have done it certainly.'

Wesley looked at his boss. 'Maybe the young man Farmer Ambrose saw running away was really a woman.'

'Aye. From that distance and with that many pints of best bitter inside him, he'd have been hard pushed to tell the difference.'

'And I've got another interesting little snippet for you, gentlemen.' Bowman leaned forward. 'Do you remember that rat you found by the body?'

'How could we forget?' said Heffernan.

'Well, I did as you asked and examined it. You were right. It had been stabbed, and probably with the same weapon.'

34

'Whoever did it must have been fast to get a moving rat with a knife,' said Wesley incredulously.

'Oh no, Sergeant. The rat was dead already . . . been dead about a day when the deed was done, I should think.'

'So it wasn't just a healthy young rat going about its lawful business when the murderer struck?' said Heffernan with a grin.

'I think it might have been poisoned. I could test for it if you like.'

'Yeah . . . if you would, Colin. Thanks.'

'So where do you think this unfortunate rodent comes into it, Gerry?'

'Wish I knew. But it didn't get there by accident and it's got something to do with why the poor sod was murdered. I can feel it in my water. But why?'

They drove in silence back to the small incident room that had been set up in Bereton village hall, contemplating this question. Why the rat?

The room the police had been allocated in the village hall had been hurriedly cleared to accommodate them. A pile of play equipment belonging to the village playgroup was pushed into a corner and the desks and computers moved in.

Wesley went through the house-to-house reports, trying not to think that at that moment Neil would be diving beneath the cold grey waters of Bereton Bay and watching the uncovering of a ship that had sailed with the Spanish Armada. He dismissed the image from his mind and returned to his own bit of uncovering. But there was nothing to discover: house-to-house had drawn a blank. The entire population of Bereton had been sitting dutifully in front of their television sets watching *Inspector Morgan*, a TV detective who, needless to say, never wasted time on useless house-to-house enquiries and who never had paperwork to catch up on. Inspector Morgan's days were filled with intriguing clues and car chases. Wesley looked around at the team beavering away at their desks and computer screens. Routine and paperwork . . . Inspector Morgan wouldn't last five minutes.

One report caught his eye. Apple Cottage. Rachel's neat, legible handwriting recorded her opinion that although the inhabitants of Apple Cottage denied having seen anything on the night of the murder, they might be worth another visit. Reading between the lines, Wesley knew that this meant they were probably lying through their teeth. He reported this to the inspector.

'What are we waiting for, Wes? Let's get round there.'

Not being of country stock, Heffernan and Wesley didn't notice the quality of the apple trees as Rachel had done. The battered door opened slowly ... first an inch, then another. A head appeared, wrinkled as a walnut and topped with fine thinning white hair. The old woman peeped myopically round the door.

'Can we have a word, love? Police,' Heffernan said quietly, showing his warrant card.

But the old woman wasn't looking at the inspector. As soon as she spotted Wesley standing behind him she fixed her watery eyes on him and started to scream. 'I'm not going. It's my house ... you're not having it. Get away ... go on ...' She let out a terrified shriek as she was grabbed from behind by a plump, shabbily dressed woman.

'That's enough, Mother. You'll have one of your turns again.'

'It's them ... the Yanks ... there's a black one there ... I ain't going ... I ain't going.' The old woman shook off her daughter and stood her ground.

Heffernan had dealt with drunks and violent armed robbers but white-haired old ladies left him lost for words. 'It's okay, love,' he tried. 'Nobody's going to take you anywhere. We've come to see your daughter, that's all.'

'It's him.' She pointed at Wesley accusingly. He too was speechless. 'He's come to put me in the truck.'

'No one's going to put you in any truck, Mother. Calm down ... come back upstairs. Shall I ring for Dr Pargiter?' The plump woman put her arm round her mother and tried to draw her towards the stairs.

'I'll not go.' The old woman's words held a finality that brooked no argument. Heffernan noticed a stream of glistening liquid running down her bare leg. The urine left a dark patch on the threadbare, patterned carpet.

'Oh, Mother, look what you've done now.' The old woman looked down as if she weren't aware of what she had done. She suddenly fell silent and acquiescent. Her daughter led her towards the stairs, crooning reassuring words in the old woman's ear.

'Quite a reception,' said Heffernan as they hovered awkwardly on the doorstep.

To their relief the woman returned after a few minutes, apologising profusely. 'You'll have to excuse Mother . . . She thinks she's back in the war half the time.' She looked at Wesley and blushed, embarrassed. 'It was you being . . . you know. The GIs . . . the Yanks . . . some of them were black and she'd not seen no black people before . . . not round here. She thought . . .'

Wesley was beginning to understand. 'So she thought we were American troops coming to move her from her home in 1944?'

The woman relaxed a little. 'It's the one thing that's stuck in her mind . . . when she was evacuated. Always on about it she is.'

Wesley nodded, feeling some admiration for this woman, who treated her senile mother with such patience. He introduced himself and showed his warrant card.

The woman was suddenly on her guard. 'Two of your lot came round yesterday. I told them I didn't know nothing.'

'If we could just have a quick word.'

'Long as it's quick. I've Mother to see to.'

'Can we come in then, love?' Heffernan said, realising the invitation wouldn't be forthcoming. The woman stood aside reluctantly to let them in.

The ceilings of the cottage were low and beamed. But this was no tastefully decorated rural retreat. The furniture was either fifties tat or cheap veneered chipboard. The settee which dominated the small room was stained Dralon. The carpet was purple nylon, spotted with filthy marks, the origin of which could only be guessed at.

'Anyone else live here?'

'My son, Wayne. He's got special needs,' the woman said almost with pride.

'And your husband?'

'He buggered off ten years back.'

'So there's just the three of you?'

She nodded. 'I've got no time for twenty questions, you know . . . I've got to see to Mother.'

'I'm sorry, Mrs . . .'

'Restorick . . . Annie Restorick.'

'We just wanted to ask you if you saw anything suspicious or unusual the night before last . . . Sunday. Between 9 and 11 pm. We've had a report of someone running out of the old chapel in this direction. Did anyone pass here at all?'

Wesley thought casual charm might work best. 'To tell you the truth, Mrs Restorick, we don't have much information . . . so anything you could give us, however small, would be of great value.'

'No, I didn't see nothing. We were watching *Inspector Morgan*.'

'Can we talk to your son?'

'He didn't see nothing. He was with me watching telly.' Defensive.

'Is he in?'

She nodded warily.

'If we could just have a quick word . . .'

'It wouldn't be any use. He was here with me all night. I don't like him going down that pub. He's not too bright, you see. People take advantage.'

'Was he at the pub on Sunday night?'

She shook her head vigorously. 'He was here all night . . . I've told you already.' She stood up, clearly anxious to be left alone. 'I've got to see to Mother now. She'll get sore.'

'You've got a lot on your plate, Mrs Restorick . . . seeing to your mum and your son being . . . having special needs. It can't be easy,' Heffernan said with sympathy.

'Wayne's not backward, you know . . . he's just a bit slow. People take advantage.'

'As you've said. Thanks for your help, Mrs Restorick. We'll leave you to it.'

She saw them to the front door, but before she had a chance to see them off the premises, a young man came down the stairs, overweight and pale. He stared at them for a moment then lumbered back upstairs again. Mrs Restorick closed the door as soon as the policemen were over the threshold.

'What do you think, Wes?' asked Heffernan as they reached the lane.

'She's hiding something.'

'What?'

'The son . . . the lady doth protest too much, methinks.'

'Eh?'

'*Hamlet*. It means she's going over the top in giving him an alibi. I reckon he was at the pub.'

'We can easily find out. He must be well known in a place like this.'

38

'And if he wasn't at the pub?'

'That's anybody's guess . . . out stabbing Americans, perhaps.'

'Whatever he was up to, I'll bet you ten quid he wasn't tucked up on the settee with Inspector Morgan.'

Rachel Tracey was a tactful young woman, good with children and beloved of elderly aunts. She was also, as Inspector Heffernan had generously pointed out to the Chief Superintendent, a good police officer. But dealing with Dorinda Openheim was stretching even Rachel's talents to the full.

She had been prepared to be sweetly sympathetic to the bereaved widow; to let her do the talking while she listened carefully for hints of guilt and provided tissues and cups of coffee. So she was abashed when Dorinda looked at her defiantly and refused to say a word; not because she was struck dumb with grief, but because she didn't want to. Grief didn't come into it.

'I'm sorry to have to ask this, Mrs Openheim,' Rachel said gently. 'I know it's an upsetting time for you.'

Dorinda shrugged.

'We'd just like to have a quick look through your husband's things. It's merely routine. Would that be all right?'

Dorinda pressed her scarlet lips together impatiently. 'Sure, honey. Do what the hell you like. Take his things if you want. He won't be needing them where he's gone.'

Rachel was lost for words. It was a well-known fact in the police force that most murders were perpetrated by a spouse or close relative of the victim. But, she thought, if Dorinda Openheim had killed her husband, surely she would have put on a show of grief to throw them off the track. And her attitude towards her late husband indicated indifference rather than hatred.

'You can be there while I look through his things if you like.'

'What's the point? You've got an honest face, honey. You ain't going to steal nothing.'

There didn't seem much point in Rachel's next question but she asked it anyway. 'Will you be all right on your own, Mrs Openheim? Is there anyone you'd like to sit with you?'

Dorinda gave her a look of contempt. 'At my age, honey, I can take care of myself. I'll get along to the bar. That okay with you?'

Rachel, speechless, nodded.

In the first-floor bedroom overlooking the sea, she looked

through the wardrobe and the drawers. She thought how her mother and her aunts would have loved this part of the job, coming as they did from a generation that kept itself to itself and thrilled at any glimpse into the private world of others.

Dorinda had brought far more clothes with her to England than her husband had: dresses, suits, skirts and sweaters filled all the available space, while Norman's clothes (a blazer, three brightly coloured shirts and two pairs of casual slacks) were pushed into a far corner of the wardrobe. The drawers told the same story: all but one contained Dorinda's things. Norman had been lucky to get one small drawer in which to store his brightly coloured golfing jumpers.

Rachel looked round. There was nothing out of the ordinary. Even the pockets of Norman's blazer contained only a handkerchief, some loose change and a couple of used ferry tickets printed with Sunday's date.

Ferry tickets. She returned to the wardrobe and took them from the pocket. What had Norman been doing on the Tradmouth passenger ferry on the day he was to die? She put the tickets in a plastic exhibit bag (she had come prepared), then she searched the suitcases beneath the bed.

Norman's underwear was well worn and washed out. Dorinda's was lacy, sexy and new-looking. Rachel allowed herself the hope that she would still be wearing pants and bras like that when she reached Dorinda's age.

The search of the cases yielded nothing of interest. Rachel was about to leave the room when she spotted the wastepaper basket pushed under the kneehole of the dressing table. Beneath the make-up-covered lumps of cotton wool and the used coffee bags, Rachel saw the telltale blue of airmail paper. The paper was crumpled into a ball, but she drew it out carefully and flattened it out on the floor. It was an air letter, postmarked Tradmouth, Devon.

'My dear Norman,' it began. 'When I got your letter I didn't know what to do after all these years. There's been a lot of water under the bridge since 1944.

'I'm a widow now with a grown-up daughter and two grandchildren. If you're coming to Devon I'd like to see you again. I still think of you as that handsome boy who used to take me to that old chapel . . . do you remember? I suppose I wouldn't recognise you now . . . or you me. Time does awful things to people, doesn't it?

'I'd like us to meet. I've got something to tell you that you should know. I still remember you fondly. I prayed you would be safe in France and I'm so relieved to hear that my prayers were answered. You were always the sweetest of all those Yanks.

'Ring me when you get here (I've put my number at the top) and we'll arrange to meet. Yours affectionately, Marion.'

Rachel looked at the address on the top of the letter: Queenswear, just over the river from Tradmouth. He had visited Marion on Sunday afternoon . . . hence the ferry tickets. She pulled another exhibit bag out of her handbag and put the thin paper carefully inside it.

It was obvious from the letter that Marion still carried a torch for her handsome young Yank, even after fifty years. She wondered if, when they had met, the reality of old age had extinguished that flame for good.

Heffernan and Wesley lunched in the Bereton Arms; a working lunch. While they were there they asked whether Wayne Restorick had honoured the establishment with his presence on Sunday night. The landlord knew Wayne well: he was sure he hadn't been in on Sunday. It had been a quiet night. Everyone had been at home watching that *Inspector Morgan*, the landlord stated bitterly. It looked as though Annie Restorick might have been telling the truth after all.

The two police officers tucked themselves away in a quiet corner with their drinks and their ploughman's lunches. The half-empty pub was a haven of peace; no piped music; no juke-box; only a flashing games machine stood incongruously against the oak-beamed wall of the lounge bar like a tart at a Mothers Union meeting . . . tawdry and out of place. Heffernan was pleased to see that no one was playing on it.

An angry shout of 'Get out . . . we don't want your sort in here . . . sling your hook' from behind the bar made them look round. A young man stood defiantly just inside the doorway. He wore a grey military overcoat, tattered and torn; his lank mousy hair was swept back into a tiny ponytail. The last time they had seen him he had been begging outside the Clearview Hotel. Bereton wasn't giving him much of a welcome.

'And don't you think of coming back . . . and tell those mates of yours the same.' The landlord, a portly middle-aged man with a military moustache, marched out from behind his bar and held open the door for the departing beggar.

Heffernan strolled up to the bar with his empty glass. 'Give you a lot of trouble, do they?'

'They've been hanging round the village a couple of days now . . . idle buggers. I can't think what they're after. I told them to get back to London where they belong.' He made the name London sound like the nether reaches of Hades.

'Has he been in here before, then?'

'No, but his mates have. Two of them . . . more strangers to soap and water. Soon as I saw them I told them to get out. I don't want the likes of them putting off my regulars. Where do they get the money from to drink anyway? Begging and scrounging most likely.'

The landlord turned towards the optics to pour himself a whisky. He had said his piece. Heffernan went to sit down.

'Wes, have you seen a list of what was found in the dead man's pockets?'

'Yeah. Nothing unusual. Handkerchief, few leaflets about local tourist attractions probably picked up at the hotel, some loose change, mints, a ten-pound note. Why?'

'Nothing. Another theory shot down in flames, that's all.'

'What theory's this?'

'Well, if he still had a tenner on him the motive wasn't theft.'

The landlord approached their table, collecting glasses. 'And another thing . . .' He bent over confidentially. 'They threatened Mrs Slater up at the Clearview Hotel. A barmaid here does breakfasts for her and she told me. One of them pulled a knife on her.'

'Didn't she report this to the police?'

'I don't know. All I know is that I don't want them anywhere near my pub.'

'I think we should have a little word with our young gentlemen of the road,' said Heffernan as they left the pub. 'I'd like to see what they find so fascinating about a place like Bereton.'

They drove the half-mile to the hotel at the edge of the beach. Wesley had wanted to leave the car in the village and walk but the inspector had said he was feeling lazy: he needed to conserve his energy for Mrs Slater.

Wesley put the car (a nondescript blue Ford, standard police issue) in the carpark near the memorial and walked towards the hotel. Heffernan nudged his sergeant and nodded towards the Sherman tank that had been dragged up from the seabed, restored and placed on a concrete platform in a far corner of the carpark as an additional reminder of the events that had taken place there during the war. Leaning against the newly painted body of the massive vehicle was the young man who'd just been ejected from the Bereton Arms. Sitting precariously astride the gun turret was another figure with a shaved head; he was pale and unhealthy-looking and dressed in scruffy grey garments that made him look like the victim of some disaster, war or famine. A third boy, aged about sixteen, with dark greasy hair and spots, crouched on the ground stroking a mangy-looking dog of dubious pedigree. The dog lay contentedly on the ground held by a lead made of dirty string.

As the policemen drew nearer, the beggars watched them, assessing how much the newcomers might be worth. Then the one with the ponytail bent down and whispered something to the custodian of the dog. They turned away. Police were bad news.

'Can we have a word, son?' shouted Heffernan.

It was the shaven-headed man on the gun turret who spoke. He looked older than the others – mid-twenties – and possessed an air of leadership. 'You pigs?'

'Pigs are supposed to be very intelligent. Did you know that?' Heffernan looked up at the gun turret enquiringly.

Shaven-head stared at him. 'You what?'

'Do you want me to shout my questions to you up there or will you come down?'

Shaven-head shrugged and stayed put.

'Fancy a chat down at the station? They make a lovely cup of tea there, don't they, Sergeant?'

'Excellent, Inspector.' Wesley was watching the reaction of Shaven-head's two companions, who were looking decidedly nervous.

'I'm not fucking thirsty.' He looked at Wesley with contempt. 'I didn't know they had black pigs in the filth round here.' He leaned forward, leering unpleasantly. Wesley stood his ground, his face impassive.

'What are you doing here?' Heffernan interrupted. 'Not much happening in a place like this?'

'What do you think, Scouse?' He turned his hostile gaze on the inspector, a sly grin on his face.

'Just answer the question,' Heffernan snapped.

'Fancied a bit of peace and quiet, didn't we.'

Heffernan seized his chance. 'We're investigating a murder . . . American tourist staying at that hotel there. Heard about it?'

'We've seen a lot of filth about,' said the spotty dog lover.

'We've heard one of you's got a knife. That true?'

'Piss off, Scouse. Who told you that?'

'You threatened a woman at the hotel.'

'Her eyes are going . . . can't tell a fucking stick from a blade.' The other two looked at Shaven-head nervously. 'That right, Snot? It was a fucking twig, wasn't it?'

Snot, the pale wearer of the ponytail, nodded eagerly. Shaven-head had quite a hold over his followers.

Divide and conquer. Heffernan and Wesley returned to the car and radioed for assistance. The unsuspecting trio were still loitering round the tank when the police car arrived. As Shaven-head's two companions were being led away, he jumped from the tank, made an obscene gesture and ran with the speed of an Olympic athlete inland towards a copse of trees.

'We can pick him up later,' said Heffernan with a confidence he didn't feel. 'We'll let our two friends enjoy the custody sergeant's hospitality for a while, then we'll have a little chat.'

'What about the other one?'

'We'll find out as much as we can about him. Information is power, remember. When we pick him up we'll have something on him. He's got away so he'll think he's untouchable. That'll make him careless.'

Wesley could just about make out some logic in his boss's arguments. He looked out to sea. 'Wonder how the diving's going . . . the Armada wreck.'

'It'll be freezing down there in March. You're better off where you are. Let's go and have a chat with Mrs Slater. We've not got a statement off her yet. I wonder why she didn't report the incident with the knife. She didn't look the type to ignore that sort of thing.'

'Perhaps it was a stick after all. What is it they say? Don't let the facts get in the way of a good story.'

'And nobody likes a good story as much as people who live in small villages where it's news if the vicar farts.'

Mrs Slater greeted them in her office behind the reception desk. It was a small, neat room painted in uniform magnolia; not a thing out of place. Dorothy Slater herself sat at her desk, a single ledger open in front of her. He suit was uncreased, her hair cropped in a style that suggested utility but not vanity. Heffernan would have described her as scrawny rather than fashionably slim. She was probably in her mid-fifties: frown lines were clearly visible despite a discreet layer of make-up. She greeted them formally and ordered tea.

At Heffernan's nod, Wesley spoke first. 'Mrs Slater, we've had occasion to take some youths in for questioning. One of them was begging outside this hotel yesterday. You told him to go.'

Mrs Slater nodded. 'They've been a nuisance.'

'We've heard they've been more than a nuisance,' Heffernan said sharply. 'We've heard one of them pulled a knife on you.'

Mrs Slater went pale.

'Why didn't you report this to us?'

'It's nothing I couldn't deal with.'

'Was it a knife?'

She nodded warily. 'He didn't mean to use it. He was just . . .'

'Is there something you want to tell us, love?' said Heffernan gently. 'Something we should know?'

Mrs Slater sighed and stared at the silver ballpoint pen laid neatly by her ledger. She picked it up and twisted it in her fingers. 'He's my nephew . . . my sister's boy. He's always been a problem, always in trouble at school . . . then with the police.'

'The one with the shaved head?'

She nodded. 'He ran away from home when he was sixteen . . . lived on the streets. No one in the family had heard from him for eight years, then he suddenly turned up here last week with two of his hangers-on. I didn't recognise him at first, not after all this time. He was always so hard . . . such a nasty little thing. He was a difficult child right from the start. I thought of my poor sister and told him to go back home and let his mother know he was all right but . . .'

'But what?'

'Some of the things he said about her . . . the words he used, about his own mother.'

'Did he tell you why he came here?'

'He said he came to see his gran. My mother was the only member of the family who ever really got on with Nigel.'

'Where does your mother live?'

'Here. She has a small flat at the back of the hotel. She's very fit . . . very independent,' she added almost with pride.

'Can we talk to her?'

'It wouldn't be any use. I didn't let him in. I told him she wasn't here . . . that she was in a home. I didn't even tell her he'd called. I was afraid she might meet him on one of her walks, but luckily she hasn't so far.'

'Would your mother be pleased to see him?'

Mrs Slater thought for a moment. 'Mother has always been a little . . . eccentric. Her obsessions have got worse with age. Not that I'm saying she's senile, you understand . . . just stubborn.'

'I see,' said Heffernan, not really understanding.

'I would prefer it if you didn't tell her Nigel was in the area. I think it's best for everyone if he just goes back to wherever it was he came from. It would upset her to see that he'd turned out like that.'

Upset her or her daughter? Heffernan wondered.

'Did your nephew and his friends have any contact with your American guests?'

'They begged from them outside in the carpark and on the beach,' she said crossly. 'But mostly they got short shrift. Veterans who've been through a world war and survived aren't the best people to scrounge from. They've seen too much to believe a hard-luck story.'

Wesley nodded. Mrs Slater's last observation was probably right. 'Did they have any arguments with the Americans?'

'There were a few angry words, but no actual arguments.'

'The sergeant, Mr Boratski, says Norman Openheim was threatened by them. Did you hear anything about that?'

Mrs Slater shook her head.

The inspector stood up. 'Thank you for your time, Mrs Slater. Just one more thing. The knife your nephew has . . . what sort is it?'

'One of those flick-knives . . . nasty, vicious-looking thing.'

'Long, thin blade?'

She nodded.

'What's your nephew's full name?'

'Nigel William Glanville . . . but his friends seem to call him Rat.'

46

Chapter Four

When the residents of this beautiful part of South Devon returned from their enforced evacuation in 1944, the first priority was to get the farmland ready for the autumn sowing. The land was swept with mine detectors; hordes of rats who had feasted in the neglected barns had to be exterminated. Our allies had left devastation behind them.

The Spanish who had come up our beach three hundred and fifty-six years before to invade those fertile fields were, fortunately, never given the opportunity to reap such destruction.

From *A History of Bereton and Its People* by June Mallindale

Rachel was glad when the inspector suggested that Wesley should go with her to see the mysterious Marion. Wesley was a contentedly married man awaiting the birth of his first child . . . and always behaved like a gentleman; not like Steve Carstairs, who lost no opportunity to practise the old hand-on-knee trick and let no *double entendre* go unexploited. Besides, Wesley was interesting to talk to, unlike Steve, a local boy whose horizons did not extend beyond the tawdry nightlife of Morbay. That's what she liked about her boyfriend Dave (an Australian who'd backpacked around a fair chunk of the world) . . . he was interesting.

'Anything new to report?' she asked as Wesley got into the car.

'Three beggars hanging about: one of them's the nephew of the hotel owner and a vicious little bastard. He's got a flick-knife and he threatened his aunty with it.'

'Charming. What does the boss say? Is he our man?'

'He doesn't seem to be in much of a hurry to find him. We've pulled his two friends in but the nephew got away. And do you know what his nickname is? Rat.'

'Hence the rat at the murder scene?'

'Could be. We've alerted all patrols to apprehend him and we've checked him out on the PNC. He's got a record for theft and possession of drugs and he's done six months for actual bodily harm.'

'Charming.'

'Who's this Marion, then? Wartime sweetheart?'

'Sounds that way from the letter. Want to see it?' She passed the letter in its plastic bag to Wesley.

'The chapel again. Seems our Norman was a bit of a lad in his day.'

'Him and Mrs O. made a good pair, then. She's hardly prostrate with grief.'

'Maybe they didn't get on. His old sergeant reckoned she was having it off with Todd Weringer.'

'I remember him . . . quite attractive for his age.'

'I didn't know you went in for older men. How's Dave, by the way?' Wesley had met Rachel's Australian six months before when he had arrested him. Dave's innocence established and his then girlfriend departed for fresh pastures, Rachel had taken advantage of the situation and offered him accommodation in a holiday flat on her family's farm.

She suddenly became serious, annoyed. 'My dad says he needs the flat for holiday lets . . . it's been put in the brochures already. I don't know what Dave's going to do. Looks like he'll be homeless if something doesn't turn up.'

'He's not the only one. Our next-door neighbours are having their house repossessed.'

Rachel's mind was fixed firmly on her own problem. 'How's Dave going to afford summer season prices? He helps my dad on the farm and Dad lets him have the flat for peanuts.'

'He'll just have to marry the farmer's daughter. Sounds like he's got his feet well under the table already.' Wesley was unable to resist a bit of mischief.

'Get lost, Sergeant.'

'Not on the cards, then?'

'Definitely not . . . I'm going to be Chief Constable by the time I'm forty.' She laughed.

They reached the ferry. Wesley drove the car slowly on to the floating platform which would chug across the glistening expanse of the River Trad to the hill-hung town of Queenswear, Tradmouth's smaller twin on the opposite bank. The ferry journey took five minutes and they drove off, past the station which served the quaint steam railway, towards the outskirts of the town. Rachel navigated; being local she knew the area well.

Marion's home turned out to be a neat whitewashed bungalow with a spectacular view over the river to the town of Tradmouth. It was on its own at the end of a track, almost the last dwelling in Queenswear before the open countryside took over.

They left the car and turned to take in the view. The water reflected blue in the March sunshine, and the steel masts of the boats glinted as they moved on the gentle swell of the river. Tradmouth stood out, pastel-coloured, against the dark green hills behind the town, an important port since the days of the Crusades; the hills and its inaccessibility had ensured the survival of its picturesque character. Tradmouth had not suffered the fate of other ports and become the victim of ugly expansion.

Somehow they had imagined Marion to be a gentle old lady who still possessed the last vestiges of faded beauty; a sad, elfin figure awaiting the return of her handsome American sweetheart . . . a sort of West Country Madam Butterfly.

The capable creature who answered the door was no romantic heroine but a well-rounded, elderly woman with straight grey hair, styled without any pretension to vanity, and a wary smile which disappeared when Wesley and Rachel showed their warrant cards. She invited them into her sitting room, which was conventionally furnished and immaculately tidy, and sat down on the edge of the tapestry sofa with nervous expectation.

Wesley spoke first. 'Am I right in thinking your name is Marion?'

'That's right . . . Marion Potter. Why? What's happened? Is it our Carole?'

'Carole?'

'My daughter.'

'Oh no, Mrs Potter. Don't worry. It's nothing to do with your daughter. Do you know a man called Norman Openheim? We found a letter from you amongst his belongings.'

Marion extracted a well-washed embroidered cotton handkerchief from her sleeve and twisted it in her hands. 'Yes,' she stated quietly. 'I knew him during the war.' She looked up. 'Is he all right? What's happened?'

Rachel spoke sympathetically. 'I'm sorry, Mrs Potter . . . he's been killed. That's why we're here. I'm sorry to have to bring you such bad news.'

'But I only saw him on Sunday . . . was it an accident?' Her voice trailed off to nothing.

'No, he was murdered . . . I'm sorry.'

Marion sank back on to the sofa cushions, her face shocked.

'Would you like a cup of tea, Mrs Potter?' Rachel nodded to Wesley, who went out to put the kettle on. Pam had trained him well domestically, and Rachel was very good with elderly ladies. Marion would be telling her life story before the tea was in the cups.

'He came on Sunday . . . he rang me first. I didn't recognise him, do you know that?' She smiled, trying hard to fight back tears. This woman showed more grief for Norman Openheim than his wife had, Rachel thought. 'I don't know what he must have thought of me. I was pretty back then.'

She went to the oak sideboard and took out a battered photo album. She opened it at an early page and passed it to Rachel.

'Is that you?'

'Yes. That's me with Norman . . . there.'

Rachel looked carefully. The two youthful faces, fresh and apparently untroubled, looked back at her shyly. Marion had been a rosy-cheeked, healthy-looking girl. Norman, with his shock of dark hair and open smile, had been very good-looking – and very young, little more than a boy: a boy with the prospect of death hanging over him. Rachel almost felt like crying herself.

'What happened to him?' She looked at Rachel in realisation. 'I heard it on the radio . . . an American tourist found stabbed in Bereton chapel. It was him, wasn't it?'

Rachel nodded.

'You're not safe anywhere these days. We used to meet there . . . do our courting.' She turned away, tears in her eyes. 'It's spoiled all those memories now. To think that some young thug . . .'

'I know.' Rachel put a comforting arm round Marion's shoulder. 'You think it was a young thug who killed him? Any particular reason?'

Marion looked at her, surprised. 'Who else would it be? Those young tearaways are everywhere nowadays . . . nowhere's safe. You see it on *Crimefile* all the time. I always keep my windows and doors locked . . . my son-in-law put some good locks on for me. Nobody locked their doors round here once. We never had to, not round here. . . .'

'When Norman came to see you, how did he seem? Was he worried about anything?'

She shook her head. 'We hadn't seen each other for fifty years. It was so wonderful to see him again . . . talk about the old times.'

'In the chapel?'

Marion blushed. 'We were young . . . so young.' She dabbed at her eyes with her handkerchief. 'And Norman had real film star looks . . . you can see that from the pictures, can't you?'

Rachel nodded. 'I'd have fancied him myself.' She smiled.

'Oh, you would, my luvver, you would.' At least Marion was smiling again.

Wesley came in quietly with three cups of tea and put them on the coffee table, taking care to find coasters for them first: Marion would be worried about the hot cups leaving rings on the wood.

'You said in your letter to Norman that you had something to tell him.'

Marion looked nervously at Wesley. 'You'll find biscuits in the top cupboard on the right, my luvver,' she said. Wesley, now so used to the familiar Devon endearment that it had ceased to cause him the amusement it had when he had first arrived from London, took the hint. This was woman's talk.

When he had gone, Marion leaned towards Rachel. 'You have to understand how it was in the war. It wasn't like today . . . young girls were taught to respect themselves, if you know what I mean. But when Norman and I used to go to the chapel . . . well, we didn't know if we'd be dead the next day or . . .'

'You slept together?'

She nodded, blushing. 'After Norman had gone . . . when they'd gone to Normandy, I found I was going to have a baby. He'd said he'd come back . . . they all said that, the Yanks, but I never saw him again. Then I read about this veterans' association in the local paper and how they were planning to visit Bereton. So I wrote to them and asked them if a Norman Openheim was a member . . . I didn't even know if he'd got back alive from

Normandy, you see. They wrote to me and said he was and that I could contact him through them . . . so I did. I wanted him to know he had a daughter.' Marion's eyes filled with tears again. 'My husband was a good man . . . took us both on. We never had children. He brought Carole up as his own.'

'How did Norman feel about having a daughter?'

'He was so pleased . . . I showed him all the photographs. He wanted to meet her, couldn't wait. But I said I'd have a word with her first. I expected him to ring today. He said he would. Our Carole said she wanted to meet him. I never forgot Norman . . . not in all those years.' She looked up. 'He's a long time with those biscuits.'

As if on cue, Wesley pushed the door open. He had arranged the biscuits carefully on a plate. Pam was a lucky woman, Rachel thought; Dave would have brought the packet.

'Does this have to all be written down?' said Marion, worried. 'Nobody round here knows that my Carole wasn't my husband's.'

'Don't worry, Mrs Potter. The worst that can happen is that we'll need a statement about when you last saw him . . . probably not even that. Isn't that right, Sergeant Peterson?'

Wesley nodded with his mouth full of custard cream.

'And he didn't mention if he was afraid of anyone? Anything out of the ordinary?'

'He said his wife was a bit – how did he put it? – cold. That's all . . . nothing that would help you.'

'Could we have your daughter's address? We might want a word with her.' Marion looked wary. 'When did you tell her who her real father was? Was it just in the past few days?'

'No . . . it was a couple of years back.'

'How did she react?'

'How could she react? She's got kids by two different men herself . . . she's on to her second husband.' She rolled her eyes in disgust. Carole's morals, it seemed, were a bone of contention between mother and daughter. 'We were talking about the war and it just came out . . . I never meant to tell her. I was saying what it was like to think that every day might be your last . . . the things you do that you wouldn't normally do . . .' She suddenly looked Rachel in the eye. 'Did Norman suffer . . . when he died, did he suffer?'

'He didn't suffer . . . died instantly. He was stabbed from

52

behind and his hearing aid was broken. He wouldn't have known a thing about it.'

Marion nodded, a faint smile on her lips. When Norman had been standing there alone in the chapel, his last thoughts would have been of their meetings . . . of their gentle lovemaking on a borrowed blanket on the hard chapel floor under the stars. Marion hoped – knew – that Norman Openheim had died happy.

The address Marion had given them for her daughter, Carole, was on the council estate which straddled the steep road into Tradmouth. Wesley decided that as it was five o'clock – and they still had to interview the two beggars currently enjoying the custody sergeant's hospitality back at the station – their visit to Norman Openheim's daughter should wait until the following day.

They drove back to Bereton to pick up the inspector, who had been talking to Openheim's old comrades and their wives. What effect Gerry Heffernan would have on Anglo-American relations Wesley did not care to contemplate.

He was waiting for them in the hotel bar. Mrs Slater scurried through and nodded to them in her usual businesslike way.

'Anything to report?' Heffernan asked.

They told him about Marion.

'What was it they used to say about the Yanks? Overpaid, over-sexed and over here.'

'Oh, I don't know, sir . . . I think it's quite romantic,' said Rachel.

'Like one of those weepy films, eh? Reunited after all those years, then he goes and dies.'

'I didn't know you were familiar with weepy films, sir,' Rachel said, half teasing.

'You can't be married for twenty-two years and avoid the things altogether.'

Rachel immediately regretted her remark. She knew that, even three years after her death, the inspector still missed his wife, Kathy, deeply. She knew he still kept her picture in his office drawer.

'Anything new, sir?' She changed the subject.

'Most of them seem to have watertight alibis . . . they all back each other up. And there are more reports of Dorinda Openheim carrying on with Todd Weringer.'

'At their age?' Wesley said with disbelief.

'Let's hope we've all got their energy when the time comes.' Heffernan grinned, Rachel's remark forgotten. 'And it seems to be the unanimous opinion that Norman Openheim was what is known in the colonies as a "regular guy". I gather that's good. They all said they liked him and that he didn't seem to have any enemies.'

'So it's still the beggar we're after. Any sightings yet?'

'Nothing yet. But I reckon he'll come back here. He wants to see his old gran, doesn't he? Some of the nastiest villains I've known have been fond of their grans,' he added philosophically.

'Motive?'

Heffernan shrugged. 'Perhaps Openheim had caught him up to some mischief, or he intended to rob him and was disturbed, or just for the sheer hell of it . . . who knows? We'll get him. In the meantime let's have a little chat with his mates, shall we?'

When they arrived at the station Wesley rang Pam to say he'd be late. She had a parents' evening: at the mention of this he remembered that she'd given him dispensation to have a drink with Neil in her absence. He told her not to bother leaving any dinner in the microwave for him. He'd get something at the Bereton Arms. He wished her luck with the parents' evening, not doubting that she possessed the tact and acting ability to carry it off successfully and send the parents of the little darlings away happy.

Heffernan and Rachel elected to interview the young man who went by the name of Snot, while Wesley and Steve interviewed his young friend, Dog. Dog's actual dog, Fang, was being given a bowl of meaty chunks by Constable Carver, who had just come on duty and was an incorrigible lover of man's best friend.

'Any idea where your mate might head for?' Heffernan asked casually.

'Which mate?'

'Rat. That's his name, isn't it?'

'Yeah . . . so?'

'He's come here to see his gran, so I've heard. Very nice . . . a lad wanting to see his gran.'

'Piss off, Scouse.'

'Treating you all right down in the cells, are they? Food all right? Bed comfy enough for you?'

54

Snot sniffed and shrugged.

'You've come a long way, haven't you, Snot? London, was it? How old are you?'

'Old enough.'

'So what's the story, then? Let me guess. All your life you've been in care . . . nobody wanted you so you thought you'd try the streets. At least you had mates on the streets . . . comrades in adversity. You stick together, is that right?'

Rachel was watching the boy carefully. His expression had softened somewhat. Heffernan had touched on the truth.

'I've met lots of lads like you in my time, Snot. Not bad lads . . . not deep down. They've just never had a chance. Do you do drugs?'

Snot looked wary. 'Sometimes.'

'The trouble with your – lifestyle they call it on the telly, don't they? – is that you can get in with some bad company, get led astray a bit. Rat's bad company, isn't he?'

'How do you mean?' Snot looked up, attentive. The inspector was getting through.

'His aunty described him as a bad 'un . . . vicious little bastard who threatened her with a knife. He's got a record that shows he's been a busy lad in the villainy department. Have you got a record?'

'Don't have nothing to play it on.' Snot laughed out loud at his own joke.

'Very funny. You might as well tell us if you're one of our valued customers, you know. We can take fingerprints, get an ID that way.'

'Okay . . . I've been pulled in by the filth a few times. But I never done nothing . . . I was innocent.'

' 'Course you were. What's your full name? We'll have to check.'

'Snot.'

'Your real name.'

'Kenneth John Jenkins.'

'Date of birth?'

Snot reeled off the date. Heffernan nodded to Rachel, who went off to summon up Snot's details on the computer.

'Bring us some tea back, will you, love? How many sugars, Snot?'

Rachel slammed the door of the interview room rather more forcefully than usual. The inspector obviously hadn't been reading the Chief Constable's memos on sexism: she would have to put them in a more prominent place on his desk. After accessing the computer and getting the relevant details, she made the tea resentfully. It was hardly her job as a CID officer to act as tea lady: Steve wouldn't be expected to do it. She returned to the interview room balancing the cups on a tray. The inspector would have the one that had spilled in the saucer – a punishment.

Heffernan looked at Snot's print-out: petty stuff. 'Hardly Mr Big, are you, son?'

'You can't keep me here . . . I've not done nothing.'

'What about murder?'

Snot's grey eyes widened in disbelief. 'What murder? I never killed no one. . . .'

'One of those Americans. I told you when you were by that tank near Bereton Sands . . . remember? He was killed on Sunday night up at the old chantry chapel in Bereton. Know it?'

Snot shook his head.

'He was stabbed . . . possibly with a knife like your mate, Rat, carries. You're not always together, are you? You go your separate ways?'

'We can make more that way.'

'Where was Rat on Sunday night, about ten o'clock?'

'Dunno.'

'Was he with you?'

'Sunday? Don't think so . . . no. We went to Tradmouth that night, me and Dog. See if we could get anything when the pubs chucked out.'

'Was Rat with you?'

'No. He stayed in Bereton . . . said he was going to have another go at seeing his gran. We left him about 5. Didn't see him till the next day.'

'And did he see his gran?'

'He said he hung round for a bit. Don't think he got to see her. He never said nothing about that night.' There was something in his voice which hinted to Heffernan that Snot thought Rat was quite capable of having spent the evening knifing Americans. But even if he admitted his thoughts to them, supposition was not evidence.

'We've heard that the American who died had a row with one of you when he refused to give you money. Is this true?'

'Nah . . . can't remember that. A few of them yelled at us, told us to get our hair cut, that sort of thing.' He smirked. 'There wasn't no aggro . . . no proper aggro.'

This confirmed what Heffernan had suspected: the argument between Norman and the beggars had been exaggerated by Litton Boratski, probably more out of prejudice than malice.

'Right, Snot . . . you're free to go.'

Rachel looked at the inspector with surprise.

'Unless you'd like to stay for dinner, and a bed for the night . . . central heating and *en suite* bucket, all mod cons.'

'Could I?' Snot looked pathetically eager. Heffernan's offer was better than a derelict building or shop doorway in the March winds.

'Okay. I'll swing it with the custody sergeant . . . say you're still helping with our enquiries. Only tonight, mind. I'll extend the invitation to your mate and all . . . and Fang's being well looked after, munching his meaty chunks as we speak.'

Snot grinned, showing a missing front tooth; the first time they'd seen him smile.

'Was that wise, sir?' said Rachel anxiously when Snot had been led away. She believed in doing things strictly by the book.

'There but for the grace of God, Rach. If the cells aren't full that poor little bugger might as well have a hot meal and somewhere warm to sleep.' He looked at his watch. 'I'm late . . . choir practice. Get off home, Rach, tell that feller of yours to stop playing with his didgeridoo and get an early night.'

Heffernan grabbed his anorak, tore down the stairs and out into the darkening narrow streets. The top storeys of the medieval shops jutted out above him, obscuring any available light. When he reached the porch of St Margaret's church he stopped to catch his breath. There was no sound of singing from inside: they hadn't started yet.

St Margaret's was a large handsome church, built in the fourteenth and fifteenth centuries by the generosity of the prosperous merchants of Tradmouth, who had made their fortunes from the wine trade with Bordeaux. Their tombs lined the aisles; self-satisfied, self-made men – mayors and aldermen of the then great port. The screen between nave and chancel was a thing of beauty: Heffernan had been unable to take his eyes off it on his first visit to the church all those years ago when he and Kathy had gone there to arrange their wedding. It was elaborately carved and painted in subtle ancient shades. That it had survived all the upheavals of English ecclesiastical history was a miracle in itself.

Behind the screen the ladies and gentlemen of the choir chattered away. Heffernan strolled slowly into the back of the church, collecting his thoughts, before he joined them. Hanging on the oak panelling to his right was a tiny typed notice in a plain black frame. He must have passed it hundreds of times but never bothered to read it. He screwed up his eyes to decipher the faint print. 'The carved timber used in this gallery came from the Armada flagship the *Nuestra Señora del Rosario* which was captured by Sir Francis Drake in 1588 and brought back to Tradmouth for refitting.'

'Well, well . . . Wesley'd be interested in that. Refitting, eh? Seeing what he could nick more likely.'

With his mind successfully taken off the problems of the case, Gerry Heffernan was in fine voice that evening. So fine that the grey permed ladies in the front row looked at each other and smiled knowingly.

Wesley's special dispensation from his wife was to last until ten o'clock; the time she estimated she'd be home. He looked at his watch . . . an hour and a half to go.

The Bereton Arms was fairly full that evening. The clientèle was what could be described as 'a good social mix': farmers; arty types settled in Devon in search of inspiration; a clutch of young professionals in search of the authentic rural experience. Even the young vicar sat in the corner clutching his half-pint tankard, talking earnestly to a man with an alarming handlebar moustache. Wesley drank low-alcohol beer: he was driving. Neil, bed-and-breakfasting in the village, had no such restraints and had just been to the bar for his third pint of best bitter.

'You should have been there, Wes. The finds we're bringing out . . . pewter plates, and a silver crucifix. . . . We've used this machine to blow the sand away from the timbers . . . the whole ship's down there . . .'

'I've never done any diving.'

'There's always a first time.'

'I won't get the chance. This case'll drag on . . . I can feel it in my water.'

'I'm not surprised if you're drinking that stuff. You mean you've not arrested some innocent member of the public yet?'

Wesley shook his head. 'Not even a guilty one.'

'When can we start on the chantry?'

'We'll let you know . . . couple more days maybe.'

'Mind you, we're getting so much down in the bay that it's probably good that we can concentrate on that for a while. You'll have to meet the team, Wes. They're a good lot.'

'On the boat?'

'Don't let that worry you. I never thought they'd get me off dry land. I used to think Jane was just posing when she went on about diving but now I'm really getting into it.' Neil delved into his pocket. 'I've brought you a present . . . something to read when you're sitting round all day in a lay-by in one of those souped-up patrol cars.'

Wesley took the book. It was slightly thinner than the average paperback and had a picture postcard photograph of Bereton church on the cover. It bore the words *A History of Bereton and Its People* by June Mallindale in large white letters.

'You wanted to know about the chantry . . . it's all in there. There's a lot about the Armada and the D-day rehearsals as well. It's a bit flowery but it seems to be fairly well researched. Let me have it back when you've read it, won't you.'

Wesley smiled. Neil had always been too impecunious to go round giving impromptu gifts. 'Thanks. I'll read it when I get the chance. Another pint?'

Silly question. Neil's eyes lit up and he presented his empty glass for refilling. While Wesley was waiting for the beer to be pulled by the homely-looking barmaid in an over-short skirt, he surveyed his fellow bar leaners. A few eyed him curiously but most studiously avoided his eyes. In the corner at the far end of the bar Wayne Restorick was standing, drink in hand, talking to a youth with a similarly vacant expression.

Wayne looked up and caught Wesley's eye. His vacant look changed to one of fear. He abandoned his glass and pushed his way through the groups of standing drinkers and ran towards the door. Wesley watched him with interest, wondering what there was about an off-duty detective sergeant that Wayne had found so disturbing.

The anthem the choir had rehearsed for next Sunday's evensong ran through Gerry Heffernan's head as he lay alone in the big double bed. The window was partly open: he had slept with the window open since Kathy's death; she had always liked it closed. He could hear the water lapping against the quayside and the soft chug-chug of the fishing boats as they left port.

He was just starting to drift off to sleep when the phone by his bed exploded with sound, disorientating him for a moment as he was thrust back into consciousness. His hand missed the receiver on the first attempt. When he had succeeded in picking it up he grunted into it, still more than half asleep.

The voice on the other end sounded disgustingly awake: the night duty sergeant. 'Just thought I'd let you know, sir . . . there's an American tourist gone missing from the Clearview Hotel. A Mrs Johnson . . . her husband's in a bit of a state.'

'Right . . . I'll get over there.'

He looked at his watch: half past one. He would have liked Wesley to go with him but he didn't want to disturb Pam at that time of night, not with the baby so close. Rachel was second choice. He told her to meet him at the hotel in half an hour.

Chapter Five

Wherever American troops were stationed, the local girls seemed to find them irresistible, especially with their own young men away in the forces. Our area here in South Devon was no exception. Many local girls married American servicemen and swapped the rolling fields of Bereton for the adventure of living on the other side of the Atlantic Ocean.

From *A History of Bereton and Its People* by June Mallindale

Heffernan got a patrol car to drop him at the hotel. He met Rachel in the foyer, brightly lit in view of the current crisis. Dorothy Slater greeted them wearing a substantial pink dressing gown. For the first time the inspector wondered if there had ever been a Mr Slater, and if so what had become of him.

'A Mr Johnson rang in after his wife had failed to return from a drive,' Rachel began, sounding remarkably alert considering the late hour. 'Apparently she'd hired a car on Saturday afternoon from a garage in Tradmouth so she could do some sightseeing.'

'She's probably got lost, Rach . . . or run out of petrol. Any accidents reported?'

'None, sir. And I've checked all local emergency hospital admissions . . . nothing.'

'Okay. Tell all patrols to keep a lookout for the car. Got the number?'

'Yes, sir. It's been done.'

'She'll be lost down some country lane. You know what they're like round here . . . like a maze when you can't see over the hedgerows. She'll meet up with some farmer on his tractor out for the dawn milking.' He turned to go. 'Nothing more we can do, Rach . . . all been seen to. Have you talked to the husband?'

'He's very upset, sir . . . especially after the murder.'

'What did you say to him?'

'More or less what you've just said. If you don't know the lanes you can easily get lost, especially in the dark.'

'Fair enough, then. She'll turn up safe and sound in the morning. Let's get back home for some kip, eh?'

'There's one more thing, sir. She's not a stranger round here . . . not really. She was brought up locally . . . married Mr Johnson in the war and went over to the States in 1945. A GI bride, I think they called them.'

Heffernan, hovering by the door, turned round. 'Right, then. Let's have a word with the husband, shall we?'

Ed Johnson sat in the empty lounge on the edge of a faded chintz armchair. He was a small, wiry man with steel-grey hair. His face, as he looked up at them, was heavily lined, indicating that he'd spent a good proportion of his life out of doors. His eyes, a piercing blue, were rheumy with unshed tears. 'Have you found her?' His voice cracked with anxiety.

'Not yet, sir. But there's been no accident report. It's our guess that she's got herself lost. Did she say where she was going exactly?'

Johnson shook his head. 'She just said she was going for a drive.'

'What time was this?'

'After dinner . . . half past eight.'

'How did she seem?' Johnson looked at Heffernan blankly. 'Was she upset about anything? Did she seem unhappy? Was there anything different about her behaviour?'

Johnson shook his head. 'She just went for a drive, that's all.'

'Did she know this area well?'

'She did once, I guess. It don't seem to have changed that much.'

'Where exactly did she live before she left England? Is there anywhere she talked about wanting to see again?'

'She lived in Maleton . . . little place a couple of miles from here. Her pa ran the village store. But her folks died some years back.' He looked up challengingly. 'What are you going to do to find her?'

'We've put out a message to all our patrols to look out for her car. We'll check Maleton in case she's gone back there on a sentimental journey. But I'm sure she's got herself lost or run out of petrol somewhere.'

'Petrol?' Johnson looked puzzled.

'Gas,' translated Rachel.

'No, the tank was nearly full . . . I checked this morning.'

Heffernan looked at Rachel. Another theory gone out of the window. 'There's probably nothing to worry about, Mr Johnson. She'll turn up in the morning, you'll see. In the meantime try and get some sleep. Just one more thing . . . has she taken any luggage with her?'

Johnson looked at him blankly.

'Perhaps DC Tracey here could help you check.'

Rachel waited until the man rose slowly to his feet and then followed him from the room. After a few minutes she returned and caught Heffernan about to doze off on the sofa.

'Sir.' He came to with a jolt. 'There's something you should know. Some of Mrs Johnson's clothes and one of her cases are missing. Mr Johnson's in a bit of a state. He's taken one of his pills.'

'At least we know that wherever she's gone she's gone there of her own free will. Got a description of her?'

'Better than that . . . I've got a photo.'

'There's nothing more we can do here. I'd get home to bed if I were you.'

When Rachel had driven off, Heffernan wandered back into the hotel foyer where Dorothy Slater still kept her lonely vigil behind the reception desk, studying some forms, although her eyes were hardly focusing on them.

'Mr Johnson's gone up to bed,' he began. 'I'm sure there's nothing to worry about . . . probably just got herself lost. Seen anything of that nephew of yours?'

'No. I'm hoping he's gone back where he came from.'

'We've got his two mates down at the station. Giving them a hot meal and a bed for the night . . . looked like they could use it.' Mrs Slater looked unsympathetic. 'If you see your Nigel, you will let us know, won't you? We'd like a word.'

'I'll do that, Inspector.'

'How's your mother?'

'Fine. I've not told her about Nigel. It's best that way.'

'Does he know where her flat is?'

'Of course not. Why?'

'Nothing . . . just being nosy. Goodnight, then. I'd get to bed if I were you.'

When Heffernan left he walked the half-mile up the lane to the incident room at the village hall. He had a key, given to him very reluctantly by the formidable woman caretaker, so he let himself in, trying hard not to make a noise and awake any village vigilantes.

The room they were using was in darkness. Heffernan switched the fluorescent light on and it flickered into life. The file he was looking for lay neatly on Wesley's desk. He flicked through the statements taken from the American veterans and their wives until he came to the one he was looking for . . . Sally Johnson's. Between nine and eleven on the evening of Norman Openheim's death, she had been taking a walk along the beach. She had seen nobody except another woman walking her dog: she did not know whether the woman had seen her.

Sally Johnson had gone missing . . . and she had no solid alibi for the murder of Norman Openheim. Heffernan picked up the phone and rang for a patrol car to take him back to Tradmouth . . . back to his bed to think.

Rachel came into the incident room yawning, surprised to see her boss so alert after their disturbed night. 'Any news of Mrs Johnson?'

'Nothing yet . . . but have a look at this.' He flung the statement on to the desk in front of her. 'She's got no alibi.'

'Doesn't mean she's guilty, sir.'

'But it's worth a look, isn't it . . . seeing she's gone missing.'

'I'll check the house-to-house statements . . . see if anyone with a dog was walking it on the beach that evening.'

'Good. Seen Wes?'

'He's around somewhere. We're meant to be going to see Norman Openheim's daughter. She's over in Tradmouth . . . on the estate.'

'Before you do that can you pick up Openheim's things from the hospital and take them to the widow. I want her to see if anything's missing. Then you can have a chat to the veterans about Sally Johnson . . . find out what you can about her and what her relationship was with Norman Openheim. She was a GI bride: find out if she talked about seeing anyone while she was over here . . . or visiting any particular place. Get her old home checked as well . . . village store in Maleton.'

'If it still exists. Lots of village shops have closed down.'

'Well, find out. Openheim's love child can wait till tomorrow.'

'That's an expression you don't hear much . . . love child.'

'Probably not politically correct . . . not many things are nowadays. Take Wesley with you to the hotel. I know Steve'd prefer an armed stake-out but I'll get him to go through these statements instead . . . see if we can find a woman who walked her dog on the beach on Sunday night.'

After driving to Tradmouth for Norman Openheim's belongings, Wesley and Rachel drove back along the coast road, quiet at this time of year before the tourists began their annual invasion.

When they reached the hotel they were told that most of the veterans had gone over to Tradmouth to have a look at the town and its church. Dorinda Openheim, however, was in the lounge reading the morning paper and sipping a cup of strong black coffee. Todd Weringer sat in an adjoining armchair, his face hidden behind a broadsheet.

'Sorry to disturb you, Mrs Openheim.' Wesley glanced at Weringer, who had put down his paper and was now peering at the newcomers over half-moon reading glasses. 'If we could have a word in private.'

'It's okay, honey. I've no secrets from Todd. I'd like him to stay. He's been a tower of strength since Norman passed away . . . don't know what the heck I'd have done without him.' She smiled sweetly as she spouted the clichés, determination in her eyes. Wesley didn't bother to argue. Todd Weringer's presence could do no harm.

Rachel produced the plastic bag that contained Norman Openheim's personal belongings. 'I wonder if you could go through these, Mrs Openheim . . . see if anything's missing or if there's anything unusual. Take your time . . . there's no rush.' She emptied the contents of the bag on to the coffee table carefully.

Dorinda looked at the items without much interest. A handkerchief, clean; a couple of leaflets, one about a nearby castle and one describing the delights of a local museum – there was a whole rack of such material in the hotel reception and Norman had probably picked these up as he passed. There was some loose change, a ten-pound note and a half-eaten packet of strong mints.

'Is this all the money he had with him?' Rachel asked.

'I guess so.'

'Anything missing?'

Dorinda shook her head. Then she studied the objects again with renewed interest as if she'd remembered something that had been eluding her. 'Yeah . . . the lighter. It's not here.'

'What lighter?'

'He definitely had it . . . never went anywhere without it. He said it was his good-luck charm. He swore he never actually used it but he couldn't fool me.' She snorted with derision. 'Guess he thought I couldn't smell the filthy stuff on his breath . . . ate mints to cover the stink. Must have reckoned I was dumb or something.'

'No one could reckon that, honey,' Todd Weringer said smoothly.

'Maybe he left it behind. Have you checked?' asked Wesley.

'Sure. The lighter was in his pocket before he went out, and a packet of cigarettes.'

'You searched his pockets?' asked Rachel sweetly. She could well believe it.

'I was looking for some change.'

'And you didn't mention the cigarettes to him?'

'Why should I? He could do what the hell he liked . . . so long as he didn't do it near me.'

'Can you describe the lighter? Was it an expensive one?'

'Sure. It was real silver . . . old, pre-war. It had been a gift from his pop and it had his initials on . . . and a buffalo engraved on it, quite distinctive. He was real fond of that lighter.'

'Sure was,' Todd Weringer interrupted. 'He was showing it round in the bar to some of the guys the night we arrived here. Said it had seen him through the war.'

'So a lot of people knew he had it?'

'You're not saying he was murdered for some darned lighter?'

'People have been murdered for less, Mrs Openheim,' Rachel said seriously. 'Just who was in the bar when he was showing it round?'

'Look, Officer, you can't possibly suspect any of our guys.' Todd Weringer sounded indignant.

'Oh no, Mr Weringer.' Wesley was at his most tactful. 'But they might be valuable witnesses. Someone else in the bar could have overheard.'

'There was no one else. Just a minute.' Todd Weringer frowned with concentration. 'There was an English couple . . . respectable-looking, I guess, young.'

'How young?'

'Say forty-five . . . fifty.'

Rachel smiled to herself. 'Anyone else?'

'The young girl behind the bar . . . and Mrs Slater, the owner: she was there part of the time, I guess. She came in to ask us if everything had been okay at dinner. And there was a lady with her.'

'What lady?'

'I don't know. I'd never seen her before.'

'Can you describe her?'

'About my age.'

'Middle-aged,' Dorinda chipped in helpfully.

'White hair . . . quite an elegant lady, I guess.'

'Have you seen her since?' Weringer shook his head. 'And you don't know who she was?'

'No idea. Is it important?'

'Probably not, Mr Weringer. But in our line of work we've got to think of everything.' Wesley gave him a brief, businesslike smile. 'We'll keep our eyes open for this lighter, Mrs Openheim. It'll probably turn up. By the way, do you know that Mrs Sally Johnson's gone missing?'

'Yeah . . . we heard. Is there no news of her yet?' Dorinda Openheim looked concerned: whether this was real or feigned, Wesley couldn't tell.

'Not yet, I'm afraid. How well do you know her?'

'Not that well . . . only saw her at our annual reunions. Seemed like a nice girl . . . very English.'

'Did she know Norman?'

'I guess so. He said he remembered her from the war . . . when she was dating Ed. They had a lot of dances . . . I guess the girls round here didn't know what had hit 'em.'

'Probably not,' Rachel said with understanding. The influx of a horde of lively, generous young men who possessed the added glamour of coming from the land of movies and plenty must have made quite an impact on the sheltered girls of the English countryside. 'Did she know Norman well?'

'Neither of them spoke about it if she did. I didn't get the impression they'd had a thing going, if that's what you're getting at. They were just friendly . . . sociable.'

'Rather like you and Mr Weringer?' Wesley couldn't resist testing for a reaction. Rachel shot him a warning look.

Dorinda blushed under her thick foundation. 'Yeah . . . I guess so.'

'Old comrades, Sergeant,' said Todd Weringer earnestly. 'There's always a bond there.' He stood up to go. Dorinda looked at him appealingly, fluttering her eyelashes in a way that Rachel considered quite inappropriate for a woman in her mid-sixties.

'Just one more thing, Mrs Openheim,' she said. 'Do you know anyone called Marion?'

Dorinda turned to face Rachel, her eyes wide with fear. She quickly composed herself. 'Who?'

'Marion. A local woman who was friendly with your late husband during the war. He went to see her on the afternoon of the day he was killed.'

'It's news to me. He told me he was going to look at Tradmouth Castle.'

'Didn't you offer to go with him?'

'He knows I hate that sort of thing.' Norman had chosen his lie carefully.

'Did you know about Marion?'

'You might as well tell them, Dorry, or they'll think we've gotten something to hide.'

'Mr Weringer's right, Mrs Openheim,' Rachel said gently.

'I found this letter in his case. I screwed it up and threw it away. It was from a Marion.'

'When did you find it?'

'After he was killed.'

'Why didn't you tell us about it?'

'Pride, I guess. If he'd been carrying on . . .'

'It was fifty years ago, Mrs Openheim. Didn't you read the letter properly?'

'No. Why should I? I could see it was from some broad . . . I could guess what was in it.'

'If you'd read it properly you'd have discovered that they hadn't met since the war. Hardly a reason for concern.'

Dorinda glared at Rachel, who suddenly saw it all. Norman had provided the money and done as he was told while Dorinda was free to spend and enjoy herself as she wished. It was the danger of the worm turning, the faithful dog biting its mistress, which had worried Dorinda Openheim. Marion, a shadowy love from the past, could have been a considerable threat. If Norman had abandoned his wife for a more comfortable woman, where would Dorinda have stood financially? Would Todd Weringer have offered her any security for her old age? They only had her word that she'd found the letter after his death. Was the discovery of Marion's existence worth murdering him for?

Wesley decided to leave the car at the hotel and walk back up to the incident room. It was a beautiful day . . . too good to waste. Rachel, who was still having pangs of conscience about what her bathroom scales had told her so bluntly that morning, agreed. Exercise would do both of them good.

Gerry Heffernan was wrestling with an ever-increasing pile of paper. 'Forensic reports have come back. Nothing much found at the murder scene. Rubbish mostly . . . nothing to do with Norman Openheim except a half-smoked fag. Probably smoking it when he died. They say smoking kills you, don't they?'

'Did they find the packet it came from?'

'No.' Heffernan looked interested. 'Funnily enough, they didn't.'

'Anything else?' Wesley asked.

'Empty lager cans, crisp packets, used condoms . . . lab asked us if we wanted a DNA analysis of their contents. I said no thanks. Whatever Norman was up to in that chapel it wasn't fornication.'

'Not this time anyway.'

Heffernan looked at his sergeant expectantly.

'It's where he used to meet Marion for a bit of how's your father. But that was fifty years ago.'

'See, Wes, sex wasn't invented in the 1960s.'

Wesley thought it best to change the subject. 'Any word on Mrs Johnson?'

'Car's not been sighted yet.' Heffernan buried his head in his hands. 'Of all the places in all the world, why did those Yanks have to come here . . . specially in the middle of a crime wave. There was another break-in last night . . . weekend cottage near Tradmouth. Same MO, usual things taken . . . tellies, videos, small high-value items. There was an ornamental dagger nicked this time . . . can't think why someone'd want a thing like that in their weekend cottage. Let's hope nobody thinks of using it . . . one murder's enough to be going on with.'

'Any news of our friend Rat?'

'No, but it's my guess he hasn't gone far . . . not if he wants to scrounge off his old gran.' Heffernan stood up. 'I fancy having a look at the murder scene. I could do with a bit of inspiration on this one. You coming?'

'Can we give the go-ahead to start the dig yet?'

'Don't see why not. SOCO have been over it . . . they won't have missed much. And if your mates come across a knife, they can hand it over like good citizens, can't they?'

They walked the short distance from the village hall to the chantry, passing through the heart of the village with its pretty pastel cottages.

The parish church of St John's stood to their left, set in the spacious green of its churchyard. A long path led between the gravestones up to its ancient porch.

'Have you been in the church, Wes?'

Wesley shook his head.

'I thought I might have a quick look round this lunch-time. Nothing like an old church for a bit of peace and quiet . . . and it's right next to the pub. Whoever planned these villages had the right idea.'

They reached the chantry, half hidden within its copse of trees and bushes. It was much tidier there than when they had last seen it. All the litter had been taken away for examination. The blue-and-white tape cordoning off the area still flapped in the breeze. Heffernan strolled over to where Norman Openheim's body had been found.

'Bet this place has seen some action in its time. Norman would have been standing here having a quiet fag remembering his bit of it.' He turned his back on Wesley. 'Come up behind me as if you're going to stab me.'

Wesley obliged.

'How did you feel? What was going through your mind?'

'How do you mean, sir?'

'What would be your biggest concern?'

'That you might turn round? You might start fighting back?'

'But if you knew I couldn't hear you, that my hearing aid was broken, you'd feel a lot safer, wouldn't you?'

'Unless I was much younger and stronger . . . and remember, I've got the knife and you haven't, and I've got the advantage of surprise.'

'You're right, Wes. That's my theory out of the window. Just a thought. If we could find the weapon . . .'

'Or the lighter. And it looks like whoever killed him pinched his cigarettes too.'

'All points to our friend Rat.'

'Doesn't everything . . . including his calling card.'

'That dead rat's not his style, surely, Wes. He'd just stab, rob and run.'

'We've got to pull him in just the same. He's the best we've got and he hasn't even got his mates to give him an alibi . . . he went off on his own merry way on Sunday night. Are we going to hold his mates?'

'Nothing to charge them with. We'll let 'em go and if they meet up with Rat again that'll make him easier to find. As a group they're pretty visible, the four of them.'

'Four?'

'Don't forget Fang.'

'How could I?' Wesley said with feeling. The dog's smell had been memorable.

There was a scuffling at the other end of the chapel. Neil stood there, slouched against the ruined arch that had once been the great doorway. 'They said you were up here.' He addressed the inspector. 'Look, is it okay with you if we start here now? We've got equipment booked and . . .'

'Yeah, I don't see why not. As long as you don't entice my sergeant away from his duties. We've got a murderer to catch, you know.'

'Great.' Neil looked round the site with hungry anticipation. 'I'll tell the others.'

'Just let us know if you find the murder weapon buried anywhere, eh?'

Neil ignored Wesley's ignorant boss and continued, 'We'll try

71

and locate the graves of these Spaniards . . . check out all the local stories. And there's documentary evidence of a whole range of buildings round the chapel . . . a sort of mini-monastery.'

'For very small monks.' Heffernan had had enough of the intellectual stuff, and he could see that his sergeant was becoming increasingly fascinated. 'Come on, Wes, we've got work to do . . . come back to the twentieth century.'

Wesley raised a reluctant hand in farewell and followed Heffernan back to the incident room. At that moment dead Spaniards seemed a lot more appealing to him than dead Americans.

Steve Carstairs got out of his car and put his hands in the pockets of his leather jacket. He strolled casually up to the small village shop just as he had seen the DCs on television police dramas stroll up to the entrance of a gangster's haunt in the seedy centre of some decaying metropolis. Oh, for the excitement of the Met: he'd be off to London like a shot if his mum wasn't quite so good at providing for his every need. It would be impossible to keep the hours Steve did at work and play and still do your own washing.

WPC Trish Walton, young and new to the job, followed Steve warily, secretly excited at being put with someone from CID . . . especially someone attractive from CID. She adjusted her hat and followed Steve into the shop, standing behind him as he flashed his warrant card at the shopkeeper.

The thin, balding man suddenly looked indignant. 'That's three days I've waited. They sent some young PC who didn't look as though he'd been out of school five minutes . . . he didn't seem interested. I told him. I said . . .'

'Sorry, sir, I'm not with you.'

'Shoplifter . . . pinched some cans of lager from over there. Ran off . . .'

'Sorry, sir, we've not come about that. Have you seen this woman at all?' He produced a fuzzy photograph of Sally Johnson, the best her husband had been able to provide. 'She used to live at this shop fifty years ago . . . name of Sally Johnson. It's thought she might have come back here.'

The shopkeeper looked annoyed. 'I'm not interested in some woman who used to live here. What are you doing about my lager? I can't afford shoplifting . . . it's hard enough to keep this place going as it is.'

Steve looked around at the shop, laid out like a miniature supermarket. The shelves were half filled with the bare necessities . . . hardly the place to buy your smoked salmon and sun-dried tomatoes.

'I suggest you keep all the drink behind the counter, sir. That's what they usually go for.'

'There's normally no problem. I know all my customers . . . mostly old folk who've got no cars and can't get to the hypermarket outside Tradmouth.'

Steve took out his notebook – better show willing. 'So who was this shoplifter? Some old dear getting a bit forgetful?' He smirked.

The shopkeeper wasn't amused. 'It was some young tearaway with a shaved head, dressed like a tramp. I knew he was trouble as soon as he came through that door.'

'Anything else you can tell me about him?'

'In his twenties, I'd say. Vicious-looking character . . . dirty . . .'

'We'll keep an eye out, sir.'

'Four cans, he stole.'

'As I said, sir, we'll keep an eye out.' Steve pushed the photograph of Sally Johnson forward. 'Has this woman been here at all?'

The shopkeeper shook his head.

'And you've not seen her in the village or hanging around outside the shop?'

'I've got no time to notice who's outside the shop. I'm open till ten most evenings.'

The shop door opened and a woman came in, smiled at the shopkeeper and picked up one of the wire baskets at the door. A customer. The shopkeeper's manner changed. 'Morning, Mrs Penrose. Nice day again.'

'We'll leave you to it,' Steve said as he pushed the photograph back into his wallet. 'If you see the woman, let us know, won't you.'

The shopkeeper was about to answer when Mrs Penrose placed her basket containing a lonely box of teabags on the counter in front of him.

Steve, hands in pockets, sauntered back to the car. 'Another blank . . . CID work isn't all glamour, you know, Trish. You stick with me and you'll learn a thing or two about detection.'

WPC Trish Walton wasn't so sure about Steve's last statement.

Rachel rubbed her eyes as she went through the statements. She had not had much sleep after her disturbed night. She had lain awake thinking of Dave and what he would do when he had to leave the flat on her family's farm. She prided herself on being an independent young woman, ambitious to progress in the police force, but the thought that Dave might take his eviction as an opportunity to move on, to move away from Devon, made her feel curiously heavy-hearted. He was backpacking around England, after all. There was no reason for him to stay once he lost the use of the out-of-season holiday flat.

She tried to put these thoughts from her mind and picked up the pile of statements on her desk, gleaned during their house-to-house visits. There had been something . . . a nagging thought. She came eventually to the one she was looking for. A Mrs Sweeting . . . a tiny bird-like woman who lived in a pink-washed cottage near the church. She had welcomed them eagerly, talking non-stop about the war and how they'd been moved out of their homes. She had spoken without resentment: it had been a great adventure for her and her friends as they had been treated and flattered by the American servicemen. She hadn't remembered Norman Openheim . . . there had been so many of them, she said. But one thing she said had stuck in Rachel's memory. One of Mrs Sweeting's sister's friends, she claimed, had been raped by one of the Americans. Mrs Sweeting had only mentioned it in passing to illustrate that life back then had its dangers. Rachel had hardly thought it relevant after all this time . . . but it was something. What, she thought, if Norman Openheim had not been the sweet young man Marion had remembered through the rosy glow of time? What if there had been a darker side to his nature . . . a member of an occupying army exercising a subtle *droit de seigneur* among the native girls? What if somebody, even after all these years, had sought revenge?

It was an unlikely scenario, Rachel admitted to herself – almost in the realms of fantasy – but it was a possibility. She would pay another visit to Mrs Sweeting . . . just for a friendly chat.

While Rachel was reading her reports an earnest young woman sat herself down at Heffernan's desk and waited, fiddling with the strings of coloured beads which dangled around her neck.

Wesley looked at her. When she had been announced, the inspector had disappeared into the toilets, telling Wesley firmly that he wasn't in. The woman sat there waiting. She was in her twenties, about Wesley's own age, and wore the uniform of the alternative society: clumpy boots, long Indian skirt and threadbare black jumper. Her nose was pierced with a gold ring and more gold hung from her stretched earlobes. Wesley approached her, cautious.

'Can I help you? The inspector's . . . er . . . otherwise engaged at the moment. I'm DS Peterson.'

'I want to see Inspector Heffernan. He's in charge, isn't he?'

'Yes, but I can pass a message on. I'll make sure he gets it.'

'He knows me. I've worked with him before. I'll wait.'

'I'll see if I can find him for you.' Wesley made straight for the village hall toilets, where he found the inspector leaning on a chipped washbasin.

'Has she gone?'

'She won't move . . . said she'll wait. Who is she?'

'Fern Ferrars. A clairvoyant . . . lives in Neston.'

'That figures.' The pretty walled town of Neston, eight miles upstream from Tradmouth, was the local capital of the alternative society. It was said by the locals that the incense could be smelt on the breeze as you approached the town. 'She said she worked with you once.'

'She made some guesses that proved to be right on a murder case a couple of years ago.'

'Don't you think you should see what she's got to say?'

'You see her, Wes.'

'She wants you. She won't talk to me.'

Heffernan sighed. 'Okay . . . but I've not got time for all this mumbo-jumbo.'

The young woman rose to her feet when she saw Gerry Heffernan. 'Ms Ferrars, what can I do for you?'

'Inspector . . .' She twisted her beads nervously. 'I felt I had to come and see you. I've had these pictures in my head . . . ever since I read about that American being killed.'

Heffernan glanced at his sergeant and rolled his eyes. 'What pictures, love? I've only got a minute . . . we're a bit pushed right now . . .'

Fern Ferrars sat down, trying to block out the inspector's scepticism. What she had seen was so real: somehow she knew that she had to convince the police to take her seriously . . . somehow. 'It happened the first time I saw the photograph of Mr Openheim in the local paper. I felt fear . . . real fear.'

'Come on, then, what did you see?' A tiny spark of interest was creeping into Heffernan's voice. Wesley sat forward, fascinated.

'I saw a boy . . . a young man, aged about sixteen, seventeen . . . with dark hair, wet, coming out of the sea. His clothes were ragged and soaking . . . he was terrified, and silver . . .'

'What kind of silver?' asked Wesley, remembering the missing lighter.

'I don't know . . . something small. And Armada . . . somehow that came into my head. Armada boy.' Fern Ferrars's face was screwed up with concentration and emotion.

Heffernan glanced at his sergeant and raised his eyebrows.

Fern Ferrars looked at him. There was a distance in her eyes that was vaguely disturbing. 'The Armada boy . . .' she whispered urgently. 'Find the Armada boy.'

The call came through. Sally Johnson's hire car had been found, locked and neatly parked in a lay-by just outside Neston. There was no sign of Mrs Johnson or of her belongings.

PC Miles, who radioed through from his newly acquired patrol car, also told Inspector Heffernan about the stains on the front passenger seat. They looked, he said undramatically, rather like blood.

Chapter Six

How those girls from the villages of Devon who married their dashing American sweethearts fared in their new country we can only imagine. Some were homesick, no doubt, in the way of exiles throughout the ages. Many must have longed for the familiar sights and sounds of their native land.

From *A History of Bereton and Its People* by June Mallindale

The car was being taken away on a low-loader for forensic examination when Steve Carstairs arrived.

'No joy at Sally Johnson's old shop, sir,' he reported to the inspector, who was staring at the small hatchback in hope of inspiration.

'Well, check all her relatives and known associates in this country, then . . . get a list off the husband.'

'Is that her car, sir?'

'Yeah.'

'Abandoned?'

'Mm . . . looks like bloodstains on the passenger seat.'

Bloodstains . . . that was what Steve Carstairs liked to hear – better than petty shoplifting. Though perhaps he should mention the shoplifting just in case it was that Rat character the inspector was so interested in. 'There's one thing, sir. This shop I went to in Maleton . . . a shoplifter spotted there matches the description of that beggar we're after.' Steve looked pleased with himself.

'When was this?'

Steve looked down, embarrassed. 'I don't know exactly, sir . . . I got the impression it was some time over the weekend.'

Heffernan rolled his eyes. 'You got the impression? Find out. Was it reported?'

'Yes, sir.'

'Well, if you look it up it'll save you the embarrassment of having to go back there seeming completely incompetent. You know what to do, don't you?'

Steve Carstairs turned round to see WPC Trish Walton looking at him enquiringly. His face flushed, he drove his car away too fast down the main road to Tradmouth.

Someone had to break the news to the Americans that they wouldn't be able to leave for London that day as planned. The only cat they would see that week was Mrs Slater's old black-and-white tom. London and Lord Lloyd Webber's musical extravaganza would have to wait for another day.

Heffernan thought he ought to be there himself to tell the party that they would be enjoying the bracing sea air of Bereton for longer than expected. The reaction was mixed, but it was the women who complained most vociferously, until Colonel Sharpe, the undoubted leader of both genders, pointed out that they could hardly leave while Sally Johnson was still missing: it would be a gross dereliction of duty.

The inspector left the party to it, to moan and argue amongst themselves. He had told them how things were . . . done his bit. He was about to make a strategic exit when he saw Colonel Sharpe approaching. The colonel, tall with smooth, steel-grey hair, possessed the self-confidence that accompanies rank. He would eat a police inspector for breakfast if necessary, but today he was in a conciliatory mood.

Heffernan went into the attack. 'Morning, sir. Sorry we've got to keep you here like this . . . but it can't be helped.'

'I understand, Inspector. You've got your job to do. I'm sure I speak for all of us when I say we want Norman's killer to face justice . . . and to find Sally safe and well, of course. I knew Norm as a kid back in '44. There's a real bond between all of us who came out of that lot alive, Inspector . . . a real bond.'

'I'm sure there is.' Heffernan took a deep breath: he could feel wartime reminiscences coming on. He was mistaken, however. The colonel took him by the arm. 'Say, Inspector, is there somewhere we can talk . . . privately?'

'Certainly, sir.' Heffernan looked around. The veterans and their wives were chattering in groups. 'The bar's empty, I expect . . . not opening time for another ten minutes.'

The colonel glanced back sheepishly as they entered the deserted bar. The smell of stale beer and tobacco hung in the air. Heffernan had always liked the smell of early morning pubs . . . no doubt a sign of his misspent youth. He breathed in deeply.

'Well, Colonel, what did you want to tell me?' He sank down into a comfortable armchair.

The colonel hesitated.

'To be honest, Colonel Sharpe, we'd be very grateful for any information you can give us, however insignificant it seems. And if it's about one of the veterans I can assure you we'll deal with anything you tell us tactfully. Is that it, sir? Have you got something to tell me about one of the men who served under you in the war?'

The colonel nodded, still reluctant to speak; he wished he had never raised the matter.

'If this man's innocent he's got nothing to worry about, and if he's not . . . would you want to see a murderer get away with it, even if you happened to be posted here with him fifty years back? Well?'

'You're right, Inspector. If he's innocent he's gotten nothing to worry about. And I'm sure he is . . . positive he is.'

'But you know something about him that's made you suspicious?'

'Not suspicious exactly . . . just uneasy.'

Heffernan sat with his head tilted expectantly. The colonel would speak in his own good time.

'It was on the Sunday evening . . . when Norman died.' He hesitated again. 'About 9.30. We'd eaten and most folk were in the bar or had gone back to their rooms. I felt like I needed some fresh air so I went outside. I intended to walk over to the war memorial, pay my private respects . . . have a quiet time to remember the men who didn't come back out of that sea alive. You understand?'

'Yeah.' Heffernan nodded.

'I did just that. It was strange being on that spot without the barbed wire and the noise of the guns. There's a theory that ghosts are some kind of recording of events . . . emotions, imprinted on a location. If that was true, boy, would there be some ghosts on Bereton Sands.' He lowered his voice. 'There were one hell of a lot of casualties. Some general made the decision to use live ammo . . . men fell like ninepins as they came up from the sea. It was all hushed up . . . bad for morale. There are some things the war memorials don't tell you.' He shook his head disbelievingly. 'Then a German E-boat attacked. Seven hundred died in terror in those freezing waters. Their landing craft were sunk, covering aircraft shot down . . . men were trapped inside their tanks and vehicles. It was a slaughter . . . we lost more men here on Bereton Sands than we did in the real thing in Normandy.' He paused. The memories still had the power to bring him to the verge of tears. 'I was a young captain at the time . . . in charge of some of those men. You can't imagine what it was like . . . such a waste. Have you seen the tank?'

'Yeah. Brought up off the seabed, wasn't it?'

'That's right. It says it all, that tank. Some poor mothers' sons were sitting in it on a landing craft, waiting to drive it up the beach. They went down with it . . . trapped inside. I can still hear the screams, the shouts for help . . . then that terrible silence. But I guess that's war.'

'At least we won, sir.'

'We sure did.' His face lit up with pride. 'You should have seen the armada of boats coming out of Tradmouth harbour on D-day. That was some sight . . . some sight.' He smiled sadly, preferring to remember the glory rather than the pain.

The colonel had been sidetracked but Heffernan had no wish to rush him. In this mood he'd be more likely to share his confidences. 'So, er, you went to the war memorial . . .' he prompted gently.

'Yeah . . . and when I was coming back I saw them sneaking out of the hotel.'

'Saw who?'

'They sure looked like they didn't want to be seen. I hung back . . . didn't want to embarrass them.'

'Where did they go?'

'They took the road up to Bereton village. They were linking arms. He was under my command back in '44 . . . always one for the ladies back then too. Look, Inspector, forget it. They can't have anything to do with Norman's death.'

'Possibly not, but you were right to tell me.'

'It was probably quite innocent . . . they went for a walk.'

'Probably. Just one thing, Colonel . . .'

'What?'

'Who are we talking about?'

The colonel swallowed hard. 'Didn't I say? It was Todd Weringer . . . and Norman's wife. It was Todd and Dorinda.'

Heffernan made for the Bereton Arms. Wesley was waiting for him.

'Am I going mad, Wes? Remind me . . . where did Todd Weringer and Openheim's wife say they were on the night of the murder?'

'In their respective rooms if I remember right, sir.'

'All night?'

'That's what they said, but I did suspect there might have been a bit of hanky-panky going on . . . but then I might just have a dirty mind.'

'So why would they leave the hotel and walk up to Bereton?'

'Did they?'

'So the colonel says.'

'We'll have to have a word with them, then. Shall we invite them down to the station?'

'No, Wes. I think it might be better to have a little chat with them on home ground.'

'Excuse me.'

They looked up. Standing before them was the young vicar of Bereton, an earnest man of medium height with a shock of fair hair. He smiled awkwardly as if he were afraid he'd just made some dreadful social gaffe.

'Hello, Vicar,' said Heffernan heartily. 'Please join us. Fancy a pint?'

'Not for me, thank you. I came to introduce myself. Simon Bradshaw.' He held out his hand. Heffernan took it and shook it heartily.

'You're the inspector in charge of this murder investigation, I believe.'

'For my sins,' answered Heffernan appropriately. He turned to Wesley. 'This is Detective Sergeant Peterson . . . he's into archaeology. He's a mate of the bloke who's digging up your chapel.'

'Oh, it's not mine, Inspector. The Church abandoned that site many years ago. I understand Henry VIII had something to do with it. Pleased to meet you, Sergeant.' He shook Wesley's hand.

'You took the memorial service for the American veterans, didn't you?'

'That's right. Colonel Sharpe wrote to me a while ago and asked if I would do it. I was delighted to, of course.'

'Did you get to talk to any of the Americans?'

'Yes. The colonel came up to the vicarage to see me when they arrived and I spoke to quite a number of the others after the service. I'd hoped to see some of them in church on Sunday but . . .'

'I don't suppose they thought of it . . . the church being out of action last time they were here.'

'That's true, Inspector. They did rather a lot of damage to the south transept, so I'm told. That's when the tomb was discovered, of course.'

'What tomb?' Wesley leaned forward, interested.

'That of a Spanish sailor, I believe . . . from the Armada. It had been covered by some heavy item of furniture – I'm not sure what – and when everything was moved for the repairs it came to light, as it were. It's covered again now with a hymn-book cupboard but . . .'

'I thought all the Spaniards were buried up at the chapel,' said Wesley, puzzled. 'Didn't the locals object to sharing a churchyard with them?'

'That's what I'd always thought. I haven't seen the tomb myself but one of my churchwardens mentioned it the other day. His father was churchwarden just after the war . . . a hereditary office, obviously.' The vicar smiled. 'If you're interested in finding out more I'd ask June Mallindale . . . she's the authority on local history round here.'

'Don't encourage my sergeant, Vicar. I've got my work cut out keeping him out of that chapel as it is.'

Wesley, slightly embarrassed, changed the subject. 'You must know the people round here pretty well, Vicar. Is there anyone you think we should have a word with?' He tried to phrase the question tactfully. He could hardly ask the vicar bluntly if any of his flock were in the habit of committing brutal murders.

'Alas, Sergeant, I don't know all the people of Bereton as well as I'd like. I've only been here two years and not all my parishioners are regular attenders.'

'Is there anyone you can think of who might be able to help us?'

'I don't know what you mean exactly, Sergeant. But if I were you, I'd start with the beggars who've been hanging round the village for the past few days. Not that I'm saying they had anything to do with it, of course, but they're out and about . . . they might have seen something.' The Reverend Simon Bradshaw was hedging his bets.

'Have you met them yourself?'

'I did make a point of talking to one of them . . . he had a shaved head. I'm afraid all I got for my pains was a mouthful of foul language.'

'Never mind, Vicar. You're not the only one,' said Heffernan.

'And of course the chantry is a haven for courting couples. It may be that someone who was up there . . . er, courting . . . saw something.'

Heffernan nodded. In the house-to-house enquiries they had tended to speak to the householder rather than any teenage children with the rampant hormones necessary for uncomfortable courting on the cold ground of a ruined building.

The vicar looked at his watch and was about to bid them farewell when Wesley remembered something that had been troubling him. 'Do you know a young man called Wayne Restorick?'

The vicar looked wary. 'What about him?'

'I just wondered if you could tell me anything about him.'

The vicar, gossip being against the principles of his calling, chose his words carefully. 'You must ask the young people of the village. That's all I can suggest. Now if you'll excuse me, I've got a funeral in half an hour.'

The vicar left.

'Nice one, Wesley,' said Heffernan, shaking his head. 'Now all we've got to do is round up the spotty youths of Bereton. Will you do it or shall I?'

Rachel put the phone down. Things were moving. Nobody at the station, she knew, actually enjoyed going down into the bowels of the building and sifting through acres of dusty files, but she had managed to charm Bob Naseby into sending some new recruit down there. Bob made the excuse that he couldn't go down there himself and get his uniform dusty: he was the face of Tradmouth police station; the person the public encountered first in their time of trouble. Appearances must be kept up.

It would probably be some time before the file was located so she decided to have another word with Mrs Sweeting . . . find out what she could. She told Steve she was going out and that she wouldn't be long. He was too busy staring at WPC Walton's black-stockinged legs to take much notice.

Mrs Sweeting's cottage near the church was the type that could be seen on many a picture postcard proclaiming the attractions of beautiful Devon. It was thatched and pink: the rose bushes in the tiny front garden, budding now, would give a fine show in the summer months.

Mrs Sweeting was glad of the company. Her arthritis prevented her getting out as much as she used to, she explained. Rachel knew that the ceremonies had to be observed: the tea, the biscuits, the chat about the weather and matters of local concern. It was fully twenty minutes before she managed to steer the conversation round to the past . . . the war.

'It was very interesting what you were telling me the other day, Mrs Sweeting, about the Americans and the war . . . the dances.'

'Oh yes, my luvver, those Yanks . . . we'd never seen nothing like 'em before. We were staying with our aunt in Tradmouth when we were evacuated from here . . . threw us all out of the village they did, and bombed the hell out of the place. We'd go to the dances the Yanks held on a Saturday night . . . spent all Saturday getting ready we did. We put gravy browning on our legs . . . we must have smelled like the Sunday roast. No wonder the Yanks kept giving us stockings. Very generous they were.'

'But your friend got attacked.'

Mrs Sweeting looked confused. 'My friend?'

'You told me last time I was here . . . she was attacked by one of the Americans.'

'Oh dear, yes . . . it wasn't my friend. It was my sister's friend.'

'What was her name?'

'I don't know . . . I don't know who it was. Things like that weren't talked of in those days. You just heard a whisper . . . just a hint and a few raised eyebrows. All I know is that I overheard that someone had been . . . you know . . .'

'Was it reported to the police?'

'I really don't know.'

'Do you know what became of the girl?'

Mrs Sweeting shook her head. 'My sister might know.'

'Could we ask her, do you think?'

'I could mention it in my next letter.'

'Letter? Where does your sister live?'

'Australia,' said Mrs Sweeting with pride. 'She went out there to live with her son eight years ago. I've got some photographs here. I'll just get them.'

Rachel sat back, resigned to spending the next half-hour gazing at images of Sydney sunshine.

'Do you want the good news or the bad news?'

Everyone stopped what they were doing – sorting statements, tapping away on computer keyboards – and looked at the inspector as he stood in the middle of the room, shirtsleeves rolled up, to address them.

'The bad news is forensic's just been on. The stains on the car seat were blood.'

One of the young WPCs looked away, unable to contemplate another violent death ... or more overtime. The phone on Heffernan's desk rang. He picked it up. The rest of the room waited in expectation.

He put the phone down. 'More bad news. There was another holiday cottage done over last night. That makes two in one night. Looks like they're after a Queen's Award for Industry. I told Stan Jenkins I couldn't spare anyone from here at the moment so he's sending some of his lot over.'

'People are getting their places ready for the summer ... bringing new tellies and videos down, that sort of thing,' said Wesley thoughtfully.

'Trouble is, Wes, you're not the only one to realise that. Our villains have as well, which shows they're putting some thought into their work. I don't like it when the criminal fraternity start using their brains.'

'So what was the good news, sir?'

Heffernan, sidetracked for a moment, looked round at the expectant faces. 'Oh yeah ... the blood's a different group to Sally Johnson's. We checked with her husband. She's O. The blood in the car isn't hers. The question is,' he said quietly, 'whose is it?'

Wesley took the file of statements from Steve Carstairs.

'No sign of any woman walking a dog, Sarge. Maybe she wasn't from the village.'

'All the farms and cottages round about have been checked, haven't they?'

'Yes, Sarge. There's nothing. Looks like Mrs Johnson wasn't telling us the truth.'

Wesley contemplated the implications of Steve's last remark as he walked outside to his car. He looked at his watch. It confirmed what his stomach was telling him: it was time to eat.

But Pam wouldn't be expecting him on the dot, not during an inquiry like this. There was time to pay a quick visit to the chantry to see how Neil's work was progressing.

The site of the chapel had been fenced off from public view; a requirement of the Home Office when an excavation involved human remains. Wesley found his way in without too much trouble. Neil was glad to see him, surrounded as he was by a group of first-year archaeology students indulging in a bit of work experience and needing supervision. Matt and Jane were still diving. Neil had been assigned to dry land.

'I believe we're sharing an office.'

Wesley looked at Neil, puzzled.

'We've been given a room in the village hall. They're installing the computer today. We needed somewhere near the dig . . . we were having to shift all the finds to Tradmouth every night. I asked the vicar if there was anywhere in the village we could work from. If you don't ask, you don't get.'

This was good news. Wesley could keep an eye on the progress of the dig without absenting himself from the incident room too obviously.

'How's it going?' He surveyed the chapel. A small digger had been brought in to remove the top layer of a large trench in what would have been the nave. The students, of assorted sexes and eight in number, burrowed with small trowels in a marked-off area, their faces earnest with concentration.

'The geophysics indicate some disturbance in the area where we've started digging. We're hoping those are the graves: there's no record of any other burials in the chapel. And we've located what look like the foundations of various outbuildings . . . trouble is, we're going to have to clear a lot of vegetation away from the outside of the chapel before we can start digging.' He grinned. 'Students have their uses. I'm issuing them with scythes tomorrow and they can make a start. Dr Parsons is coming down to have a look.'

Wesley remembered his old tutor – a lady of eccentric ways and equally eccentric grey hair which she wore in a half-demolished bun. 'I'll try and get up here to see her. It's been a long time.'

'How's Pam?' Neil asked, a hint of anxiety in his voice. He had gone out with Pam in their university days until she had met Wesley. He was still fond of her, still concerned.

'She's fine. She's had no trouble with being pregnant at all. I suppose she's been lucky. We deserve a bit of luck after all the time it took.' Wesley and Pam had attended an infertility clinic until nature had decided to buck up her ideas and take her course. The mention of his wife had awakened Wesley's conscience. She would be delighted if, for one evening at least, he arrived home at a reasonable time and enjoyed his supper straight from the cooker rather than heated up in the microwave.

'I'd better get home, Neil. Pam's been seeing little enough of me as it is.'

'How's the murder going? Arrested any innocent people yet?'

Wesley, familiar with his friend's jibes against the authorities that had once arrested him for possession of a small amount of an illegal substance in his student days, responded with his usual 'No . . . not even any guilty ones.' Then he added, 'But if you see a young bloke with a shaven head who looks like he's been sleeping rough, you'll let me know, won't you?'

'Might do.'

Wesley knew better than to argue. He changed the subject. 'Did the vicar tell you that there's a Spanish sailor buried inside the church?'

'Yes. He did mention it. But it's not referred to in the book I lent you and I can't see the villagers allowing one to be buried inside the church. It was a bloody great honour to be buried inside . . . the plebs had to make do with the churchyard. I think someone got hold of the wrong end of the stick in all the rush to repair the church after the war. And the thing's covered with some ten-ton cupboard so it's not easy to have a look.'

'Will you check it out?'

'Sure. . . I'll try and go through the church burial records if I've got time. There are bound to be some documents up there referring to it. They got quite good at writing things down by 1588.'

Wesley had been watching the students digging as Neil spoke. They hadn't uncovered anything of interest as yet – fallen masonry from the chapel building and a medieval floor tile were the total haul. Something, a thud of a shoe on wood perhaps, made him look round at the hastily erected fencing that hid the excavation from public view. A head peeped over the fence, supported by two elbows. When the figure saw Wesley looking, the head disappeared and the sound of running feet on the packed earth of the footpath receded rapidly into the distance.

Neil rolled his eyes. 'Not him again. He's been watching us all day, but when I try to talk to him he just legs it. I'd hoped some of the locals might lend a hand when we get to the buildings. Don't know what he thinks we're going to do to him.'

'He's a bit slow . . . you know, special needs.'

'You know him?'

'Sort of. His name's Wayne Restorick . . . lives in the village.'

Neil shrugged. If Wayne Restorick wanted to peer at them from behind the fence, it made no difference to him.

Pam Peterson was surprised to see her husband arriving home so early. She had work to do – record cards to fill in. Supper wouldn't be ready for at least another hour, maybe two. Wesley felt a little peeved that his good intentions weren't appreciated – peeved that he wasn't greeted with a delighted kiss and his supper steaming on the table.

The dining table was covered with paper – exercise books and forms. Pam resumed her work while Wesley sat himself down on the sofa and read the paper, annoyed with himself for feeling annoyed – Pam had her work to do after all, and a man shouldn't feel resentful when his wife gave her attention to her career. This is what his head, his conditioning as an educated man of the modern age, told him . . . but it would have been nice if she could have had his dinner ready when he returned from a tough day. Wesley found he couldn't concentrate on the paper and its stories which seemed to swing between the boring and the scandalous. After fifteen minutes of silence he decided to speak.

'How are you feeling?'

'Fine. This one's kicking away, though. I find the kids watching my stomach. You can see him moving through my clothes . . . like something out of *Alien*.'

She patted her stomach and laughed softly. Wesley took pity on her, working her way through the piles of paperwork. Tomorrow he could well be working late again: he really ought to do his bit when he got the chance.

'Shall I make the supper?'

Pam grinned at him. 'I thought you'd never ask. Look through the freezer. There's bound to be something.'

Wesley obeyed. A frozen shepherd's pie found its way into the oven.

'Any news on Sue and Jim?'

'I haven't seen them.' Pam sounded concerned. 'And I hardly like to go round. Sue said they've got till next week.'

'Let's hope something turns up for them.'

'Not much chance of that. Let's not talk about it, eh? I hate even thinking about it.'

Wesley indulged her. He didn't want to think of their neighbours being made homeless any more than she did. Twenty minutes to supper. Wesley discarded the paper which contained nothing but politics and sex with a seasoning of violent crime. He looked round for something that would take his mind off the problems of everyday life and eagerly seized upon Neil's book about Bereton which was lying on the cluttered coffee table.

He flicked through it, not reading properly – that could wait till he had more time – but scanning the pages for anything interesting that caught his eye. He saw a section on the local girls who had married American GIs in the war. There were no names: Ms Mallindale's writing was high on generalisation and short on specifics, a style that Wesley found intensely irritating. He flicked backwards, past the eighteenth century and the Civil War to the section that described the events of 1588.

He read the flowery speculations about the thoughts of the Spanish sailors as they stumbled up Bereton Sands. He craved hard facts based on well-conducted research, not romantic suppositions. There was a mention of the burials in the chantry but only an oblique reference to one of the sailors, a young boy in his teens, who had been sheltered by a local family with tragic consequences: no hint was given of what these consequences might have been. It was all too much for Wesley. He threw the offending book to the other end of the sofa and got up to see how the shepherd's pie was faring.

But something in June Mallindale's overdramatised account reminded him of Heffernan's visitor, Fern Ferrars, the inspector's self-appointed psychic consultant. She had spoken in the same terms as June Mallindale; maybe she had read the book. What was it she'd said? A boy coming up from the sea . . . the Armada boy. Find the Armada boy. Maybe Neil would do just that.

It was nine o'clock. Gerry Heffernan had no qualms this time about ringing Wesley. He was hardly likely to have put himself to bed yet.

Heffernan was one of that rare and unregarded breed of human being who didn't possess a car. Parking was a virtual impossibility at his small whitewashed cottage at the end of Baynard's Quay, and Tradmouth's steep, narrow streets had been difficult to navigate by horse and cart, let alone carriages of the horseless variety. Heffernan used whatever public transport was available or, when on duty, relied on another police officer to get him to his destination.

Wesley picked him up at exactly 9.30, trying hard to contain his curiosity. 'Where are we going?'

'Seddon Hotel, Neston.'

'Am I allowed to ask why?'

' 'Course you are. But I was going to keep it as a surprise.' Heffernan was grinning widely. He was in a good mood.

'Well?' said Wesley impatiently, turning the car on to the Neston road.

'It's good news, Wes. A call came through at five to nine from reception at the Seddon. Someone there who'd been listening to the local news on the radio when they should have been working said she'd just checked in.'

'Who?'

'Sally Johnson, our GI bride. She's alive and well and stopping in Neston.'

Chapter Seven

The parish church of St John, Bereton, has been the jewel of our village for over six centuries.

During the Second World War the church's treasures were taken away for safe-keeping when our village was evacuated. The largest item to be moved was our magnificent rood screen, dating from the fifteenth century. Whatever could not be removed from the church was sandbagged. The Bishop of Exeter left a touching message on the church gate explaining to our allies what the church meant to our community and entrusting it to their care. But war is a destructive business: the church received a direct hit which blew out the south wall.

From *A History of Bereton and Its People* by June Mallindale

The Seddon Hotel had been built in the age of coach and horses, that much was obvious from the archway leading to the cobbled courtyard, big enough to let through a carriage of Dickensian proportions. The Seddon, half timbered with its leaded windows twinkling golden in the night, evoked pictures of Mr Pickwick and Merrie England . . . a suitable retreat for the home-coming exile.

Wesley and Heffernan stepped up to the monumental oak reception desk. An efficient-looking young woman in a severe grey suit greeted them with a corporate smile. They showed their identification and the smile was switched off.

'It was the new girl, Inspector. She was typing up some invoices in the back office and she happened to be listening to the radio. She recognised the name . . . Sally Johnson. She checked in this afternoon.'

'Right. Thanks for telling us. Can we speak to Mrs Johnson?'

'I'll just ring up to her room.' The phone in Sally Johnson's room was answered promptly. 'She's on her way down,' the receptionist said almost in a whisper when she'd put the phone down.

Wesley and his boss fixed their eyes on the fine oak staircase, deeply carpeted in claret red. A woman appeared at the top. Wesley looked away in disappointment. She glided down the stairs, tall, elegantly dressed in a simple blue dress that flattered in all the right places. Her ebony skin was skilfully made up to enhance her fine cheekbones and her hair, straight and shining like jet, was pulled back in a knot. She was stunning, Wesley noted, a little older than him perhaps . . . early thirties. She approached Wesley, smiling confidently. 'You wanted to see me, Officer . . . not another speeding ticket, I hope.' Her voice was well bred, Home Counties. She held out her hand. 'Sally Johnson.'

Wesley stared at her for a moment. 'I'm sorry?'

'Sally Johnson . . . you wanted to see me.' She tilted her head expectantly.

'I'm terribly sorry, madam. I think there's been some mistake. We're looking for a missing woman . . . a Mrs Sally Johnson. An American lady.'

'And quite a bit older than you, love,' Heffernan chipped in bluntly. 'Sorry to have bothered you.'

'That's quite all right.' She looked Wesley up and down, reluctant to let him go. 'As a matter of fact I'm down here covering the Neston Arts Festival for the *Daily Bugle*. I've heard about this missing woman . . . GI bride, wasn't she? If there's anything you can tell me about the case . . .' She gave Wesley a meaningful look. 'I'm sure my editor would be very grateful . . . and so would I. After all, the festival happens every year and one controversial playwright is very much like another.' She smiled. She was a very good-looking woman . . . and she was pointedly ignoring Heffernan. 'How about you join me for a drink, Sergeant?'

'Put him down, love. He's a married man.'

Wesley looked at his boss gratefully. Sally Johnson was a woman who was not used to taking no for an answer. At that moment all he wanted to do was to get home. 'I'm sorry, Mrs Johnson. . . .'

'Miss.'

'I'm sorry, Miss Johnson, but there's been a misunderstanding. We really must be going. Sorry you've been bothered.'

Wesley made a rapid exit.

'I think you clicked there, Wes.'

'Not my type, sir. Too pushy.'

'Very wise. Beware of journalists offering drinks. I wonder if she did it on purpose.'

'What?'

'Called herself Sally Johnson . . . same name as the missing woman. I wonder if this was all planned.'

'It's a common name.'

'It was just a thought. Good way of getting a bit of inside information, though . . . get one step ahead of the opposition.'

'It didn't work, though, did it?'

'Only 'cause I've got no manners. Get on to the *Daily Bugle* tomorrow. Ask them if they've got a Sally Johnson down here covering the arts festival.'

'And if they haven't?'

'We just remind her that wasting police time's an offence and give her the press release like everyone else.'

'That doesn't give much away, sir.'

'Precisely. Fancy a pint?'

It was 9.30 the next morning when Gerry Heffernan entered the double-glazed portals of the Clearview Hotel. He had been disappointed the previous evening when Wesley had insisted on sticking to a single half-pint and getting back home early; now he saw the wisdom of his sergeant's strategy. He told himself he should have taken note of the sermon he had sat through the previous Sunday and considered the needs of others: just because he had to return to a cold, empty house, he had to understand that Wesley's circumstances were different.

They had rung the *Daily Bugle* offices and checked out Sally Johnson: she was who she said she was – arts correspondent down to cover the annual arts festival at Neston. Wesley was relieved that he wouldn't have to seek her out and interview her: he had found her unsettling, though he would never have mentioned this to Pam.

Now they came in search of another unsettling woman. They

93

asked for Mrs Openheim and Mr Weringer at the reception desk, and Dorothy Slater, ever efficient, sent a young girl who was sitting at a computer behind the desk up to their rooms. The girl left her post, a bored look on her face. Mrs Slater explained that she was there on work experience. She obviously wasn't finding the experience to her liking – not even a murder investigation evolving around her could lift the blanket of tedium.

The girl returned after a few minutes and announced that there had been no answer when she had knocked on their doors. She resumed her seat behind the computer, resigned to another day of mind-numbing boredom. Mrs Slater handed Wesley two keys. 'You might as well go up and check.'

'Very public-spirited of her,' commented Wesley as they climbed the stairs.

'She doesn't want any of her staff walking in on a couple of corpses, more likely. Didn't you notice she looked nervous?'

'Not really, sir. She always looks like that.'

'As if her knickers are too tight, you mean?'

Wesley smiled. 'Something like that.'

The work experience girl had been correct in her deductions. The rooms were empty. Heffernan undertook a swift search of Todd Weringer's belongings.

'Should we be doing this, sir?'

'Doing what, Wes? I'm just being nosy. I'm a nosy person.' He flicked through the diary that he found in the inside pocket of Weringer's jacket. 'Let's see . . . what does it say about Sunday night?'

'What do you expect it to say, sir? Murdering N.O. 10 pm . . . old chapel?'

'You're right as usual, Wes . . . nothing. Still, I'll be interested to see how Mr Weringer explains himself. He's lied to us. Colonel Sharpe saw him leaving the hotel with the grieving widow. I don't like it when people lie to us.'

'It's an occupational hazard, sir.'

'Not if we're talking to innocent people with nothing to hide it isn't.'

Wesley couldn't argue with that. They went back down to reception.

'Seen anything of that nephew of yours, Mrs Slater?' asked Heffernan in a voice the whole hotel could have heard.

She shook her head. 'I don't want to either. Mother's not been well since the weekend so she's stayed indoors. If she'd been out to the village she might have met him, then heaven knows what might have happened.'

'What would have happened? Wouldn't she have told him to sling his hook as well?'

'Oh no, Inspector, she's got a soft spot for him. He ran away from home when he was sixteen and turned up here. She wanted to let him stay but I insisted that he went back. If Mother had her way he'd get his feet well and truly under the table . . . and he'd take her for every penny she's got.'

'I've heard his friends have moved on to Morbay. Would he join them, do you think, or would he go back to London?'

'I couldn't say, Inspector. As long as he's far away from here, I don't care what he does.'

Wesley and Heffernan left the hotel: there was nothing to stay for. They would come back later to talk to Todd and Dorinda. The Americans were strangers in a strange country . . . they wouldn't have ventured far.

They were nearing the carpark when they heard running footsteps behind them. They turned to see the work experience girl, her face uncharacteristically animated, the bored expression gone; when there was interest in her eyes she looked quite pretty.

'Excuse me.' She was breathless from running. 'I heard you were looking for Mrs Slater's nephew . . . that beggar. I saw him yesterday.'

'Where?'

'He was hanging around the hotel a few days ago with his mates. He always made remarks to me as I came into work so I recognised him. He was running towards the trees at the back of the hotel . . . over there.' She indicated with a sweep of her arm.

'What time was this?'

'When I left work . . . five, it'd be.'

'Did he see you?'

'Oh no . . . he was in a hurry.'

'Alone?'

'Oh yes.'

'Do you know Mrs Slater's mother?'

'I've seen her around.'

'And you don't know if this nephew of Mrs Slater's managed to see his grandmother?'

The girl shrugged. 'I don't know. Shouldn't think so.'

'Thank you . . . er . . .'

'Melanie . . . Melanie Cookson.'

'Thanks, Melanie. You've been a great help.'

Melanie smiled shyly and ran off back to the hotel like a startled deer.

'Well, at least we know he's still about, sir.'

'Oh aye . . . I don't think he'll be going far if Granny's such a soft touch. Has Steve checked up on that shoplifting yet? It's a long shot but it could take our friend Rat out of the frame for the murder if he was three miles away without the benefit of the infernal combustion engine to whisk him to the scene of the crime.'

'We'll ask Steve when we get back . . . if he hasn't been too busy dreaming about fast cars and loose women he might have had time to have a butcher's at the reports for Sunday night.'

'Oh, Sergeant Peterson . . . who taught you to be so optimistic?'

Wesley's optimism was justified. Steve had tracked down the report of shoplifting over at Maleton. The offender, fitting Rat's description, had walked into the village store just before the shopkeeper was closing up. The time had been about quarter to ten on Sunday night.

'How far did you say Maleton was from here?'

'Three miles, sir.'

'And the shopkeeper's sure he had no transport?'

'According to the statement, the offender ran off. It was dark so he couldn't see where he went. He definitely didn't hear a car engine.'

'Three miles in fifteen minutes . . . unless he ran or walked at a cracking pace it'd be impossible without transport. Next step is to show the shopkeeper Rat's photo and see if we can get a positive ID. Ask around the local bus and taxi companies too . . . find out how he got to Maleton in the first place. He could have walked, I suppose.'

This gave Steve Carstairs more than enough to be going on with. He sighed and winked at Trish Walton. She looked away.

Wesley was sorting through reports of sightings of Sally Johnson. They were coming in from all over: Scotland, Wales, every conceivable corner of the British Isles including Northern Ireland. He ignored most of them: cranks, the well-meaning – they all had to get their two-pennyworth in when it came to a missing person. Wesley had a strange suspicion that Sally Johnson was to be found not far away . . . if she was still alive. Devon was all she knew, after all. He looked up from his reports to find Rachel standing there. He noticed that dark shadows had formed beneath her eyes. She looked as if she hadn't slept for several nights. 'You all right, Rachel? You look tired.'

She perched on the edge of his desk, showing an expanse of shapely leg. Wesley averted his eyes.

'I'm okay, thanks. It's just . . .'

'Just what?'

'It doesn't matter.'

Wesley wasn't going to push it. She would talk about it in her own good time if she wanted to.

Rachel resolved not to let her personal life affect her work. 'I thought it'd be a good time to go and see Carole Martin . . . Norman Openheim's daughter. That okay with you? Shall I take a PC or . . .'

'No. I'll come with you. I'd be interested to meet her.'

'Yeah . . . all that high romance. The result's probably plain, overweight and wears a beige cardigan.'

Wesley laughed. But Rachel's prediction would prove to be correct. They parked outside the whitewashed council house in the middle of the estate on the outskirts of Tradmouth. The net curtains at the window were respectably white and the front garden was neat but not the work of a keen gardener.

Carole Martin answered the front door: plain, overweight and draped in an old beige cardigan. Her hair, mousy brown peppered with grey, was swept back in an untidy ponytail. Her face, before it had acquired its double chin, would once have been quite pretty. But Carole Martin had let herself go many years back. She had inherited her tendency for weight gain from her biological father and had done nothing to struggle against nature.

Wesley introduced himself and Rachel. Carole showed them into the living room nervously and asked them to sit down.

'It's about my real dad, isn't it?' Her voice was high-pitched and didn't match her appearance. 'My mum said he'd been killed. She was really upset.'

'I'm very sorry about your father,' said Rachel genuinely. 'It must be very upsetting for you . . . even though you never met him.'

'That makes it worse, really . . . that I'd never met him. He'd not got any other children, my mum said. It would have been nice for him to see me before he . . .'

'Yes . . . yes, it would.' Wesley spoke quietly. 'As Constable Tracey said, we're very sorry. Now we're trying to find out who killed him.'

Carole nodded earnestly. 'Oh yes . . . you must. I'll help in any way I can. But I can't really tell you anything. I never met him, see.'

'Did your husband meet him?'

'Oh no. Kevin wouldn't be interested in what my mum got up to in the war.'

'Or your children . . . did they know about their grandfather?'

'My son was keen to meet him. He's got this idea that all Yanks are rich, see. Thought he was going to get a rich granddad. I heard him boasting to one of his friends about it over the phone.' She smiled indulgently at the naïve ideas of the young. 'I told him, I said I bet he's as poor as we are. They're not all rich, you know.'

'Norman Openheim was fairly well off . . . he owned a garage business.'

Carole's eyes lit up, greed overcoming grief. 'Do you think we're entitled to anything, then? I am his daughter.'

'I really couldn't say, Mrs Martin. You'd have to consult a solicitor about that. There is a widow.'

'But no kids, you said.'

Wesley thought how the need for money swept aside all else . . . especially in those who didn't have any. And by the look of Carole Martin and her house, money was in short supply here. 'Does your husband work, Mrs Martin?'

'No . . . been unemployed five years now.'

'And your son?'

'No jobs round here for the young ones . . . only a bit of seasonal work and that.'

'Your son lives with you, then?'

'Oh no. He's got a flat over in Morbay,' she said with pride. 'He's eighteen now. Too old to live with his mother . . . so he says.'

'Have you any other children?'

'I've got a daughter up in Newcastle. She's got three kiddies. I hardly see them though . . . too far away.'

'Did your son know when his grandfather was arriving?'

'Oh yes. He said he was going to try and see him.'

'And did he?'

She thought for a moment. 'He would have told me, wouldn't he? If he'd seen his granddad he would have told me.'

Not if he'd killed the goose that was expected to lay the golden egg and refused at the last moment, Wesley thought to himself.

'Can we have your son's address, Mrs Martin? If he did see Mr Openheim by any chance we'd like to speak to him.'

Carole suddenly looked wary, realising the direction in which the detective's thoughts were turning. But she could hardly refuse to give him the address. She wrote it down on the back of a discarded envelope.

'Let's get over there before she has a chance to warn him,' said Wesley as they got into the car.

But the phone is faster than the car, especially when that car has to cross the river on an agonisingly slow car ferry in order to reach the other side. Wesley drove too fast on the road out of Queenswear, hurrying past farms and spring fields until they reached the outskirts of Morbay. Rusticity yielded to suburbia. The landscape became manicured, dotted with bungalows. Then, as Morbay drew nearer, the bungalows yielded to pebbledashed semis and rows of shops; the semis yielded to stuccoed Edwardian terraces – hotels or flats. Then at the centre of the resort came the promenade and the sands which had attracted summer visitors for the past century.

Morbay had once been considered rather swish. The elegant white villas still stood in their lush gardens, though many were now converted into flats. In recent years amusement arcades had begun to appear where there had once been tea rooms; the small hotels that had catered for the middle-income families who now patronised the campsites of Brittany had started taking benefit claimants to stay in business. The palm-lined streets now saw the homeless sleeping rough in shop doorways. Those summer visitors who still holidayed there tended to stay in the large and unsightly caravan parks on the edge of the town. Morbay, as the older residents would tell anyone prepared to listen, was not what it was.

Kevin Martin's flat was on the top floor of a crumbling semi-detached villa on the down-market side of town. Other villas on the street served as fancifully named hotels – the Paradise, the Bella Vista. Many had faded notices in their windows proclaiming that benefit claimants were particularly welcome. Wesley thought of Sue and Jim, his neighbours. In a short time they would inhabit this shabby world. It had only taken a bit of bad luck. He pushed this thought to the back of his mind and parked the car in the street where seagulls were busy pecking at the litter on the ground.

'Let's hope his mum hasn't rung him,' said Rachel, matter-of-fact. 'We wouldn't want him to have his story all worked out, would we?'

There was no answer when they rang the doorbell with his name on it, one amongst several. A grey net curtain twitched back in a ground-floor window.

Rachel caught Wesley's eye. 'Shall we talk to the neighbours?'

'Best not. It'll panic him if he hears the police have been asking questions. Round here they'll be able to smell police a hundred yards away as it is. We'll let him relax, then we'll come back another time.'

'You're the boss, Sarge,' answered Rachel with a twinkle in her eye. She could see the merits of Wesley's argument.

Wesley drove the car some way down the road to allay any neighbourly suspicions, then radioed through for a check on the police national computer.

The reply came back to him within minutes. Kevin Martin had convictions for shoplifting, burglary and possession of cannabis.

'No wonder his mum looked uneasy. Old Norman would hardly have been proud of his grandson,' observed Rachel.

'Good job he never met him.'

'What if he did?'

'We're in the realms of speculation here, Rachel.'

'It's possible.'

Wesley sighed. 'Anything's possible.'

Gerry Heffernan reached a natural break. He was awaiting some information which wouldn't come for another hour at least. It was a good opportunity to take an early lunch. He suggested this to

Wesley, who had just arrived back from Morbay, and the idea met with no opposition. A ploughman's lunch in the Bereton Arms was a tempting proposition.

The church door stood open when they passed. It wouldn't take long to have a quick look inside. Both men enjoyed mooching round old churches, Wesley's motives being more academic than his superior's. Without a word they walked down the long straight path that ran between the graves of Bereton's dead and entered the church.

The great oak door was remarkable in itself, studded with elaborate metalwork with a huge iron ring set in its centre. The inspector touched it. 'Quite a knocker . . . probably to wake 'em up if they fall asleep in the sermon.'

'It's a sanctuary ring.'

The two policemen turned round. The woman who had spoken was slim with long straight blond hair. The lines around her eyes, mouth and neck were the only things that betrayed her age; without them she would have passed for a young girl in her long diaphanous skirt. She carried a huge bunch of spring flowers clutched to her chest as if for protection.

'And what's a sanctuary ring when it's at home?' Heffernan asked, interested. Wesley could have told him but he left it to the woman, not wishing to intrude on her territory.

'If a wanted man got to the church and touched it, he was allowed sanctuary from his pursuers.'

'Good job they don't have 'em today, eh, Sergeant? It'd make our life harder if all the villains started making for the churches.'

'You're policemen?' She didn't sound surprised.

'That's right, love. We're investigating the death of that American tourist found in the chantry chapel. I suppose you've heard about it.'

'Oh yes. I had two policemen round the day after it happened. Do you know who did it?'

'We will,' said Heffernan with a confidence he didn't feel. 'You've not seen a scruffy individual . . . mid-twenties . . . shaved head?'

'Is that who you're looking for?'

'Let's just say we'd like a chat with him . . . share a cup of tea and a plate of biccies. . . .'

'You're from Liverpool,' she said accusingly.

101

'Does it show?'

The woman smiled – a warm, sunny smile.

'Gerry Heffernan . . . Inspector.' He held out his hand. 'And this is my sergeant, Wesley Peterson. He's the station intellectual . . . degree in archaeology.' He made the last fact sound like a secret vice.

'So you'll be interested in the dig at the chapel, Sergeant.'

Wesley nodded. 'A friend of mine's in charge . . . Neil Watson. Have you met him?'

'No . . . but I'm interested in the history of this place.' She looked down modestly. 'I wrote a little book a couple of years ago . . . about the village and its history.'

Wesley smiled. 'You're not June Mallindale by any chance?'

'That's right.'

'Neil Watson's read your book and he's lent it to me but I've not had a chance to . . .'

She looked mildly embarrassed. 'It's not very scholarly, I'm afraid . . . not what you'll be used to. I wrote it mostly for the tourist market. I hope your friend didn't find it too . . .'

'Oh no . . . he said it gave him a flavour of the place before he began the dig,' Wesley said tactfully.

'Has he found anything yet . . . the skeletons?'

'It's early days . . . these things take time. You must go up there and introduce yourself. Do you know about the Spanish sailor buried in the church?'

The smile disappeared. 'I did hear something. Do come and have a look at the rood screen . . . it's one of the finest in the district.'

Politeness dictated that they did the tour of the church and dutifully admired its architectural features. But something was unsettling Wesley – in addition to his rumbling stomach, which was anticipating the ploughman's lunch waiting at the Bereton Arms.

As they stepped outside into the spring sunshine, Gerry Heffernan spoke. 'She didn't want to talk about that grave inside the church, did she?'

'I thought it was just me imagining it.'

'She was definitely rattled.'

'Probably forgot to mention it in her book.'

102

'That'll be it . . . professional embarrassment.' He paused. 'Er, she's very . . . attractive, isn't she, Wes?'

Wesley smiled to himself. 'Very, sir.'

Rat pushed his body down firmly against the back wall of the cellar of the Clearview Hotel. He was hidden by the drums of cooking oil. He couldn't be seen by anyone who came down to the cellar to fetch supplies for the kitchens, he was certain of that.

The cellar door opened, showing a rectangle of daylight at the top of the short flight of steps. A fluorescent light flickered on. Still . . . he must keep still. He held his breath.

Whoever it was didn't stay long – just found whatever it was they were looking for and left.

Rat emerged from behind the drums, his eyes adjusting to the dim light from the high, barred windows. Half the cellar was above ground, half below, with an entrance that led on to the yard at the back of the building. The door had been easy to force. He wondered if anyone had noticed yet that the lock was broken.

He felt in his pocket for the knife: it was still there, reassuring. The pigs wouldn't get him . . . not before he'd found Gran. He knew they'd got Snot and Dog but they could look after themselves: they'd only come with him to Devon for a change of scene anyhow. They had no ties. They could head back to the smoke any time. But Rat had things to see to . . . unfinished business. His aunt – that bitch – said Gran didn't live there any more, that she was in a home, but he didn't believe her: she was lying. Why did they always lie to him? He'd got so mad that he'd pulled out the knife, but the cow still wouldn't tell the truth.

He walked about, exercising his limbs. He was hungry. He crossed the cold concrete floor to where he knew the boxes of ice cream wafers were kept. He had already raided the store. He located the opened packet and pulled out a handful of the crisp, insubstantial wafers. As his teeth bit into them the sound of crunching echoed round the cellar. They tasted good but failed to fill his empty belly. He took another handful, then another.

He was tired of waiting: tired of the tedium that was stretching seconds into minutes and minutes into hours. And it would only be a matter of time before someone discovered the broken lock on the cellar door and searched the place to see if anything had been taken.

He helped himself to another handful of ice cream wafers and padded quickly towards the door. He opened it a few inches and listened: there was no sound in the courtyard. Emboldened, he opened the door wider. The courtyard was deserted.

Rat stepped outside into the fresh air. The sun felt warm on his shaved head after the chill of the darkened cellar. He looked around, still on his guard. The last person he wanted to encounter was his aunt, the ever-efficient dragon at the gate. Gran must be somewhere here . . . he knew it.

He scanned the upstairs windows. The interiors of the guests' rooms were obscured by crisp net curtains. Nothing. Then he raised his eyes to the top floor, the family's quarters, where there were no net curtains. A few ornaments graced the windowsills; one caught his eye. It was a long way to the second floor but Rat's eyes were sharp. He could make out the vase. He remembered it from childhood visits – quite distinctive with red and yellow flowers swirling dramatically around it. His mother had said it was hideous; his aunt had agreed. But his gran had loved that vase. It had been given her by someone special, she had told him that: someone who was no longer with us, was how she had put it. Where the vase was, Gran wouldn't be far away: he knew that for a fact.

Then he saw a shape flit across the window behind the vase, a tantalising flash of snow-white hair. Gran. He looked around the cobbled courtyard, desperate for something to throw up at the window; some gravel that would catch her attention, just like they did in the films. But the yard was swept clean . . . there was nothing. He couldn't shout – that would bring everyone out to investigate the commotion.

He knew it now. His aunt – that old bitch – was lying. He had to think, had to make plans.

Rat ran silently across the courtyard and made for the sheltering trees behind the hotel.

Snot and Dog sat on the concrete plinth in the shadow of the restored Sherman tank above Bereton Sands. They didn't know what had made them return there after their release from police custody and a day's lucrative begging in Morbay. They couldn't put the decision into words. Loyalty, perhaps . . . the comradeship of shared hardship. They felt it, whatever it was, but couldn't put a name to it. They were worried about Rat.

They watched the hotel. Fang sat patiently by their side and watched with them. They looked on as people went in and out: they seemed like Americans, old and garishly dressed. A couple passed them and Dog asked politely for the price of a cup of tea. A coin was tossed. Ten pence. You couldn't get a cup of anything for ten pence.

It was a sunny day but a stiff breeze blew off the sea and set the gulls wheeling overhead. Snot stood up and leaned against the tank, watching the hotel.

'There he is . . . there's Rat.'

Dog looked up in time to see a grey figure dashing into the trees that backed the white building. 'Are you sure?'

'Yeah. It was him.'

They left their post and ran towards the trees, Fang following enthusiastically behind. They arrived at the trees, bent double, breathless. Snot called Rat's name . . . then again. They went further into the trees and called again, their voices echoing in the green dimness.

A voice answered. 'Snot . . . that you?'

'Yeah . . . where are you?'

Rat appeared from behind a tree. 'I thought it was the pigs . . . thought you'd moved on.'

'We didn't want to leave without you. The pigs got us.'

'What did you tell 'em?' He leaned towards them threateningly; his hand went to his pocket. They knew he kept the knife in that pocket.

'Nothing . . . honest. We didn't tell 'em nothing. You seen your gran yet?'

'I've seen her. She's on the top floor . . . I've seen her at the window. I knew she wasn't in a fucking home . . . that cow was fucking lying.'

'Are you going to go in and see her, then?'

'I can get in, no problem. But it has to be night . . . too many people around in the day.'

'Don't give the old girl a heart attack. If she sees you climbing through her bleeding window . . .'

'I'm her favourite grandson, ain't I? She'll be pleased to see me,' Rat said, trying to convince himself that his plan had no drawbacks.

'Why are you so keen to see the old bird?' enquired Dog as he examined Fang for fleas.

Snot laughed. 'He's after getting something in her will, ain't he.'

Rat swung round, his eyes ablaze. He grabbed Snot by the arm and spun him until he held him fast, his arm twisted up his back. With his spare hand Rat held a knife at Snot's throat. Snot, feeling the hard coldness of the blade, whimpered. Dog looked on, paralysed. Even Fang, sensing the tension, stayed silent and still.

'Let him go, Rat. He ain't done nothing.'

'Shut up, Dog. He's fucking crazy.'

The knife was pressed closer to Snot's throat.

Snot was gaining in courage. 'We can help you get back to the smoke. The pigs are looking for you ... we came back to warn you. They know you did for the Yank. They'll get you if you hang around here. Forget your gran. You can come back another time.'

The knife stayed pressed to his throat.

'He's right ... Snot's right. We didn't have to come back. We came to tell you about the pigs. Let's get back to the smoke, eh?' Dog, the youngest, looked at Rat nervously.

Rat stood, impassive, his knife held firmly at Snot's throat. Then, slowly, he eased his grip. Snot took his chance. He ducked under Rat's arm and ran to Dog, sheltering behind the younger boy.

'We've fucking covered up for you ... we didn't tell the pigs nothing. You're fucking mad ... you're crazy.'

'Okay, okay. I'm sorry ... I lost it. Sorry. How about a drink, eh?'

'Who's going to let us into a bleeding pub round here?'

'There's other ways to get a drink ... come on.'

Rat put his knife back into his pocket. Dog and Snot still regarded him warily, but Rat grinned at them as if all were normal between them; as if he had never held a knife to his friend's throat and pressed the blade into the vulnerable flesh.

Snot and Dog looked at each other, disturbed by the sudden change. They knew Rat had a temper but they had never before been at the receiving end. The experience had frightened them. They would be back to the smoke at the first opportunity. Let the pigs get Rat. He had killed the Yank ... he was bad news.

They followed him through the trees towards the village, humouring him, waiting till they could safely escape. They hoped he wouldn't make trouble when they reached Bereton ... but they wouldn't have liked to have laid bets on it.

106

Chapter Eight

The Spanish sailors were buried in consecrated ground. The chantry chapel, disused and crumbling since its abandonment in 1545, was an ideal place for the burials as it meant that the invaders would not share the churchyard with the dead of the village.

The later 'invasion' of Bereton in 1944 left over seven hundred dead as a result of the tragic events that unfolded during the final rehearsal for the D-day landings. A convoy of eight landing ships (rather like our modern car ferries only intended to carry tanks) which were making for Bereton Sands as part of Operation Lionheart were attacked by German E-boats which had somehow found their way into the area. The accounts of eye-witnesses make for disturbing reading. The sea was thick with bodies as far as the eye could see. The dead were washed ashore still wearing their life-preservers and backpacks. Many bodies were never recovered from the sea; those that were were buried secretly, as a tragedy on such a scale could hardly be mourned or acknowledged openly at such a sensitive time in the progress of the war. Death was bad for morale. My own grandmother witnessed some of these clandestine burials and was ordered never to talk about what she had seen.

From *A History of Bereton and Its People*
by June Mallindale

Rachel rang another doorbell . . . the fifteenth that day so far. PC Burrows, a middle-aged, homely officer, usually assigned to give road safety talks to primary school children, was aiding her in her search for the hidden teenagers of Bereton. The young of the village seemed to have gone to ground since the investigation had begun. They had even abandoned their usual posts at the bus shelter and the telephone box, kept in by anxious parents who feared a murderer was at large and seeking a second hapless victim.

Number 36 Church Street was an unattractive grey pebbledashed cottage adjoining the village mini-market. Its windows were new double-glazed units which destroyed any charm the house may once have possessed. Rachel saw a shape approaching behind the steel-framed frosted glass of the front door – another unsightly home improvement.

The door was opened slowly by a girl, aged about sixteen. The faded jeans she wore showed off a fine pair of pink furry slippers. She shuffled her feet self-consciously as though she had just realised that her footwear was ruining the image she wanted to project to the world. Her shaggy hair was dyed an alarming shade of red, and her nose and ears shone with golden studs.

Rachel showed her identification and asked if she could come into the house for a quick word. The girl looked confused.

'Me mam said I wasn't to let anyone in.'

'Where is your mother?'

'She works in the mini-market till seven. You come about the bike?'

'What bike?'

'My mum rang your lot on Monday morning. My dad had his bike nicked. She's not heard nothing.'

Rachel smiled sweetly. 'It's not about your dad's bike, I'm afraid. We want to talk to some young people . . . see whether any of them hang around the old chantry. Do you know anyone who does?'

The girl snorted, unable to suppress her giggles. 'Only one reason for going up there.'

Rachel sensed that confidences wouldn't be forthcoming in the avuncular presence of PC Burrows. 'Would you talk to me on our own?'

The girl looked Burrows up and down, then made her decision. 'Okay.'

'If you'd give us a minute, thanks, Constable.' Burrows took the hint and strolled off down the road, looking every inch the village bobby on his well-trodden beat.

The girl, who reluctantly parted with the information that her name was Sylvia Chard, let Rachel into the living room. Rachel sat expectantly, waiting for Sylvia to speak.

'What did you want to know about the knocking shop?'

'Knocking shop?'

'That's what we call the old chantry. It's good for a bit of . . . you know . . .'

'Can't you find somewhere a bit warmer?' The teenagers of Bereton were obviously a hardy lot.

'It's okay in summer . . . better than behind the bus shelter.'

'I thought everyone these days did it in cars,' said Rachel, trying to sound worldly-wise.

'Who can afford a bleeding car?'

There was no answer to that. Rachel continued, 'Have you been up there recently?'

'Not me. It's a bit cold.'

'Any of your friends?'

'Yeah . . . me mate Kerry, she went up there with Craig last week.'

'And did she see anything unusual?' Sylvia smirked, about to answer with a ribald comment.

Rachel rephrased her question. 'Was there anyone up there who wasn't . . . er . . .' She hesitated to use the word 'courting', which sounded quaintly archaic even to her twenty-five-year-old ears. 'Anyone on their own hanging about?'

'You mean Wayne? Oh aye . . . he likes to watch. Can't get any himself so he watches everyone else at it.' She laughed, a cruel laugh.

'Wayne Restorick hangs around the chantry watching couples? Is that what you mean?'

'Everyone knows. We take the piss – "see any good live shows last night, Wayne" – that sort of thing.'

'Were any of your friends up at the chantry on the night of the murder . . . last Sunday?'

Sylvia shook her head. 'Nobody's said nothing to me . . . I would have heard.'

'Might Wayne have gone up there, hoping to . . . er . . . catch someone at it?'

'Wouldn't surprise me.'

Rachel stood up to go.

'Is that all?'

'Have you got anything else to tell me?'

Sylvia shrugged her shoulders. 'Not really.'

'Can I have the names of your friends who might have been up at the chapel? Don't worry. I'll be discreet. I won't mention anything embarrassing in front of their parents.' Rachel smiled at Sylvia conspiratorially. She knew that sex and parents were oil and water – unthinkable that the two things could possibly mix.

Sylvia decided that Rachel could be trusted: she wrote the names on the back of a used brown envelope.

The national press coverage of the missing GI bride caught the public imagination, so much so that Sally Johnson was sighted all over the country. But Gerry Heffernan doubted if she'd have gone far – not of her own accord anyway. It was the other alternative that worried him – if she had not gone of her own accord; if someone had forced her to go somewhere she hadn't chosen to go. Rat was still at large . . . and he had a record of violence.

But it wasn't her blood on that passenger seat, so Heffernan preferred to take the optimistic view. He contacted the hospital at Neston.

The receptionist in the Accident and Emergency department sounded harassed, but she was able to confirm that a total of seven people had come in on the relevant night with injuries that required treatment. Heffernan took pity on the woman, who sounded as if she had a queue of anxious patients demanding her attention. He thanked her and said he'd send someone down.

He was about to call Steve over when WPC Walton appeared round the partition that separated his desk from those of the lower ranks.

'Sir,' she said breathlessly, 'she's here. Sally Johnson . . . she's here.'

'Is she okay?'

'Oh yes, sir, but . . .'

'But what?'

'Well, see for yourself, sir.'

Heffernan stepped out from behind his partition. His heart sank. Sitting there, crossing her elegant legs, was the Sally Johnson they'd encountered at the Seddon Hotel: Sally Johnson the journalist.

110

'Miss Johnson . . . er . . . I didn't expect to see you here. I think the WPC took you for the missing woman. You're a bit young for a GI bride, I think that's what threw her. What can I do for you?'

Sally Johnson fluttered her long black eyelashes. 'Just wondered if you had anything for me, Inspector?'

'Sorry, love. Nothing. You'll have to make do with the press releases like everyone else. If there're any developments we'll let you know, eh?'

'Don't you want to know a snippet of information I picked up on my travels?'

'What's that, love?'

'Oh, come on, Inspector. You scratch my back, et cetera . . .' She uncrossed her legs, clad in sheer nylon that any GI would have been proud to give his girl in the days when such things were hard to come by.

'Withholding information is an offence, madam.' This woman was too sexy by half and Heffernan was not going to fall for it.

'Okay. I suppose it's my public duty, but anything you get . . .'

'I'll make sure you get the first look at the press release, if that'll keep you happy. I thought you were covering the Neston Arts Festival . . . what's happened to that? There'll be a lot of alternative poets crying into their beer without the oxygen of publicity, you know.'

'Oh, missing GI brides are far more appealing than alternative poets, don't you think, Inspector?'

'I won't argue with that. What have you got to tell me, then?'

'Just that someone fitting Sally's description was seen with a young man drinking in the bar at the Seddon. That's all.'

Heffernan sat forward. 'You're sure?'

'Oh yes. I heard the barman talking about it, so I got chatting to him.'

'Why didn't he report this to us?'

He just said how this woman looked like the missing woman's photo. He didn't think it was her. She was with a young man.'

'So what makes you think he was wrong?'

'Instinct.'

'Fair enough. What about this young man? Description?' Surely Rat would be somewhat conspicuous in an establishment such as the Seddon.

'Fair-haired, early twenties, very good-looking; drank lager.'

Heffernan felt some relief . . . this was no description of Rat. 'And he had a bandaged hand.'

'Bandaged hand?'

'That's what I said.'

'When was this?'

'On the night she went missing . . . near closing time.'

Heffernan sat back and chewed the end of his pen. It was the first time in his experience that a journalist had been anything but a complete waste of space.

Wesley and Steve entered the Clearview Hotel and nearly collided with Dorothy Slater, who was rushing through to the lounge with a tray of coffee. She gave the policemen an unwelcoming look.

'When are these Americans going to be allowed to leave?' she asked Wesley, her eyes desperate. 'They do nothing but complain about being kept here. I feel like a prison governor. And they're so demanding . . . coffee, coffee, coffee. And everything must be just so. It's a strain on the staff. I've one waitress threatening to leave. They keep sending things back to the kitchens . . . not how it's cooked back home.'

Steve was about to give out the benefit of his wisdom but Wesley, tactfully, got in first. 'I'm very sorry, Mrs Slater. We won't keep them here any longer than necessary. You can appreciate that they are vital witnesses, and with Mrs Johnson going missing . . .'

'Oh, of course, you're right, Sergeant, but we've got some people booked in next week for a spring break.'

'We'll do our very best, Mrs Slater.'

Mrs Slater had said her bit. Now she came to a matter she found more personally distasteful. 'I don't suppose there's any news of my nephew?'

'Not yet. Sorry. We'll let you know when we hear anything.'

Mrs Slater had no choice but to be satisfied with this impasse, but she was uneasy. The longer Nigel – or Rat, as he called himself; goodness knows why – was at large, the more likely he was to make trouble. He hadn't come all this way from London just to slink back quietly with his tail between his legs.

But she didn't confide her fears to the two policemen. She just confirmed that Mrs Openheim and Mr Weringer had returned half an hour ago and were now in the bar.

Steve began to march purposefully towards the glass door that separated the bar from the foyer. Wesley put a restraining hand on his arm. 'Not so fast, Steve. We don't want to frighten them, do we?'

Steve hung back sulkily.

Wesley went first, strolling into the bar and acknowledging Todd and Dorinda casually, as if they were old acquaintances. He smiled and asked if he could join them. Steve drew up a stool and sat down, studying his fingernails.

'Been out anywhere interesting today?'

Wesley's friendly enquiry put Todd at his ease. 'Yeah, as a matter of fact we have. We caught the bus to Tradmouth and took a cruise up the river to Neston. Lovely little place . . . and did you know there's a market there and all the stallholders dress up in Elizabethan costume? It's really something else.'

'Did you enjoy it, Mrs Openheim?'

Dorinda nodded, still somewhat on her guard.

'It's good to see you getting about after your sad loss.'

Dorinda pressed her lips together, catching the irony of Wesley's remark.

'Mr Weringer, we'd be grateful if we could speak to Mrs Openheim alone.'

Todd stood up and put an encouraging hand on Dorinda's shoulder.

'There's just one thing I'd like to ask you, Mrs Openheim,' said Wesley quietly when Todd had gone over to the bar.

'What's that, honey?' She looked wary.

'We have a witness who saw you and Mr Weringer walking towards Bereton village on the night of your husband's death . . . about 9.30.'

Wesley said no more: he watched Dorinda's face carefully. She was giving nothing away.

'Will you tell me what you did on the evening of your husband's death, Mrs Openheim?'

Dorinda stayed silent.

'If you have nothing to hide there's nothing for you to worry about. If what you have to tell us is embarrassing, I can assure you we'll be discreet. If you'd prefer to come down to the police station in Tradmouth . . .'

'No, honey. I don't want to end up in the county jail. I'll tell you. You're sure this won't get out? These old soldiers sure like to judge folk who step out of line, and I . . .'

'Don't worry, Mrs Openheim, anything you tell us will be confidential.'

Dorinda nodded, businesslike. 'Todd and I planned to spend the evening someplace else. We were going to check into a hotel in Tradmouth . . . come back around midnight.'

'And did you?'

'Yeah . . . yeah, we did.'

'How did you get to Tradmouth?'

'We rang for a cab from the hotel and asked it to pick us up in the lane that leads to the village. We didn't want no nosy pokes seeing us going off and putting two and two together.'

'Why didn't you . . . er . . . stay at this hotel?' Steve asked incredulously. Discretion wasn't really in his nature.

Dorinda looked at DC Carstairs as if he was a particularly stupid child who needed the very basics of everyday existence explained in detail. 'For a start, Norm might have walked in on us at any moment, and these old comrades watch each other like hawks . . . and the walls in this place are so thin. You get my drift?' She smiled knowingly at Wesley. 'So you see, Sergeant, Todd and I were being discreet.'

'And your husband? Wasn't he suspicious?'

'Oh, Norm lost interest in . . . er . . . the physical side of marriage some years back.'

'Surely he would have wondered where you were?'

'Doubt if he noticed I'd gone.'

'Where was Norman when you last saw him?'

Dorinda shrugged. 'Down in the bar, I guess. I didn't go looking for him. Now, if that's all . . .'

'That's all. I'll have to confirm this with Mr Weringer, of course, and if you could give me the name of the hotel . . . and the taxi firm . . .'

'Sure, Sergeant. Anything you say.' She looked Wesley up and down. 'You sure are cute, Sergeant. Anyone ever told you that?'

Wesley noticed that Steve Carstairs was smirking.

'Oh, one more thing, Sergeant. We didn't use our own names in the hotel. Mr and Mrs Smith. Todd said that's traditional over here.'

'Yes, madam,' said Wesley stiffly. 'That's very traditional.'

* * *

114

Rachel volunteered to go to Tradmouth to confirm Dorinda Openheim's story. In all the years she'd lived and worked in the area, she had never entered the Tradmouth Royal Marina Hotel, an establishment frequented by the upper echelons of the town's yachting fraternity.

She had imagined it to be much more palatial, like the interior of one of the more exclusive ocean liners. The faded sixties splendour disappointed her. But this was where Todd and Dorinda had chosen to consummate their adulterous liaison. That much was confirmed by the receptionist and the entry in the hotel register: Mr and Mrs Todd Smith of Buffalo, USA. Todd and Dorinda had arrived at 9.45 and had departed at 11.30, causing much speculation amongst the staff. Couples there for a bit of the other, the receptionist explained seriously, were usually younger.

With Dr Bowman pinpointing the time of death at ten o'clock, it looked as though the alibi of Norman's unfaithful wife and her lover was firmly established. It was always possible, of course, that they had slipped out of the hotel and back to Bereton: anything was possible.

Rachel had ideas of her own. Norman was a harmless tourist: he wasn't robbed and he wasn't involved in a fight of any kind. But he had been in Bereton before, albeit half a century ago, and Rachel had a feeling that his death was connected somehow with that distant past . . . with something that had been stirred up by his return like sand churned up on the river bed.

She left her car in the hotel carpark and walked along the quayside to the centre of the town, admiring the display of daffodils in the Memorial Park. Boats bobbed contentedly on the shimmering river while a brass band played on the park bandstand, getting some practice in before the tourist season started in earnest. A Royal Navy minesweeper floated proudly in the centre of the river, its neat, blue-uniformed crew looking like models as they carried out their well-rehearsed duties. Rachel could have sat herself down on one of the benches that dotted the quayside and watched the world and the boats go by for the rest of the afternoon, but, conscientious by nature, she made for the police station.

Bob Naseby greeted her like a long-lost friend. 'How are you doing out there in the wilds, my luvver? Rum lot up at Bereton . . . too much inbreeding.'

'We're surviving, Bob . . . not been sacrificed by the natives yet. And what do you mean, inbreeding? From what I hear the Yanks put a stop to all that in the war.'

'I bet they did.' Bob winked. 'Any progress?'

'The usual . . . we're following a few leads . . .'

'As the dog handler said to the actress.' Bob Naseby chuckled at his own joke. 'Any sign of this missing woman? GI bride, wasn't she . . . from Maleton?'

'We're still looking. Have you got me that file, Bob?'

For a moment the desk sergeant looked confused, then he remembered. 'Oh, *that* file . . . from the war. It was a bugger to find.'

'Did you go down there yourself, Bob?'

'Me? Never. I got a young constable to go and look . . . new lad.'

'Hope he didn't ruin his uniform . . . all that dust.'

'There's worse than dust down there . . . but it'll clean.' He reached under the desk and pulled out a package encased in a new brown envelope. 'I'll give the lad his due, he used his initiative . . . couldn't have been an easy thing to find. He'll be joining you lot in CID, you mark my words. You going to let me into the secret?'

'What secret?'

'Why I've had one of my men delving in the cellar for wartime files.'

'I'll tell you when I know more myself. It's a bit of a long shot.'

'Well, I won't tell that to young Constable Jones . . . I told him it were dead important.'

Rachel leaned over the desk and gave Bob Naseby a kiss on the cheek. 'Thanks, Bob. If there's anything I can do for you . . .'

'Cricket season's starting soon. You could have a word with Wesley Peterson . . . see how he's fixed for the team. His great-uncle used to play for the West Indies, you know.'

Rachel smiled, knowing full well what Wesley's answer would be. 'I'll see what I can do, Bob.'

She walked quickly out of the station clutching the file to her breast. When she got back to her car she sat there for a while just looking at it, savouring its musty odour, anticipating the secrets it contained. She wouldn't look at it yet. She would save it for later, when she had more time. She was certain that she would find the name of Norman Openheim somewhere in that file.

Neil Watson and his team had certainly got their feet under the table at the village hall. The ladies of the Mothers Union had even made them a pot of tea – which was more than the police got: they had to attend to their own catering arrangements.

Wesley was surprised to see Neil drinking from a china cup and saucer of the classic village hall design. 'How did you manage to get that?' he asked.

'Some lovely ladies couldn't resist my charm. Some of us have got it and some haven't.'

'I thought you'd be at the dig.'

'Jane and Matt are there. The local divers say the tides are wrong for diving in the bay at the moment. Dr Parsons has arrived, by the way. She's up at the chapel now. She said she's looking forward to seeing you again ... wonders why you joined the police force. I said I'd no idea.'

'Sometimes I wonder myself.'

'She thinks you're a great loss to the world of archaeology and she said that when you showed your face I should tell you to get up there.'

'How can I refuse an invitation like that? I've got half an hour. I'll nip up now. You coming?'

'No ... paperwork. You know how it is.'

Wesley knew how it was, all right. He told the boss he was going up to the murder scene for half an hour. Heffernan nodded knowingly and told him to knock off for the day. He'd see him tomorrow first thing unless something turned up in the meantime.

Wesley, released from the concerns of the day, strolled up Church Street past the mini-market and the church towards the chantry. There were various cars parked in the lay-by, mostly of ancient vintage and wearing their rust spots with pride. He pushed open the temporary wire gate which now gave access to the site.

'Wesley Peterson ... how wonderful to see you.' A lady of a certain age, round and with grey hair that was trying to make its escape from an untidy bun, came running up to him and planted a hearty kiss on his cheek. 'Neil tells me you've joined the boys in blue. Hardly the career I would have predicted for you. I always

117

expected you to come back as a postgraduate student . . . I would have put money on it. There was always a place for you in the department, you know, especially with your first.'

Wesley looked sheepish, hoping nobody had overheard. The fact that he had obtained a first-class degree was not something he talked about in his present line of work, and to air it in the atmosphere of the dig would sound boastful. 'It's great to see you again, Daphne. How's it going?'

'We've started to uncover the first body. We located a definite grave cut and we've just uncovered what looks like a skull. Come and have a look. It's such an exciting dig . . . especially when there's been so little known about this incident apart from local legend.' She clung to Wesley's arm, her warm brown eyes twinkling with excitement. 'Wouldn't it be wonderful if we could find some artefacts in the graves? Have you seen what they've been bringing up from the wreck?'

'No . . . it's all been taken to Exeter. A body was found here, you know.'

'Of course . . . there are several of them, I hope.'

Dr Daphne Parsons hadn't changed. She lived in the time she was investigating. The past was her life, the only thing that was real to her. Wesley had always admired her single-mindedness: she had been an inspiring teacher.

'No, there was a murder a few days ago in this chapel. An American tourist.'

'Oh dear. I do hope we shall be safe, Wesley. I hope whoever did it doesn't come back.'

'There's safety in numbers. Besides, you've got police protection now.' He put his arm round her shoulder. 'Are you going to be here long?'

'I'm staying in the village for a few days . . . bed and breakfast. I tried to book that hotel by the sands but apparently it's full of Americans.'

'They were here in the war, practising for D-day. They've come back for a reunion.'

Daphne Parsons smiled knowingly. 'Oh, I remember the Yanks. I was only a little girl at the time up in Norfolk, but I'll never forget them. They used to give us children chocolate and something they called candy which would give any self-respecting dentist nightmares. They were so different, so . . .

exciting. We children thought they were wonderful . . . never seen anything like them before.'

'Yes . . . and one of them's just got himself killed.'

Dr Parsons gave a hearty laugh. 'Probably a jealous boyfriend . . . they were fiends in the war for the girls, you know. If I'd have been a few years older I'd have no doubt had a few more interesting memories than chocolate.'

She led Wesley over to where a group of students were digging under Matt's authoritative eye. There was an atmosphere of hushed expectation, of held breath, while the small area of white bone showing in the earth expanded.

Dr Parsons clapped her hands together ecstatically. 'We'll soon see it, Wesley. Soon we'll see the body of a man who sailed with the Spanish Armada.'

They watched fascinated as the skeleton came slowly into view, the earth carefully brushed away.

One of the first-year students, standing at the edge of the trench, leaned over to get a better view of the proceedings. He missed his footing and fell forward, managing to right himself at the last moment before he suffered the embarrassment of tumbling into the trench. But his foot had kicked away some loose earth, revealing something metallic embedded in the side of the trench, about two feet above the level of the bones. Matt saw it and ordered the digging to stop. Then he brushed round the object carefully until the compacted earth was worn away and a few inches of the thing could be seen. He looked up at Dr Parsons, excited.

'Bloody hell, Daphne . . . I've seen something like this before – there was one on the ship. It's gold, I'm sure of it. I think it could be the hilt of a dagger.'

Wesley was in a good mood when he returned home. Pam was there, hidden behind piles of paperwork. There was no sign of a meal being prepared – it would be the freezer and the microwave again.

She looked up and gave a half-smile. 'Didn't expect you back so early.'

'I've just been to the dig . . . saw my old tutor. They've discovered a gold-hilted dagger . . . beautiful piece. They only found it today by chance. A student dislodged the side of the trench and there it was. Dr Parsons hasn't changed . . . it was great to see her again.'

'And the boss gave you time off for this trip down memory lane, did he?' she said with some bitterness.

'We reached a natural break. How's things?'

Pam sat back and rested her hands on her bump. 'I'm shattered.'

'You should be taking things easy,' he said. He could see the dark rings beneath her eyes and the strain on her face.

She raised her hands in despair. 'How? You try telling the kids I've got to take it easy . . . and the paperwork doesn't go away.'

'Maybe you should think about giving up till . . .'

'If I give up I don't get paid. You don't want us to end up like Sue and Jim, do you?'

'It'd hardly come to that.' He went over to her and put his arms round her. She pushed him away.

'Why wouldn't it? If we had to survive on your salary . . .'

'We'd survive. It wouldn't be the end of the world.'

'And the house?'

'We'd manage . . . we'd be okay.'

'That's what Sue and Jim thought.' Tears were welling up in her eyes.

Wesley took his wife in his arms; he felt the baby move a little in her belly. 'It's terrible for them but there's nothing you can do about it.'

She started to cry. He hated it when women cried: he was always afraid that anything he said would make matters worse. He held her and said nothing, handing her a tissue when he judged the worst was over. She blew her nose and leaned against his shoulder.

'I'm sorry.'

'You sit down. I'll get supper.'

'Thanks.' She touched his face. 'I've been thinking . . . what if we let Sue and Jim have our spare room? It'd be better than one of those seedy places they put them in. . . .'

'Hang on. What about . . .'

'It was reading the work the kids had done that gave me the idea. When people were turned out of their houses in Bereton for the D-day landing practices they went to stay with friends or family in places like Tradmouth or Neston . . . places that weren't affected. Slept in their spare bedrooms, on the floors. People rallied round. That's what we should do . . . don't you think?'

'It's not a good time, Pam. You've got enough to deal with. The baby, and working, and . . .'

'Let me ask Sue. Please.'

'We really don't know them that well. When I get home I need to unwind, not have a house full of . . .'

'It'll only be till they find somewhere.'

'That could be ages. No . . . not with the baby on the way.'

'I didn't think you'd be so selfish.'

'I'm thinking of you. You're shattered as it is.'

'I'm still asking them.'

Wesley sighed: when Pam got in this sort of mood there was no arguing with her. 'Go ahead, then . . . do what you want.' He called her bluff.

She looked more unsure of her ground now. 'Okay. I'll ask them tomorrow. I'll go and put the supper on.'

'I said I'd do it.'

'No. You sit down. I can manage.' She left the room, her hand on the small of her back, a martyred expression on her face. She had had a bad day.

Wesley sat down in the chair she had vacated at the dining table and flicked through a couple of exercise books. The children had been asked to talk to elderly neighbours or relatives and recount their reminiscences of wartime South Devon. In one book he picked up something caught his eye – the word murder was printed immaculately at the head of a page of superlatively tidy handwriting. He read on. The style was immature but the content interesting.

"My grandma told me about a murder that happened in the war," it began. "A man was out shooting rabbits in Bereton and an American soldier shot him. My granddad saw it."

It was short and to the point, but intriguing nevertheless. Wesley put the book back on the pile and looked at the name of the child printed on the front – David Mallindale. Any relation to the literary June? Wesley wondered.

Rat had it all worked out; he always did. One of them would buy something small at the counter – a packet of chewing gum, something like that – while the others helped themselves to as many cans of beer as their coats could conceal. Rat made his last inspection of his troops – the final briefing, then over the top.

They had waited till dusk – easier to make a getaway if they were discovered. And it was likely they would be – any village shopkeeper would watch them closely as soon as they set foot on the premises. Things like this were much easier in the anonymity of London.

The windows of the mini-market were still brightly lit. It was very much open: people expected a village store to be open all hours. They could see inside – just a solitary woman at the till, plump and middle-aged, not one to move fast. They'd hardly needed to wait till the light disappeared – she'd be a pushover.

They left Fang tied to a telegraph pole; the last thing they wanted was an argument about dogs on the premises. Fang would slow them down, and the operation had to be quick if it was to work – Rat made that quite clear. Fang sat patiently, watching his master cross the road with his two companions and enter the mini-market, resigned to a war of nerves with a ginger cat who sat crouched on the churchyard wall near by staring at him with sly, gemstone eyes. Fang stared back: cats didn't bother him.

Dog entered the shop first, the others behind. They scattered to their separate tasks: Dog to buy chewing gum, the others to appropriate as many cans as they could without discovery. They were in luck. The beer was hidden down a far aisle. Dog was at the counter; the assistant watched him, uninterested, her only concern being what she was going to cook for tea that evening and whether her daughter, Sylvia, was still on that stupid diet of hers.

Snot and Rat busied themselves, secreting cans in the pockets and folds of their ragged coats, glad that the assistant was either too preoccupied or too stupid to realise what they were up to.

It never does to become complaisant or to underestimate the enemy.

'You put those back or I'm calling the police.'

Rat looked up to see the woman glaring at them from her post behind the counter; one hand clutched a telephone handset while the other jabbed at the number nine. Dog had left. They could hear Fang's barks outside receding into the distance. He had got away.

Snot did likewise. He dropped most of his haul but he managed to cling on to a couple of cans of strong lager as he rushed from the shop.

Rat stood, staring at his adversary. The woman put the phone down, unsure of her next move, praying silently that a couple of burly constables would burst through the door that very second and retrieve the situation. One of the thieves at least was still here . . . but it was the one who looked the most dangerous of the three. She moved warily towards the door while Rat stood by the display of beer cans staring at her. She reached the door and slipped the catch down. He wasn't going to escape . . . the police would thank her for that. She felt quite pleased with herself, with her presence of mind, relieved to see that the thief was standing statue still.

Then he made a sudden movement and she saw the flash of metal in his hand: a knife . . . he had a knife. She froze with terror. His eyes stared into hers as he came slowly towards her . . . mad, pitiless.

With an effort of will she flung herself at the door and fumbled with the latch she'd so smugly fastened a minute earlier. It wouldn't move: the door remained locked and her hands had become clumsy with panic. He was still coming towards her slowly . . . so slowly. She turned and saw the blade pointing at her, hard, shining and cold as death.

She could hear the distant siren of a police car. Her fingers, endowed with fresh confidence, managed to operate the catch. She threw open the door and ran outside into the street without a thought for the stock or the till. She thought only of escaping that sharp steel blade and the one who wielded it.

A police patrol car appeared round the corner and she ran towards it, waving her arms like a castaway sighting a rescuing ship on the horizon.

Rat followed her out, concerned not with harming the woman but with getting away. He ran in the opposite direction from the assistant, towards the church. He wasn't looking out for traffic when he ran across the road; there was never much traffic in these villages anyway. His expression when the green Land Rover hit him was one of startled disbelief. He took the impact full on, bouncing off the bonnet and on to the road. The driver, a farmer's wife delivering her daughter to the local Brownie pack, jumped from the driver's seat to see if the man she'd hit was all right while her daughter remained strapped in the front seat, howling.

The driver looked round as she heard running footsteps and was amazed to see two uniformed policemen descending on her. She looked back towards her victim to find that he was no longer lying on the ground.

He was staggering down the church path, moving fast for an injured man. The policemen stopped to mumble some reassuring words to the shocked driver before resuming their chase. Rat reached the church porch. He fell to his knees, doubled up with pain. The knife . . . where was the knife? He must have dropped it when the car hit him.

He reached up . . . reaching for the huge iron sanctuary ring in the centre of the church door. His fingers grasped it and he hauled himself up. The ring slipped from his grasp and banged against the door. He could hear the noise echoing inside the church. He grasped at it again; it fell back, louder this time . . . and again.

The vicar opened the massive oak door and stared in disbelief at the man who had just fallen across the threshold of St John's church and was lying on the stone floor in a pool of blood with two policemen watching over him like avenging angels.

Chapter Nine

During World War II relations between the people of this part of
Devon and our American allies were not always harmonious. I'm
sure Hitler's propaganda machine would have thrived on tales of
resentment, violence and even rape that the authorities of the time
tried to dismiss or cover up.

From *A History of Bereton and Its People* by June Mallindale

Gerry Heffernan arrived on the scene as the ambulance was
pulling away. The constables in the patrol car told him the gist of
what had happened. The vicar was speaking to the driver of the
Land Rover; both looked shocked. The overalled assistant from
the mini-market was being comforted by a neighbour who had
come out of her house to investigate the commotion.

Heffernan called Wesley and told him to get down to the
hospital right away, then he approached the mini-mart assistant.
She had just been joined by two other women and was holding
court, beginning to enjoy her fifteen minutes of fame.

'Hello, love. Inspector Heffernan . . . Tradmouth CID. Can I
have a word?' He looked meaningfully at the woman's entourage,
who slunk off, only to regroup a few yards down the road.

'Can you tell me what happened?'

The woman, who gave her name as Eileen Chard, was only too
ready to tell her story. The bits about facing the mad-eyed
desperado with a knife would become more polished and embell-
ished with time for the benefit of family and neighbours, but to the
police she gave the bones of the account, plain and unadorned.

'So his two mates got away? Did you see where they went?'

She shook her head. 'When they'd gone he just stood there pointing the knife at me . . . until he heard the police car siren. I reckon that's what saved my life.' She put her hand to her heart as if to calm its frantic beating. 'Is he dead?'

'No . . . but it's touch and go, apparently. Did you see the accident?'

'I'd just got outside but it all happened so quick.'

'Sir.' A young, spotty constable interrupted Mrs Chard's flow. He held out an exhibit bag for inspection. Through its clear plastic Heffernan could see a flick-knife, open, with a long, thin, lethal blade.

'Where did you find it?'

'Just in the road there, sir,' said the constable nervously. 'He must have dropped it.'

Heffernan turned to Mrs Chard, who was staring at the knife open-mouthed. 'Is this the knife he was carrying?'

Mrs Chard swallowed anxiously and nodded, imagining the thing stuck between her ribs.

'Okay, Constable. You know what to do.'

The constable turned and walked away, carrying the knife as though it were some ceremonial blade to be delivered safely to the white-coated high priest . . . the guardian of the mysteries of forensic science.

Heffernan stared after him, deep in thought. Mrs Chard brought him back to reality by muttering something about her daughter's tea. He gave her permission to go, noting that instead of going straight home to feed her offspring she was waylaid by her cronies. The daughter would have to get her own tea or go hungry.

Then he remembered where he had heard the name Chard before . . . it was the mention of the daughter that had reminded him. Rachel had interviewed a Sylvia Chard concerning the nocturnal goings-on at the old chantry. Sylvia had claimed that Wayne Restorick had gone in for a little light voyeurism in his spare time, the chapel being the time-hallowed place for that sort of thing. She had talked to some other representatives of Bereton's golden youth too. They had all told the same story: Wayne Restorick liked watching couples at it. It might be worth having a word with this Wayne – if he had been indulging in his hobby on Sunday night, he could be a vital witness . . . and they would need all the proof they could get if they were going to prove that Nigel Glanville – or Rat as he preferred to be known – had murdered Norman Openheim.

The defence would make the most of his shoplifting exploits in Maleton, but at least they had the knife: forensic should be able to prove it was the murder weapon . . . and the dead rat his calling card. There was the problem of how he got from Maleton to Bereton, but Heffernan was fairly confident the last piece of the jigsaw would turn up . . . someone who gave him a lift, a stolen car or bicycle. The inspector smiled to himself. It was all sewn up and the murderer was lying unconscious in hospital with a police guard. He wasn't going anywhere.

It was a lovely evening for the time of year . . . just the evening for a quick visit to Neston.

He walked back to the incident room in the village to see who was about. He found Rachel there, hunched over what smelt like a pile of musty old papers.

'What are you doing, Rach?'

She looked up, startled, and began to put the papers away in her desk drawer. 'Nothing, sir . . . just an idea, that's all.'

'Ready to share it with us yet?'

'I'll . . . er . . . see how it goes, sir. It might be nothing.'

Heffernan was intrigued, but he liked to see his officers using their initiative. He'd got some good results in the past by encouraging a bit of creative thinking in his team.

'Fancy driving me over to Neston? I'll buy you a drink . . . and I've got a bit of news. Our friend Rat threatened a woman with a knife and got knocked down by a car . . . how's that for divine judgement? He's been taken to Tradmouth Hospital. I reckon we've got our man. I'll tell you about it in the car.'

Rachel looked surprised. 'So we're celebrating, sir?'

'Not exactly . . . not yet. Don't go thinking this is a social drink . . . it's strictly work.'

'You're certain this Rat killed Norman Openheim?'

'Pretty sure. There's the problem of how he got from Maleton to Bereton in the time. Can you check if there were any cars or bikes nicked in the vicinity on Sunday night?'

'There was a bike nicked in Bereton on Sunday evening. A girl called Sylvia Chard said her dad's bike went missing . . . it was reported.'

Heffernan looked triumphant. 'That's it, then. Our friend Rat has certainly got it in for the Chard family . . . it was an Eileen Chard he threatened in the mini-market. Get a search mounted for this bike, Rach. If Rat nicked it and rode over to Maleton to do the shop he could have been back in Bereton in under fifteen minutes.'

'Yes, sir . . . I'll see to it. But I was thinking that if Norman wasn't robbed the motive might be something more personal – maybe something in his past, something that happened when he was over here in the war.'

'You've been reading too many whodunnits, Rach. You know as well as I do that it's usually your nearest and dearest who do you in . . . or some little toerag with a knife after money for his next fix.'

'Was Rat an addict?'

'Not that we know of . . . I was just speaking generally.'

'Where are we going to in Neston?'

'Hospital . . . where else?'

'But the suspect's in Tradmouth . . .'

Heffernan grinned secretively. 'But Sally Johnson isn't. Come on.'

They drove to Neston. Rachel listened to the tale of Rat's failed attempt at robbery in virtual silence, punctuated only by a few affirmative noises. The pitch-dark country roads needed concentration.

Neston Hospital was a modern building on the outskirts of the town, not far from where Sally Johnson's hire car had been found. The Accident and Emergency unit was built in the Roman villa style, so beloved of supermarket chains.

Heffernan, Rachel noticed, was curiously subdued as he approached the reception desk and showed his warrant card. Hospitals always had that effect on him. His wife had been a nurse, she remembered. He had met her many years ago when he had been in the merchant navy. The story of how he had been winched off his ship suffering from appendicitis, ended up in Tradmouth Hospital, married his nurse and came ashore to join the force was well known throughout the nick. Maybe the presence of so many members of his late wife's profession brought back painful memories.

It was a generous slice of luck that the doctor who had been on duty the night Sally Johnson disappeared was on duty that evening.

Dr McTaggart was a tall, red-headed Scot, who hardly looked old enough to have left school. He was pale: freckles stood out against the whiteness of his skin. His eyes were underlined with dark smudges. Dr McTaggart looked exhausted. Heffernan hoped he wouldn't have anything too complex to deal with before he got himself a good night's sleep.

The doctor looked relieved that Heffernan and Rachel appeared to be medically fit: he obviously had the same misgivings as the inspector. He sat down in a cubicle, stethoscope around his neck, head in hands.

'What do you want to know?' he yawned.

They told him. He got up wearily and led them to reception, where he dug out the records for the appropriate date. As the receptionist had said on the phone, seven people had come in that night requiring treatment. It had been a quiet night, the doctor said wistfully. There were two injuries that caused loss of blood. A farmer had cut his leg tripping over a scythe – illustrating the perils of primitive technology – and a young man had come in with a badly cut hand. It was the latter who interested Heffernan.

The doctor described him. 'Young . . . average height . . . fair-haired . . . well-spoken.

'Was anyone with him?'

'An older lady . . . spoke with an American accent. She seemed very concerned for him.'

'Did he say how he'd sustained the injury?'

'I didn't ask but he told me anyway. He said he'd cut it on some broken glass.'

'Do you think he was telling the truth?'

'He'd ripped a slice out of his hand. I had no reason to disbelieve him.'

'Have you got an address for this unlucky lad?'

The doctor nodded. 'It's all in the file.'

'And the lady who was with him . . .' He produced Sally Johnson's photo. 'Is this her?'

Dr McTaggart took the picture and stared at it with bloodshot eyes. 'Yeah . . . that's her. What's she done?'

'We don't know yet.' Heffernan returned the photo to his

wallet. He put a fatherly hand on the doctor's shoulder. 'If I were you, Doc, I'd go and get some kip.'

The doctor yawned. 'Fat chance . . . another eight hours to go yet.'

'Go and get the doc a strong coffee from the machine, Rach.' He handed her a coin. 'He looks like he needs it.'

Dr McTaggart looked up at Heffernan gratefully while Rachel stormed off indignantly in search of the drinks machine. She really would have a word with someone about the inspector's assumption that if drinks were to be provided it was always the female officer present who did the providing.

When she had gone, Heffernan turned back to the doctor. 'Now then, Doc . . . about this patient of yours. I don't suppose you'd have a name and address for me, would you?'

Friday morning dawned and Wesley Peterson was tired. Torn from his supper the previous evening and suffering from a bad attack of indigestion, he had rushed to Tradmouth Hospital to watch Rat, unconscious and sprouting tubes and wires, in case he came round.

The doctors assured Wesley that the patient was unlikely to regain consciousness for some time . . . if at all. Staying at the hospital would have been a waste of time. He put a uniformed constable on guard and returned home to Pam. Rat would be saying nothing that night. The inspector had given instructions that the injured man was to be charged with Norman Openheim's murder. Wesley had his reservations. It would all depend on what forensics came up with when they examined the knife and whether the missing bicycle – when it turned up – would have his prints on it.

The inspector was in an alarmingly cheerful mood when Wesley arrived at the incident room: a virtuoso rendition of 'A policeman's lot is not a happy one' was clearly audible through the thin partition that separated off Heffernan's inner sanctum. There were barely suppressed giggles amongst the junior ranks, and Wesley allowed himself an indulgent smile as he studied the report of Heffernan and Rachel's visit to Neston Hospital the previous evening.

Heffernan emerged from his lair. 'Thought you'd all join in the chorus.' He beamed at the assembled team. 'We had a good night last night. I reckon we've got Norman Openheim's killer and I've got a lead on Sally Johnson . . . positive sighting. I'm following that up this morning.'

Rachel, cool and neat in a yellow linen suit, spoke up. 'I'm going to see Wayne Restorick this morning, sir. There have been reports of him hanging round the old chapel watching courting couples. I thought he might have seen something.'

'I bet he has,' mumbled Steve Carstairs under his breath. Rachel heard and he was rewarded with an icy stare.

'Right, Rach, you do that. And I want someone tactful to go and do their bit for Anglo-American relations down at the Clearview. Hopefully we won't need them much longer, tell them. And find out what you can about our friend Nigel Glanville . . . or Rat, as he prefers to be known. If there's anything we haven't been told, I want to know it . . . okay? Rach . . . you go up to the hotel when you've seen Wayne Restorick. And Steve, you can organise a search for this bike that was nicked from Bereton on Sunday.' Steve nodded – surely police work should hold more thrills than tracing missing bikes.

Rachel looked longingly at her desk drawer. She hadn't had a chance to look though the old file she had purloined . . . and time might be short. If necessary she would have to stay late tonight. Dave had suggested that they go to the cinema in Morbay; he would just have to wait.

The inspector's phone rang. He jogged back to his office and picked the receiver up eagerly. It was Dr Bowman, asking him to pop along to the mortuary when he had a moment. Only Colin Bowman could make a mortuary sound like a gentleman's club.

He put the phone down and it rang again. He barked a greeting. The voice on the other end was female and sounded anxious. She spoke with breathless urgency.

'Inspector . . . it's Fern Ferrars. I've had that dream again. Every night . . . more and more vivid.'

He tapped his foot impatiently. 'Yeah . . . I'm pretty busy right now, Ms Ferrars . . .'

'Please listen. The skeletons . . . in the chantry. The answer's not there. It's somewhere else.'

Heffernan rolled his eyes. Why did they always choose him? It was always the same . . . a bus full of people and the nutter would always sit next to him. What was it about him that attracted them? He suspected it was because he was too soft. 'Well . . . er . . . thanks for ringing, Ms Ferrars . . .'

'Listen . . . please. When you find the boy then all will be clear. You must find the Armada boy.'

'Yes, love. I'll bear that in mind. Thanks very much . . . bye.'

He put the phone down and breathed a sigh of relief. Next time he'd put her on to Wesley.

As if he'd read his thoughts, Wesley appeared. 'Shall we be off to Neston now, sir? You got the address?'

'Somewhere. Hang on.' He rummaged in his trouser pockets. 'I've just had a funny phone call, Wes . . . from that clairvoyant woman, Fern Ferrars.'

'Did she tell you your future?'

'Did she heck. Now if she could finger villains for us she'd be useful. No . . . she just went on about an Armada boy again.'

'She said that before.'

'Someone should tell her the Armada's been and gone. She mentioned skeletons and all.'

Wesley looked up with interest. 'What did she say?'

Heffernan tried to think. Having dismissed Fern Ferrars as a nutcase, he hadn't been listening too closely. 'Something about not finding the answer with the skeletons . . . you've got to find the boy, the Armada boy. That's what she said.'

Wesley shrugged. 'If the skeleton of a boy turns up at Neil's dig I'll bring it in for questioning.' He grinned.

'Right, Wes. Let's see if we can find Mrs Johnson. Ready to go on the hippie trail to Neston?'

Rachel's reception the first time she had called on the Restoricks had hardly been welcoming. Now, she rang the cheap plastic doorbell and waited. WPC Walton shuffled her feet behind her, a nervous habit she had noticed before . . . only the nerves it was getting on were Rachel's.

Annie Restorick answered the door, her expression wary, even hostile.

'Could we come in for a quick word, Mrs Restorick?' Rachel said confidently, flashing her warrant card.

'No. I've got Mother on the toilet.' She was about to shut the door when Rachel put out an arm to stop her.

'We want to talk to your son, Mrs Restorick. We want to talk to Wayne.'

'He's not in.'

'Then we'll wait. It's important that we speak to him.'

Annie Restorick looked frightened. 'What's he done? He's a good lad . . . it's the others who lead him on. They think it's funny to get him into trouble.'

'He's not in trouble, Mrs Restorick. We just want to talk to him, that's all.'

Annie looked undecided. As she hesitated, considering the course of action that would get rid of her unwelcome visitors the fastest, a figure appeared in the hallway behind her. The old lady shuffled towards her daughter, her knickers draped loosely round her ankles.

'Annie . . . what you doing?' she wailed pathetically. 'You shouldn't leave me . . . not when I'm paying a visit, Annie . . .' Her voice trailed off.

Annie Restorick turned and put her arm round the old woman's shoulders. 'Come on, Mother . . . back to the toilet. Come on.' She led her gently into the house.

Rachel looked at Trish. They were thinking the same thing.

'Mind if we come in, Mrs Restorick?' Rachel called, not giving Annie the chance to object. 'Thank you,' she added firmly.

They stood in the shabby hallway, the front door closed behind them.

'We'll just wait till Wayne gets back . . . nothing to worry about,' she shouted through. There was no answer.

They stood there in the hallway a full five minutes. The only sounds that could be heard were Annie's voice crooning words of reassurance to her mother, then the toilet flushing. It was a small place to have a downstairs toilet, Rachel thought . . . probably put in for the old lady's benefit.

Then she heard another noise. It came from upstairs . . . a creaking, like footsteps. Annie had said her son was out. She had lied.

'Wayne,' Rachel shouted up the stairs. 'Can we have a quick word with you, please? Nothing to worry about. Just come on down. We can't talk to you up there, can we?'

Annie tore from the back of the house like an avenging fury. 'I've told you he's out . . . how dare you come in my house and . . .'

She was cut off in mid-sentence by the appearance of Wayne. His flabby body was squashed into a shrunken, washed-out T-shirt and jeans that looked a size too small for him. He moved awkwardly down the stairs.

'What do you want?' he asked, a vacant expression on his face.

'We just want to know where you were last Sunday, Wayne,' Rachel said gently. 'There was a man killed and we think you might be a very important witness. Do you know what that means, Wayne?'

'Course he knows what it means. And I've told you once . . . he was here all night.'

'No he weren't . . . he went out.'

Annie Restorick swung round. Her mother, escaped from the confines of the toilet, was standing behind her, a grin of pure, childlike mischief on her face.

'Don't be daft, Mother. You don't remember.'

'I do. You was watching that *Inspector Morgan*. Wayne said it were boring so he went out. I saw him. He went out . . . out to the pub.'

'Oh, shut up, Mother. You don't know what you're saying. It was another night you're thinking of.' She turned to Rachel. 'Take no notice of Mother . . . she don't know what she's on about half the time.'

Rachel was unsure of her next move. She looked at the inexperienced Trish, but it was no use seeking guidance from that quarter.

'Okay, Wayne . . . but we might want a little chat another day. Nothing to be scared of . . . just a few questions, okay?'

Wayne looked at his mother, who shook her head. 'You'll not take him anywhere. He's easily led . . . you lot'd get him saying all sorts. I know what the police are like.'

'I can assure you, Mrs Restorick, that if we question Wayne there'll be an appropriate adult present . . . you or a social worker or . . .' Whoever it was, Rachel hoped it wouldn't be the mother.

This did nothing to appease Annie, who pointedly opened the front door to let them out.

When they had gone Wayne returned to his room. He lifted up

a corner of his mattress and took out something small and shiny. His treasure . . . his shiny treasure. Whatever the police were after, they weren't going to get their hands on his treasure.

The address Dr McTaggart had given for Sally Johnson's companion turned out to be a flat above a shop near the centre of Neston. The shop, displaying a collection of brightly coloured carved wood surrounded by a selection of objects in the ethnic style, was called Carver's Emporium. It was sandwiched between a vegan health food shop and an outlet for healing crystals.

There was no sign of the flat entrance so they went round the back, where a flight of iron steps led upward to a freshly painted sky-blue door. Their footsteps clanged on the metal steps . . . a warning of approaching visitors better than any doorbell.

The door was opened by a young man. The first thing that struck Wesley was his good looks; the fair hair flopping casually over one eye, the diffident smile. Here was a young man who would charm his way through life . . . and prosper by it.

'Morning, gentlemen . . . hope you're not selling anything. I'm skint . . . honestly.' As if to emphasise the point, he turned out his empty pockets and shrugged dramatically.

They produced their warrant cards. 'Oliver Ballantyne?' The young man nodded. 'If we could just have a quick word, sir . . . won't take long.'

A flash of alarm crossed Ballantyne's face but his features composed themselves almost immediately into their habitual amiability. 'You'd better come in, officers . . . though I can assure you I was nowhere near the bank on the day in question,' he said jokingly.

Heffernan decided to play the dull copper . . . he felt it was expected of him. 'What bank would that be, sir?'

Oliver Ballantyne had the grace to look apologetic. 'Er . . . only joking. Would you care for a coffee? I've just put the kettle on.'

Wesley, forced by Pam to take an interest in interior decoration from time to time, looked round the flat. It was stylishly furnished with polished floorboards and richly coloured hangings on the whitewashed walls. Understated but expensive. Here and there a piece of modern sculpture was placed to provide a conversation piece . . . a strategy the police weren't falling for. The air smelled deliciously of sandalwood and fresh-ground coffee. Ballantyne displayed no signs of guilt. He hadn't even enquired about the reason for their visit . . . a strange thing in itself, Wesley thought.

'No coffee for me, thank you, sir. Perhaps Sergeant Peterson . . .'

'No thanks.' Wesley looked at their host. His left hand was expertly bandaged. 'How did you hurt your hand, sir?'

'Oh, this? I cut it on some glass . . . some kind person had put it on top of a wall. I was taking a short cut . . . probably trespassing. Is that why you're here?'

'Not exactly. Did you go to Neston Hospital on Tuesday night?'

'Yes. This thing was pouring with blood . . . had to get it seen to. The doctor there said it was nasty.' He tilted his head enquiringly. 'How exactly can I help you, Inspector?'

'Can you tell me what happened on Tuesday night?'

'Everything?'

'If possible.'

Ballantyne looked down and grinned like a naughty schoolboy. His fine fair hair flopped over his face. 'That would be a bit embarrassing. There was . . . er . . . a lady involved.'

'What do you do for a living, Mr Ballantyne?'

'I'm a student . . . at Neston Hall . . . fine arts.'

With a rich daddy picking up the bill, no doubt, thought Heffernan. He'd seen the type before. A few years of the alternative lifestyle with no financial worries, then, when the Arcadian idyll had palled, a place in Daddy's merchant bank. If only he, Gerry Heffernan, had enjoyed such advantages. But he couldn't grumble . . . his dad had put in a good word for him with the shipping line when he had first gone to sea. Nepotism was a wonderful thing . . . for some.

He continued, 'This lady . . . could you tell us her name?'

Ballantyne leaned forward with a 'we're all men of the world' expression on his smooth, unclouded face. 'I'd rather not . . . she is married.'

'And she's a good deal older than you?'

Ballantyne looked genuinely puzzled. 'A few years . . . that's all. You've still not told me why you're here,' he said, as if the fact had only just occurred to him.

'We'll come to that in a moment, sir,' said Heffernan, wanting to keep the advantage of surprise. 'The lady went with you to the hospital, didn't she, sir?'

For a moment Ballantyne looked blank. Then, as realisation dawned, he began to laugh. 'That wasn't the lady I . . . did you think? She was old enough to be my grandmother. Lovely lady, mind. If she'd been forty years younger . . . No, Inspector, that was my good Samaritan. She saw me standing by the road with my hand pouring blood. She stopped and offered to drive me to the hospital . . . only her car conked out and she managed to pull it over to a lay-by and we had to walk. I'm afraid I made a bit of a mess of her front seat. I told her to send me the cleaning bill but she wouldn't hear of it. Lovely lady. I thought she was American but it turned out she was from round here . . . went over to the States in the war.' He smiled fondly. Sally Johnson had made quite an impression. They showed Ballantyne her photograph. He nodded. 'That's her.'

'We're trying to trace this lady. She came over with her husband for a veterans' reunion and she's gone missing. Everyone's been very worried about her.'

'There's no need. She was fine when I last saw her.'

'When was that?'

'We went for a drink at the Seddon and she slept in my spare room on Tuesday night. I drove her to Whitely on Wednesday morning. She was planning to stay at the Wheatsheaf for a few days. She lived in Whitely once. Did you know that? She had to leave during the war because they were using it for target practice or something.'

'But Mrs Johnson came from Maleton . . . her family ran the village shop there.'

'That was later. They stayed in Maleton when they were evacuated, then when the war was over they found their house in Whitely had been shelled. They had to stay in Maleton . . . she told me all about it.'

Wesley and Heffernan looked at each other. Why hadn't they enquired more closely into Sally Johnson's past? If they'd known about the Whitely connection, they might have found her by now.

Gerry Heffernan resisted the temptation to make Oliver Ballantyne feel uncomfortable. He was satisfied that he was telling the truth. He was not there to judge the rights and wrongs of the man's dalliance with a married woman. He had the information he came for. He stood up. Wesley did likewise.

'Did Mrs Johnson seem worried about anything, Mr Ballantyne?'

'Yes . . . yes, she did. She didn't seem too happy about going back to the States. In fact . . .' He hesitated. 'Well, she seemed to think she wouldn't go back . . . not at all. She said she wanted to stay here . . . to die.'

Whitely was a large village about three miles along the coast from Bereton. It too had been evacuated during the D-day rehearsals, its inhabitants scattered to beg the hospitality of relations or provided with temporary accommodation in Tradmouth or Neston. There was no sign now of the scars of war. The village was neat and pastel-washed, and spring flowers burst from its gardens and window boxes. They made for the Wheatsheaf, an attractive inn with a fancy wrought-iron balcony which spewed forth tumbling flowers.

'Nice place,' commented Wesley.

Heffernan nodded, looking appreciatively at the floral display. He was no gardener himself, but that didn't stop him admiring the handiwork of the more talented.

They went inside and asked at reception for Mrs Johnson. A woman – from her air of capable authority they assumed her to be the landlady and from her Yorkshire accent not a local – looked through the register and shook her head. 'We've no Mrs Johnson . . . sorry.'

Heffernan showed the photograph. The landlady took off her glasses and peered at it. 'That's Mrs Beesly . . . I'm sure it is.'

'American lady?'

'That's right.'

Beesly . . . why hadn't they thought of that? Beesly had been her maiden name.

'She went out this morning . . . doing a bit of sightseeing. She said she used to live round here. She seemed such a nice lady . . . you'd never think the police'd be after her.' She leaned forward confidentially. 'What's she done?'

'Nothing that we know of, love. Her husband's just a bit worried about her, that's all.'

'I can give you a ring when she comes in if you like . . . always ready to help the boys in blue.'

'That's very good of you, madam. We'd be very grateful.'

The landlady nodded public-spiritedly. In the licensed trade it was always wise to keep on the right side of the law . . . even in such an irreproachable establishment as the Wheatsheaf.

They returned to the car.

'Do we tell the husband?'

'Not yet, Wes. Let's have a word with the lady first. After all, she might not want him to know where she is. Who knows what goes on between husband and wife? I said I'd pop round to the mortuary. Colin Bowman wants the pleasure of my company. You coming with me, Wes?'

Wesley hated mortuaries. The very smell caused the contents of his stomach to rise. If he had the choice, it was a visit he'd avoid. 'I've got things to catch up on back at the incident room . . . and I wanted a word with Rachel about this Wayne Restorick character – see if she's managed to find anything out.'

'Fair enough. Just drop me off at the hospital, then.'

Wesley was only too happy with this arrangement and bid his boss a smiling farewell when he dropped him at the mortuary entrance. Gerry Heffernan walked through the scrubbed corridors in search of Colin Bowman. He tracked him down in his office.

'Glad to see I'm not the only one buried deep in paperwork.'

Bowman looked up and a warm smile illuminated his face. 'Gerry . . . come in, sit down. I was just about to have a coffee. Will you join me?'

'I never say no if it's free, Colin . . . you know me.'

Colin Bowman went to the kettle in the corner of his office and filled a cafetière. Heffernan sipped the expertly brewed, delicious-smelling coffee appreciatively. 'You certainly know how to live down at the mortuary, Colin. Our coffee tastes like last week's washing-up water. What did you want to see me about?'

The pathologist was unprepared for the discussion of business. He had to shuffle a few files on his desk to get himself in the mood. 'Oh yes . . . the post-mortem results on that rat found by the body. It had been poisoned . . . ordinary commercial rat poison available anywhere. It'd be used on a lot of the farms round about, I should think.'

'Thanks. Any word on the knife yet . . . the one that belonged to the suspect?'

'That's the main reason I rang. When you've finished your coffee I've got something to show you.'

Heffernan hoped that whatever it was it wouldn't be gruesome, but knowing Colin Bowman it probably would be. He was led to the area where the bodies were stored. Bowman slid out the drawer containing Norman Openheim's remains as casually as Heffernan would have opened a filing cabinet. He pulled the sheet back from the body. Norman looked surprisingly peaceful . . . the effects of being released from a lifetime under the thumb of Dorinda, the Mighty Atom, perhaps.

Bowman unlocked a cupboard on the other side of the room and produced the knife, still in its plastic bag.

'I understand from forensics that there was no trace of blood found on the knife.'

'How come you know before me? I'll have a word with Gwen. . . .'

'I asked and Gwen told me . . . report's not typed up yet. I'm sure she hasn't forgotten you.'

Heffernan shrugged. Paperwork was the blight of every profession . . . forensics would be as bound up with it as everyone else.

Bowman leaned over Norman's body and gently rolled him on to his side so that his wound was visible. He held the knife against the body for comparison. 'Look at the width. Whatever he was stabbed with was at least half an inch wider . . . more like three-quarters. And the depth of the wound suggests something much longer. Sorry, Gerry. This isn't your murder weapon. I'd say something more like . . . oh, let me think . . .' He closed his eyes, his face screwed up in concentration.

'A kitchen knife? One of those you use for carving?' Heffernan suggested helpfully.

'No . . . wrong shape.' He looked at the inspector triumphantly. 'A bayonet. It's just a possibility, of course . . . I wouldn't commit myself, but that wound could have been made with a bayonet. I'll need one for comparison, of course.'

'I'll try and arrange it.'

'Tell you what. My wife and I have been invited to dine by one of the commanders up at the naval college . . . I'm sure to pick one up there.'

Heffernan smiled to himself. Colin Bowman was a welcome

dinner guest in the most unexpected places. Now, it seemed, he had penetrated the hallowed ranks of the Royal Navy.

He said farewell to the pathologist and decided, as he was on the premises, to pay a visit to Rat . . . show his face and say a few words of encouragement to the constable given the tedious task of guarding an unconscious man.

If Rat was innocent of murder – which was starting to look like a possibility – he'd better start finding some new suspects. The ones he had were proving sadly disappointing.

Wesley, back in the incident room, had come to a natural break in his paperwork. Rachel hadn't yet returned from providing a sympathetic police presence at the Clearview Hotel.

Neil had established his base just over the dusty parqueted floor of the village hall. Wesley left the incident room and strolled the few yards to the side room that the archaeological unit were using as an office. He tried the door. It was locked. Neil would be at the dig.

Wesley could honestly say that he was due for a break, so his conscience only nagged a little as he walked out of the village hall and up towards the chantry.

Neil was pleased to see him. The students needed a lot of super-vision and advice, and it was good to have someone there who wouldn't trample all over the evidence like a herd of startled elephants . . . or at least that's how Neil described the first-year students. Wesley hoped he exaggerated.

'Where's Daphne?' he asked. He had hoped to see Dr Parsons again.

'She'll be back tomorrow. She's taken the dagger we've found back to the university for conservation. Beautiful piece . . . gold hilt. Must have belonged to an aristocrat at a guess. Funny that it wasn't really buried in the grave with the skeletons . . . it's almost as if someone had placed it a couple of feet down in the freshly dug grave as an afterthought. It's strange that some villager didn't keep something like that for himself, don't you think?'

'Maybe people were more honest and God-fearing in those days.'

'Come on, Wes . . . who are you trying to kid? I bet you the crime rate was just as high in 1588 as it is now . . . and they didn't have your lot with their computers and patrol cars. All they had was the parish constable and the hangman.'

'Wonder what their clear-up rate was like,' pondered Wesley. 'When can you dive again?' he said, changing the subject.

'Probably not till after the weekend. Fancy coming down with us?'

'No thanks.' Wesley wasn't one of nature's sailors . . . a fact he'd discovered on his first trip on the cross-Channel ferry.

'We should be nearly finished in this part of the chapel by the weekend. We've had a lot of help,' Neil said, nodding towards the burrowing students. 'Not all of it expert, unfortunately. But still . . . never look a gift horse and all that.'

'What have you found?'

'Seventeen graves in all. Not much of an invasion.'

'What was the population of the village?'

'Couple of hundred?'

'But the Spaniards were trained soldiers . . . and armed. . . .'

'And knackered from crawling out of their wreck. The university pathology department are having a look at the damage, but from the state of the skulls when we got them out of the ground I'd say the poor sods were murdered. The fact that they were Spanish and Catholic would have been enough to give the self-righteous villagers an excuse for a spot of carnage.'

'Nothing new about prejudice,' said Wesley sadly: he'd experienced that unpleasant commodity from time to time at first hand.

'Sure isn't. The less appealing side of human nature, eh?'

They stood, heads bowed, thinking of the men who had spent four hundred years beneath the soil of a hostile land.

Wesley broke the silence. 'Anything found in the graves?'

'Nothing much. The villagers must have stripped the bodies of anything desirable before they were buried . . . that's what's so puzzling about that dagger we found.'

'Could it have been buried at a later date? It was on a different level from . . .'

'No, it was certainly buried in the grave – probably in the freshly dug earth – no sign of later disturbance and it's Spanish, contemporary with the wreck. Why leave something like that buried when you've nicked everything else? Come on, Detective Sergeant . . . work that one out.'

A sound behind them, a tactful clearing of the throat, made them turn round. They expected to see a nervous first-year student, plucking up courage to ask advice, but instead June

142

Mallindale was standing next to a spoil heap, her face impassive. She was, as Heffernan had remarked, an attractive woman. She wore tight-fitting jeans that showed her slim figure to best advantage, and a simple blue blouse. Her blond hair hung loose. Although middle-aged there was something youthful about her; not well preserved, but undeveloped.

'I hope I'm not intruding,' she said diffidently. Wesley introduced her to Neil, who looked at her appreciatively.

'I've read your book ... very interesting. You read it yet, Wes?'

'Er ... haven't had a chance. I think Pam's started on it, though.' He thought he owed the author a brief explanation. 'My wife's a teacher. Her class are doing a project on the evacuation of the villages round here during the war. She'll find that part of your book helpful, I'm sure.'

June Mallindale smiled, a secretive smile. 'Some of the things that went on are hardly suitable for the ears of young children.'

'You mean the Yanks and the local girls? I'm sure Pam'll leave that bit out.'

She was about to say something, then she hesitated, thinking better of it. She turned to Neil, a bright smile on her face. 'How are you getting on with the dig? I had to come and see whether you've disproved anything I wrote in my book.'

'On the contrary. Your hypotheses have proved to be pretty accurate. We've found seventeen graves – adult males – with every indication they'd died of head injuries. We're having the bones carbon-dated ... just to make sure they're contemporary with the wreck. No artefacts buried with them ... they'd probably been robbed of anything decent they might have possessed. It doesn't reflect very well on the good folk of Bereton, but that's war for you. The only thing of real interest that we found was a dagger ... gold hilt, very fine – looked as if it had been buried as an afterthought, perhaps in the soft soil of the freshly dug grave, rather than with the body as a prized possession. It's certainly contemporary with the Armada ... all a bit of a mystery why it didn't find its way into someone's pocket.' Neil noticed that June Mallindale was gazing beyond him, as if her mind was elsewhere. He hoped he wasn't boring her. 'Do you know anything about this grave that's supposed to be in the church? The vicar told Wesley that one of the Spaniards is buried up there, didn't he, Wes?'

'Yes. Under a cupboard.'

June Mallindale looked at Wesley. It was clear from her expression, from her body language, that something was making her uneasy. Professional embarrassment, perhaps ... an omission from her book?

'I really wouldn't know.'

Neil looked at Wesley enquiringly. He too had picked up on June Mallindale's discomfort. He changed the subject. 'I wish you could see the dagger, Wes. It's quite a find. And the condition's good. Should polish up nicely, as my old mum used to say.'

June was shuffling her feet, anxious to be gone, worry accentuating the lines on her face and making her look older ... nearer her true age, which must have been the mid-forties at least.

'One of my wife's pupils mentioned there was a murder round here during the war. Have you heard about it?' Wesley asked, trying to include the woman in the conversation and make her feel more comfortable.

The question had the reverse effect. 'No,' she snapped. 'There was nothing like that. I really must be going. Thank you for showing me the dig, Mr Watson.'

'It's a pleasure. We'll be starting on the buildings next week if we can get some tame students to clear the undergrowth. Come up again ... any time.'

She thanked him politely, keen to be gone. She left as silently as she'd arrived.

'Funny woman,' commented Neil when she was out of earshot. 'Not bad-looking, though, for her age. What do you think rattled her?'

'It was when we mentioned the grave in the church ... and then when I mentioned the murder during the war ...'

'Premenstrual tension ... that's what it'll be.'

'That's your answer to everything. You're becoming a crusty old bachelor, Neil.'

'Me? You're only jealous 'cause I'm not saddled with a mortgage and a kid on the way, and far be it from me to tell you how to do your job, Wes, but I reckon you should ask Ms Mallindale a few questions ... she's hiding something.'

'It can't be anything to do with Norman Openheim's murder whatever it is. She's got an alibi ... I've checked.'

'You never know, Wes, you never know. But you're the detective . . . it's up to you.'

Wesley looked sceptical.

Lunch-time had its usual effect of clearing the incident room. Rachel hadn't got much time: lunch would have to wait.

She opened her desk drawer furtively. There was only a young and inexperienced uniformed constable on the phone at the other end of the room. He would hardly be likely to comment on the presence of an ancient, musty-smelling file on her desk.

She took the file out of her drawer carefully: the thing looked as though it could disintegrate and the papers inside were brown and fragile. At some point in their history they had been kept somewhere damp, which hadn't helped their condition.

She turned the papers over carefully until she found what she was looking for. There wasn't much – just a brief report and a note that the case had been passed to the US military authorities as it involved one of their servicemen.

She read the report slowly, devouring every detail, every word. A young woman, Muriel Carmichael, had gone on a date with an American serviceman and had come home distressed with her clothing dishevelled. Her father had made a complaint to the police. Whether the US authorities followed it up Rachel had no means of knowing from the records.

Then she noticed the date – 30 May 1944. Wasn't that a few days before the D-day landings? If the case had been passed to the Americans they would have had other things to concern them . . . like liberating France. Maybe the man involved was killed. She turned the page. As she suspected, there was a communication from the police inspector of the time to the man's commanding officer; along with it was the reply. The unit had moved to France on active service. In view of the circumstances of the complaint, and the evidence of witnesses, it was suggested that the matter should be dropped.

Rachel bit her lip, angry that a war should halt justice. But, being a realist, she admitted to herself that the case could hardly be proved anyway. But the mention of witnesses intrigued her . . . and the seeming lack of a statement from the victim herself.

The printing was small and the paper wafer-thin – probably conserving supplies for the war effort. She had to peer closely to read it. Then she found what she was looking for: the man's name. Her heart began to thump as she smiled in triumph. The accused man hadn't died in France – he was alive and well and staying half a mile away. 'Yes!' she mouthed, carefully putting the file back in the drawer. It was the evidence she needed.

Her visit to the Clearview Hotel after lunch would be more interesting than she had anticipated. There was one person she wanted to question very closely and preferably without Steve being there to interfere. She knew that would be going against all the rules, but sometimes you had to break rules to get on . . . to get noticed.

Rachel was determined that she would speak to one veteran of the D-day landings alone.

Chapter Ten

Of course, Bereton wasn't the only village to be evacuated for the D-day landing rehearsals. Many other small villages in the area met a similar fate. The church at Whitely sustained a great deal of damage, having its entire west wall blown out by mortars. Now, thankfully, this beautiful church has been restored to its former glory.

From *A History of Bereton and Its People* by June Mallindale

Rachel Tracey had been brought up to be honest. Her initial determination to keep her information to herself had begun to waver after half an hour's thought. It was only right that the inspector should be told. Besides, it was insurance: she had seen officers sticking their necks out before . . . and paying for it. She'd better do this by the book.

The inspector and Sergeant Peterson had come back. She knocked on Gerry Heffernan's partition and approached his desk, the musty file held before her at arm's length.

'Hi, Rach . . . any news come through about Nigel Glanville?'

'Not that I've heard . . . Can I have a word, sir?'

'Any time, Rach. Park your backside. What's that smell . . . like something's died?' He looked at the file she held suspiciously.

'I think I've found something, sir. . . .'

The phone on Heffernan's desk rang. Its shrill cry distracted Rachel, who sat staring at the instrument, her determination to share her discovery wavering.

Heffernan picked the receiver up. 'Yeah? Right. Thanks for letting us know. We'll be down right away. Ta.'

He grinned at Rachel triumphantly. 'We've found Sally Johnson. We're off to Whitely to see her now. Wes!' he shouted.

He rushed from the room, leaving Rachel pondering her dilemma. Then she made her decision. She'd do it alone. There were too many villains walking the streets because things were done by the book.

Wesley drove at a sedate pace down the hedge-walled country roads that led to Whitely. He took each bend cautiously. The confidence needed for fast driving in such conditions – Rachel possessed it – only came from a lifetime spent amongst the fields, farms and hedgerows of the district.

When they reached Whitely the landlady of the Wheatsheaf greeted them with suppressed excitement, telling them that their quarry had left ten minutes ago to have a look at the church.

They strolled down the village's main street to the picturesque church, of a similar vintage to St John's in Bereton. They entered by the west door. The west end that had been so damaged in the war had been lovingly restored – impossible to tell that it hadn't stood undisturbed since the Middle Ages.

The church interior seemed dim after the bright spring daylight. The sun streaming though the stained glass threw jewelled patches of light on to the stone floor. A lady of the parish was busily arranging flowers by the finely carved pulpit. She nodded to the new visitors and smiled. Wesley wished her good morning.

They didn't see the other woman in the church until they were halfway down the centre aisle. She was there in a small screened side chapel, kneeling on a hassock, carefully embroidered by the Mothers Union. Her eyes were fixed on the painting of the Virgin hanging over the small, plain altar. The two policemen looked at each other, hardly liking to disturb the woman's devotions. They sat down on a pew near the front of the church and waited until she stood up.

Heffernan approached her slowly. 'Mrs Johnson?'

She nodded. 'I knew it wouldn't be long before you came looking for me.' Her voice was soft. Her native Devon accent had blended well with the one she had acquired in America. 'I feel bad about not telling Ed where I was but he'd only have wanted to come along with me and I needed time to think . . . time on my own. . . .'

Gerry Heffernan took her arm gently and led her to the front pew. He sat beside her, his face sympathetic. 'You've had us worried, love. We didn't know where you were.'

Tears began to fill her eyes. 'I know . . . I'm sorry. It's not that I haven't been happy in the States. Ed and I have had a good life there, but . . .' She began to cry. Heffernan fished in his pocket for a handkerchief, but the only one he could find was unironed and decorated with some unappealing stains. He signalled to Wesley, who produced a clean one.

Sally Johnson blew her nose loudly and wiped her eyes. 'I'm sorry for all the trouble I've caused. How did you find me?'

'A young man called Oliver Ballantyne . . . quite taken with you, he was.'

That made her smile. She must have been very pretty as a girl . . . the queen of the jitterbug at the GI socials all those years ago.

'Such a nice boy, Oliver . . . bit of a charmer, though,' she added affectionately.

'Would you like us to give you a lift back to Bereton, Mrs Johnson?' asked Wesley.

Sally Johnson looked at him and shook her head. 'Not yet . . . is that all right?'

''Course it is, love,' said Heffernan. 'You take your time.'

'I'd like you to understand . . . I really would.' She twisted Wesley's handkerchief in her hands. 'I never intended to stay away for so long but . . . I knew I couldn't go back. . . .'

'Is there anything you'd like to tell us . . . about what happened last Sunday night?'

She looked at the inspector, puzzled. 'You mean poor Norman? Is that it? I did something rather silly, didn't I? I told that policeman I'd been for a walk on the beach. I didn't think it'd do any harm . . . after all, it had nothing to do with poor Norman's death and I really didn't want Ed to find out where I'd gone. I just wasn't ready to tell him . . . I was still confused.'

'So where were you?'

'I drove here . . . to Whitely. We lived here until 1944, my parents and me – and my brother. He was killed in the war . . . in Italy. Then there was the evacuation. They gave us a couple of weeks to get out. We were lucky, I suppose . . . my aunt had a shop in Maleton so we went there, and when my uncle died my father ended up running it. We never came back to Whitely. It was just a childhood memory . . . my land of lost content.' She smiled wistfully. 'We'd lived here for centuries, my family. And there are all the memories of Mum and Dad and George, my brother. . . .'

Her eyes filled with tears again. She took hold of Heffernan's hand. 'I've something to show you . . . come and see.' She led him to the south aisle where a stone plaque stood proudly on the wall. George Beesly, Elizabeth Beesly, Francis Beesly, Jane Beesly, Matthew Beesly . . . The list went on – generations of Beeslys lay in the vault beneath the plaque. Near the family vault stood a bronze war memorial which listed the dead of both world wars. It was surrounded by wreaths of bright red poppies. Sally pointed to a name: George Beesly. 'My brother,' she whispered. 'There are more of my relatives buried in the churchyard. I feel I'm part of this village . . . even after all these years. Buffalo was just a place to visit . . . can you understand that?'

Heffernan nodded. He understood. 'What will you do now?'

'I didn't tell you where I was on Sunday night, did I?' She began to walk towards the west door, out of the church. When they reached the street Sally pointed to a pink-washed, double-fronted house; an attractive building, not large but possessed of pleasing Georgian proportions and a handsome oak door with a gleaming brass knocker. Jutting from its upper storey was a For Sale sign.

'I saw a picture in a real estate office in Tradmouth.' She used the American term, Heffernan noted. 'I came to have a look at it on Sunday night. I'm buying it,' she said simply. 'It's where I was brought up. I'm coming home.' She hesitated. 'You see, Inspector, the doctors in the States have found a tumour. It's slow-growing – they say that with treatment I might survive two years . . . maybe three, maybe five . . . they don't know. I don't want to die over there. Does that sound silly to you?'

Heffernan shook his head. It didn't sound silly at all. 'What will your husband say?'

'I don't know . . . that's why I've been so secretive. But there's nothing for him in Buffalo. The kids have moved away and he's got no other family. I was praying back there that he'll understand that I couldn't face ending my life over there . . . that I had to come home.'

'Would you like us to take you to him now?' said Wesley.

She nodded, a small, secret smile flitting across her face as she looked back towards her childhood home. Sally Johnson was content . . . she was going home for good.

They dropped Sally Johnson off at the Clearview Hotel. They asked if she wanted them to go in with her but she declined; facing Ed was something she had to do alone. They stayed outside just long enough to see Ed Johnson run arthritically towards his wife and take her in his arms, tears in his eyes.

It was lunch-time so they made for the Bereton Arms: no police force ever functioned well on an empty stomach. Half an hour later, with their hunger satisfied, they strolled slowly back past the church. The great oak door stood open and the vicar, about to leave, spotted them and waved. They walked up the churchyard path towards him as he stood in the porch wearing a benevolent smile of greeting.

'Good afternoon, gentlemen. I was going to come down to the village to ask you how that unfortunate young man was.'

'Still unconscious, I'm afraid. Did you know he was Mrs Slater's nephew . . . from the Clearview Hotel?'

The vicar looked genuinely surprised. In the enclosed world of Bereton visiting nephews normally stayed *en famille* as welcome guests – they didn't roam the streets with knives robbing village shops. 'No . . . no, I didn't know that. I know Mrs Slater, of course . . . she shows her face in church at Christmas and Easter like so many people these days. Busy woman.'

'I suppose her mother's one of your regulars?'

'Her mother? No, as a matter of fact she isn't . . . not set foot in the church since I've been here. I see her walking around the village, though . . . she tends to ignore me. Is the young man expected to recover?'

'Touch and go, the quacks say.'

'And is he your murderer, do you think?'

Gerry Heffernan had never lied to a man of the cloth. 'We did think so but now the evidence points to him not being our man.'

'So his bid for sanctuary was in vain?'

'Sanctuary?' asked Heffernan, puzzled. 'Oh yeah . . . the knocker.'

'Ring,' corrected Wesley.

'If that had happened five hundred years ago, Inspector, you wouldn't have been able to lay a finger on him . . . not once he'd touched that ring. If he managed to elude his pursuers and reach a consecrated place, then once he'd made confession and given up his weapons he was safe.'

'Churches'd be packed to the rafters if they could do that today,' said Heffernan incredulously.

'Oh, there were certain conditions, Inspector. He had to confess to the coroner within forty days, dressed in sackcloth. Then he had to flee the country, forfeiting all his possessions. He had to travel to the coast by the shortest route, wearing a white robe and carrying a cross.'

'Good idea . . . let the French police deal with 'em.'

'It might be a reciprocal arrangement, sir . . . we'd get all the French villains.' Wesley grinned. 'I hope our sanctuary-seeker didn't give you too much of a shock, Vicar.'

'Not at all, Sergeant . . . and call me Simon, please. Everyone does. Actually I wanted a word with you. I've talked to one of my sidesmen about that grave in the south aisle . . . nice old boy – he was here when the church was restored after the war. He remembers seeing it, so if you and Neil are interested I've no objection to you moving the hymn-book cupboard to have a look.' He led Wesley over to the cupboard, a monumental structure. 'It's heavy, mind . . . I wish you luck.'

'I think we'll manage to shift that. Neil's got some students assisting with the dig so we've got plenty of help.'

The cupboard, a solid construction in oak, had been built in the days of Queen Victoria, before the idea of skimping on materials had even been thought of. It stood some six feet high and eight feet wide, and behind the dingy glass of its doors were rows of tattered Bibles, hymn books and Books of Common Prayer. Some assorted theological works, probably acquired by a former vicar at the start of the century, graced the top shelf, gathering dust.

'Probably be easier if we took the books out. Is that okay with you?'

'Oh yes. In fact you'll be doing me a favour. I've been meaning to sort that cupboard out since I came here . . . just one of the things I've never got round to. Tell me, Sergeant, how did you become interested in this dig?'

Gerry Heffernan, seeing that Wesley was about to become

embroiled in a lengthy conversation with the amiable clergyman, gently nudged his arm. Wesley understood.

'Sorry, Vicar. I'll have to drag my sergeant away before he starts digging up your church floor. Duty calls.'

'I quite understand, Inspector.' He shook Wesley's hand. 'Do let me know when you want to move the cupboard, Sergeant Peterson.'

'Wesley.' He judged that reciprocal first names were appropriate. 'Sorry to rush off but, as the inspector says, duty calls.'

They walked back to the incident room in amicable silence until Heffernan said what was on his mind. 'What do you reckon, Wes? Who killed Norman Openheim? Looks like it wasn't Rat. He's a vicious little bastard who'd probably slit his mother's throat for a fiver, and if he nicked the bike he could just about have made it back to Bereton, but somehow I don't think this was his MO. He'd be more interested in the money Norman had on him than a silver lighter that he might find it hard to get shot of. And where would he get a bayonet?'

'The bayonet indicates someone with a military connection. A souvenir of the war, perhaps . . . one of Norman's comrades?'

'How do you get a bayonet through airport X-ray machines and metal detectors without questions being asked? Besides, they've all got alibis, Wes . . . backing each other to the hilt.'

'Unless they were all involved . . . an execution.'

'What for?'

'How should I know? Cowardice? Isn't that what they used to do in times of war?'

'There's nothing to suggest Norman Openheim did anything untoward in the war. And he seemed popular . . . just a regular guy, everyone said so. Popular.'

'Not popular with his wife.'

'He probably lacked excitement . . . but then most of us do after being married that long. I'd have put my bets on it being the wife for the insurance money and the chance to marry the dashing Todd Weringer, but they've got an alibi far more watertight than the *Rosie May* is at the moment. Who does that leave?'

'Madam Butterfly.'

'Who?'

'Marion Potter. The wartime sweetheart he deserted. He left her a souvenir in the form of a daughter. I've met the lady . . . she seems a lovely old dear but . . .'

'Never trust appearances . . . quite right, Wes.'

'I think we can rule out the daughter, but she's got a son who's known to us . . . bit of burglary, receiving, that sort of thing. He wasn't in when Rachel and I paid him a visit . . . either that or his mum had rung to warn him we were on our way.'

'So let's go and give him a nice surprise, shall we?'

'The daughter, Carole Martin, said he didn't see his grandfather . . . but he knew where he was staying. If he'd arranged a meeting . . .'

'He sounds more interesting by the minute. Come on.'

They reached the car. When they climbed inside Heffernan switched the radio on and found it tuned to Classic FM. 'I fancy a bit of culture, Wes,' he explained as Dame Kiri Te Kanawa gave a fine rendering of Puccini's 'One Fine Day'. 'Very appropriate this, Wes.' He smiled with satisfaction. 'Must be a sign . . . Madam Butterfly. "One fine day I'll find him . . ." Know what it's about, Wes?'

'Yes, sir. Pam and I went to see *Butterfly* at Covent Garden when we lived in London . . . birthday treat.'

Heffernan, the music lover, appeared deflated. He was looking forward to showing off his cultural knowledge by telling his sergeant the story of the local – in this case Japanese – girl who falls in love with an American serviceman and has his child, unknown to him until his return. It all ended in tears, of course. It had to: it was an opera. Had Marion's love ended, not in her death as with the unfortunate Butterfly, but with her former lover's? It was something to be considered.

'What about Wayne Restorick?' Wesley changed the subject. 'What do you make of him as a suspect?'

'Do you see him as a murderer? Would he stick a knife into someone's back?'

Wesley shook his head. 'He's a bit slow. I can see him being easily led and easily scared . . . but stabbing someone in the back for no reason – not his style. That doesn't mean he wasn't hanging around the old chantry. He might have seen something, but we've no proof . . . not yet. It's hard to question him . . . the mother's very protective.'

'We could take him down to the station . . . get a social worker to sit in.'

'I don't want to frighten him, sir. He might clam up altogether if we did. The station might not be the best place.'

They had reached Morbay, driving down its palm-lined seafront where mothers with small children to entertain were now venturing on to the beach in coats and shivering in the watery sunshine while their offspring mined for buried treasure.

They turned left at a large and once prestigious hotel and drove into Morbay's back streets. Young people hung around street corners dressed in shades of black and grey. There were two shabby figures, loitering outside a run-down fish and chip shop sharing chips from a greasy sheet of paper, whom Heffernan recognised immediately. He told Wesley to stop the car and strolled up behind them. They didn't turn round but their dog was studying him in a quizzical manner.

'Give us a chip, lads. I'm starving.'

The two young men swung round. Their first instinct was to flee, but Fang began to jump up at Heffernan, licking his hands playfully, greeting him like a long-lost friend.

'It's okay, lads. Nothing to worry about. I'm not going to pull you in this time. Do you know your mate's in hospital?'

They shook their heads, dumbstruck, wary.

'It wasn't our idea . . . it was Rat. He's crazy. We just went along . . . we had to make sure he didn't do anything stupid,' Snot snivelled ingratiatingly, trying to convince the inspector of his innocence.

Heffernan had no real intention of arresting them. They'd be in trouble soon enough and provide some young PC with a couple of notches on his truncheon.

'Is Rat okay?' Dog looked younger and more vulnerable than Heffernan remembered. The inspector had a son of his own. He felt sorry for the boy who stood there, dirty and pathetic. The streets – even the streets of Morbay – held dangers for kids like Dog.

'We don't know yet, son,' he replied gently. 'He's still unconscious.'

Snot drew his own conclusions. He began to approach Heffernan threateningly. Dog put a warning hand on his arm but Snot shook it off.

'You pigs beat him up. I know what you fucking pigs are like . . . beat him fucking unconscious. Suppose you said he fell down some stairs. . . .'

He put up his fist but Dog clung on to his sleeve. Wesley, seeing what was happening, got out of the car and grabbed Snot, holding the struggling youth in an armlock.

'Nobody beat him up, Kenneth,' said Heffernan calmly, using Snot's real name. 'He was run over . . . ran out in front of a Land Rover. It was his own fault . . . nothing to do with us, okay?'

Snot looked at the inspector, the fight fading from his eyes. Wesley gradually released his grip.

'You okay now?'

Snot nodded. Dog began to stroke Fang, who had watched the proceedings with interest.

'I've got a couple of things to ask you, then you can go. I could arrest you for being Rat's accomplices when he pinched the beer from that shop, but I'm a soft old bugger so I should take advantage of it if I were you. If you tell me what I want to know – tell the truth – I'll give you another chance . . . okay?'

Snot nodded, suspicious. 'What is it? What do you want to know?'

'Did Rat say anything about where he'd been on Sunday night?'

'He said he nicked a bike and went to a village . . . nicked some booze from a shop and kipped in a barn. That's what he told us. We met up with him the next day.'

'Have you ever seen Rat with a knife?'

'Yeah. He had a knife . . . you know he did.'

'Is that the only one he had? Did he have another knife? Something bigger . . . like a bayonet that fits into a rifle?'

Snot laughed and shook his head. The question was easier than he had expected. 'Nah . . . nothing like that.'

'You sure?'

'Positive,' said Dog confidently. 'He didn't have nothing like that.'

'Thanks.' The inspector put his hand in his pocket and took out a ten-pound note. 'Here. Get yourselves something to eat . . . don't spend it on booze or dope, okay?'

Snot studied the note suspiciously as if there must be a catch to this policeman's generosity.

'Have you got anywhere to sleep?'

'Night shelter on Warren Road.'

'Gordon Street's better . . . Sally Army place. I know Captain

Wells who runs it. I can give you a lift there if you like . . . introduce you. Going back to London?'

Snot shrugged. 'Dunno . . . can't really leave Rat here.'

'Look, Kenneth . . . word of advice. Rat's bad news. Either stop round here or go back to the smoke, but forget about him. Do yourselves a favour . . . keep away from the likes of Rat. Get in the car.'

Wesley looked at his boss enquiringly.

'Come on, Wes, give us a hand with Fang.'

Wesley, unused to dogs, took the string that served as a lead and held on to Fang, who looked up at him appealingly and wagged his tail while Heffernan settled the lads in the back seat. The sergeant drove to the old school building which served as a hostel for the increasing numbers of homeless in Morbay and waited in the car.

Heffernan emerged from the hostel grinning. 'I've sorted them out,' he said, getting back into the car. 'Captain Wells says he might be able to get them some seasonal work and all.'

'Isn't this a bit . . . er . . . beyond the call of duty, sir? They've got records and . . .'

'What's the alternative? Back on the streets under the fatherly guidance of the likes of Rat, adding to our workload?'

'Point taken, sir. It's very . . . er . . . enlightened of you,' Wesley said, having his doubts about the wisdom of his boss's actions. 'Where to now?'

'Kevin Martin's place. You've got the address.'

When they arrived and parked outside, the place looked a little more lively than it had when Wesley had last been there with Rachel. The front door stood open, revealing a dingy interior of chipped paintwork, tattered woodchip and a filthy linoleum floor.

'Des res,' commented Heffernan as they climbed the worn stone steps. He studied the names above the plastic bellpushes. 'Here we are . . . K. Martin. Flat three.'

They stepped inside, their nostrils assaulted by the stench of unemptied bins. Flat three was on the first floor. They knocked on the flaking door. There was a noise inside, someone closing a cupboard or drawer, then footsteps.

The first thing that struck them about Kevin Martin as he opened the door was that Norman Openheim's genes had battled with rivals to give his grandson his nose, eyes and mouth . . . but nature had subtly rearranged them so that Kevin lacked the young

Norman's good looks. Kevin even had his grandfather's reputed shock of dark hair . . . or would have done if it hadn't been scraped back into a ponytail.

'Hello, Kevin. We've come to have a word about your granddad. I take it you know about his death?'

Kevin Martin looked nervous. He nodded and stood aside to let them in. The inside of the flat was as gloomy as the rest of the house. Peeling wallpaper and bare light bulbs bore witness to the fact that it probably hadn't been decorated since the 1970s. The landlord, whoever he was, was running the place on a shoestring . . . and probably driving round in a Jag on the profits, Heffernan thought fleetingly.

'We're sorry about your grandfather,' Wesley said formally. 'You understand that we want to find out who killed him?'

Kevin nodded.

'Did you meet him?'

'Er . . . no, I didn't.'

'Did you know he was staying at the Clearview Hotel on Bereton Sands?'

'Yeah . . . er, my mum mentioned it.'

'Weren't you curious . . . to see the grandfather you never knew existed, all the way from America?'

'Yeah . . . suppose I was.'

'Did you get in touch with him?'

Kevin looked nervous. He didn't answer.

'May we sit down?'

Kevin had sat in the only chair. There was only the bed. A balding green candlewick cover was spread on top of a series of angular lumps and bumps. Kevin looked at it, sudden panic in his eyes. He stood up, crossed to the bed and pushed whatever it was under the cover back so that the edge of the bed could be used to sit on. He took great care to keep the mysterious objects covered, but Wesley saw that the bedspread had slipped in the corner, revealing something hard, black and square. He looked towards the inspector, who was busy studying the décor. Kevin Martin was watching Wesley warily as he sat down.

'So, Kevin, did you say you managed to get in touch with your granddad?'

Kevin looked round at Gerry Heffernan, who was still standing by the door.

'No . . . no, I didn't.'

'Where were you last Sunday night?' asked Heffernan.

'Dunno.'

'Think.'

'At the pub,' Kevin said mechanically.

'Which pub?'

'Can't remember.'

'Were you with anyone?'

'No.'

'Did you see anyone? . . . anyone you know?'

'Dunno.'

Wesley look the opportunity to tweak the candlewick bedcover aside. 'Are these yours?'

Kevin Martin looked round in horror. He opened and closed his mouth, goldfish style. 'Er . . . yeah. I'm . . . er . . . looking after them for a friend.'

' 'Course you are, Kevin. Mind if I have a look? I'm after a video myself.' Heffernan strode over and pulled the cover off the bed. Beneath it lay a number of video recorders, along with a couple of camcorders and a trio of mobile phones.

Wesley looked under the bed: more video recorders and a cardboard box which, on investigation, contained a selection of jewellery and small silver objects. Among the shiny objects was a long ornamental dagger with a jewelled handle. Heffernan turned to look at Kevin Martin, who sat, transfixed with terror.

'They're not mine . . . they're nothing to do with me.'

'You're looking after them for a mate . . . 'course you are, Kevin. What's your mate's name?' Heffernan opened the cupboard beside the fireplace. Staring blankly at him were the screens of five portable televisions.

'Quite a little electrical shop you've got here, Kevin. What's your mate's name?'

'I don't know. I met him in a pub.'

'Very generous of you to allow a stranger to take up all this room in your flat with his stuff.'

'He's paying me.'

'What pub?'

'I can't remember . . . one in the middle of town.'

'Kevin Martin, I'm arresting you for possession of stolen goods

159

'. . .' Heffernan recited the caution while Kevin Martin stood like a naughty boy before the headmaster, eyes downcast.

'Let's get him back to the station, Wes. Get a patrol car down here. I'm putting my money on these things coming from the weekend cottages that have been done over. Come on, Kevin, let's have a nice cup of tea back at the station.'

Kevin, resigned to his fate, allowed himself to be led down to the car. Wesley was surprised by his acceptance of the situation . . . that he didn't protest his innocence. Unless he would rather be done for receiving stolen goods than for murder.

A call came through to say that Mr Chard's bicycle, stolen on Sunday evening, had turned up in some undergrowth near the war memorial: Rat's fingerprints were all over it. But Heffernan felt little triumph at the news. Colin Bowman had used his influence with the Royal Navy to confirm that a bayonet was the most likely murder weapon. That, and the fact that Norman's money had still been in his pocket when he was found, meant that Rat was hardly his prime suspect.

The inspector asked Rachel to try to have a word with Wayne Restorick. Wayne could well have seen something, but getting at the truth would need tact and sensitivity: Heffernan had thought Rachel was the person for the job, but today she was preoccupied, not her usual efficient self. Steve Carstairs noticed this.

She hardly said a word as they walked to Apple Cottage. Annie Restorick told them that Wayne was out. Rachel, unprepared to challenge this, turned round and walked meekly back to the village hall.

'Anything wrong, Rach?' Steve asked, wary of her new and unfamiliar mood.

'I don't know.'

'Feel like telling your Uncle Steve?'

She winced. Patronising bastard. If she'd been with Wesley, say, she would have been tempted to share her knowledge; instead she told Steve she wanted something from the village mini-market: she would see him later back at the incident room.

She made for Mrs Sweeting's cottage. The old lady was pleased to see her and hobbled off into the kitchen to put the kettle on without asking the reason for her visit.

'Mrs Sweeting,' Rachel called through to the kitchen. 'Do you know a woman called Muriel Carmichael?'

There was no reply. Perhaps Mrs Sweeting hadn't heard. Rachel repeated the question when her hostess brought the tray of tea and chocolate biscuits through.

'She was a friend of my sister's,' the old lady said as she put the tray down. 'I didn't know her well.'

'Can you tell me anything about her?'

'I never repeat tittle-tattle, my luvver. It ain't Christian to go gossiping about folk behind their backs now, is it? And I never really knew her . . . she was a few years older than me.'

'Whatever you can tell me might be important, Mrs Sweeting. It might help us catch the person who murdered that American up at the chantry.' Rachel leaned forward, pleading.

'I don't see how . . . but I suppose it can't do no harm, as long as you keep it to yourself and remember I'm only guessing. Muriel still lives round here . . . I shouldn't like it to get out that. . . '

'I'll be very discreet, I promise.'

Mrs Sweeting hesitated, then she began quietly. 'I was evacuated to Tradmouth. I'm only saying what I heard when the war was over, and that was only snippets . . . my sister never said nothing. There was some talk of her getting into trouble. She went away and didn't come back till the war was over. It's all a bit hazy but I remember hearing my sister say that Muriel was going out with some Yank . . . mind you, that wasn't unusual in those days.'

'Think carefully, Mrs Sweeting. You mentioned someone being raped during the war.'

'It's all hazy. I was a child . . . I overheard things, things I shouldn't sometimes. I remember my mother telling my sister someone had been raped and to watch herself . . . I remember her laughing and saying it was nonsense. Of course, when they realised I was listening they shut up. It wasn't like it is nowadays . . . there were things that were never spoken of in front of children.'

'You said Muriel still lives round here. Do you know where?'

'I don't want her to think I've been gossiping.'

'Your name won't be mentioned. I promise.'

'She lives at Seafield Farm, on the road out of Bereton past the chantry. She married Cyril Napp. He's dead now, mind; died last year. Her son runs the place.' She put her teacup down and looked up at Rachel. 'So what are you thinking, then, my luvver? That Muriel got raped by a Yank in the war, then murdered him last Sunday for revenge?'

Rachel's mouth fell open. The old lady was sharper than she'd given her credit for. Mrs Sweeting started to laugh. 'Oh, you're way off the mark there, my luvver. Muriel would never do a thing like that . . . not Muriel Napp.'

'What makes you so sure?'

'You'll see for yourself. You go up to Seafield Farm and see for yourself.'

Rachel, pride wounded, bade Mrs Sweeting a polite goodbye and resolved to do just that.

Wesley was home early. Heffernan had told him to go and get something to eat and check on Pam. He was due back at Tradmouth HQ at 6.30 when they'd interview Kevin Martin. Kevin was on the lower rungs of the ladder of crime, Wesley thought to himself: burglary, receiving. Inadequate and dishonest . . . but murder was a different thing altogether. Had Kevin moved from one league into another?

When he arrived home, Pam was on her way out. She was going to see Sue next door. For the past couple of days her idea about having them to stay hadn't been mentioned: Wesley hoped it had been quietly forgotten.

The dining table was covered with Pam's schoolwork again. Wesley was becoming concerned about her: she should be taking it easy. But whenever he mentioned the subject he was accused of fussing – of being unaware that pregnancy and childbirth were the most natural things in the world. But they'd waited so long for this baby. Wesley couldn't bear to think of anything going wrong now. He resolved to be firmer with her . . . to enlist the help of his mother-in-law if necessary. After all, she wasn't far away; only in Plymouth. It was time Pam began to put her feet up and rest.

The sight of the pile of exercise books on the table jogged something in his memory. Mallindale . . . a child's account of a wartime murder, a child called David Mallindale. Wesley silently cursed himself for not asking June Mallindale if David was any relation. But then, was it important? Probably not.

He searched through the pile of books until he found the one he was looking for. He reread the account. A man out shooting rabbits was shot dead by an American soldier. There must be a record of such an incident, even after all this time. And there must be someone still alive who would remember. It might be nothing to do with Norman Openheim's death but, on the other hand, it meant that there might – just might – be somebody in the district with a festering grudge against the US forces. He dismissed it from his mind as he went into the kitchen to open a tin of tuna for supper. He was allowing his imagination to escape and trample all over the bare known facts. However, he would make enquiries, see if any records existed at headquarters . . . to satisfy his own curiosity if nothing else.

He opened the tuna and put it on two plates, then set some oven chips to cook – the limit of his culinary skills.

When Pam returned she found her husband asleep on the sofa dreaming of rabbits shooting murderous Spanish sailors with sawn-off bayonets. Like everything else, Wesley's dreams made no sense.

Chapter Eleven

'Overpaid, oversexed and over here.' Reportedly that's what the men of England used to say about the Americans posted here in the war. The first two items on the list might merit some discussion but the third was indisputable: over here they certainly were, and their impact on the locality in the war years cannot be over-estimated.

From *A History of Bereton and Its People* by June Mallindale

Rachel put the phone down. Dave had sounded cool, resentful. She had only told him that she couldn't go to the cinema with him that evening, that she had to work late. The film was only about the war anyway . . . hardly her taste. He'd have to understand that her work came first, took priority over everything. Besides, once he'd lost the flat on her family's farm she might be seeing a lot less of him: she'd have to get used to that.

She pushed any regrets firmly to the back of her mind and called across the room. 'Steve, are you doing anything that can't wait?'

'Why?' When Rachel put on the charm, Steve got suspicious.

'I wanted someone to come with me to the Clearview . . . have a word with a witness.'

'Okay.' A visit to the Clearview, a walk to clear his head, might be just what he needed. He was still suffering from the effects of too much beer the night before. 'Who are you going to see?' he asked, wondering what the normally-so-efficient Rachel was up to. He had never found her secretive before: usually everything was above board, by the book.

'You'll see.'

'Going to surprise me, are you?' Maybe it wasn't work. Maybe she fancied him. Maybe his luck was changing. He wouldn't mind getting his leg over with Rachel Tracey; he'd often thought that.

'Look, Steve, if this doesn't work out, don't mention it to the boss, will you?'

Better and better. He could use this to his advantage. She was confiding in him: there was something, a secret, they would share; a bond between them, the first step on the way to the bedroom. Maybe she'd suggest a drink after this was over, then back to his flat. He turned and saw that she was looking at him.

'Don't get any ideas, Steve. This is purely business.'

Steve was resigned to his irresistible charms not working every time. There were plenty more pebbles on the beach . . . a good simile, he thought, for a walk by Bereton Sands.

It was dusk. The residents of the Clearview were about to go into dinner. The American party had been told earlier that they could go on to London the next day, provided they left details of their whereabouts. Ed Johnson had been reunited with his wife: they'd have to sort out their problems themselves. Nobody else could dictate what went on between husband and wife.

Rachel went into the bar. She looked around: sitting at the bar was the man she was looking for. She could hear her heart beating. She had to speak to him alone.

She looked at Steve standing behind her and began to regret the decision to bring him with her. But she was stuck with him, so she'd better make the best of it. She stepped forward.

'Litton Boratski?' He nodded. 'My name's Detective Constable Tracey. Can I have a word with you, sir?'

'Sure, why not.' He smiled at her, friendly, unsuspecting.

Rachel was about to wipe that smug smile off Litton Boratski's face.

'I'd like a word in private, sir.'

'Why?'

'I think it would be best, sir.'

Dorinda Openheim and Todd Weringer chose that moment to enter the bar. Rachel cursed silently. But Dorinda and Todd, engrossed in each other, ignored her, and steered themselves towards the bar to order drinks.

Rachel led Litton Boratski through into the deserted lounge;

Steve followed, looking slightly puzzled. Rachel, less sure of herself now, took a deep breath and began.

'Mr Boratski, certain allegations were made against you in June 1944.'

'June '44. I was mighty busy in June '44. We all were . . . liberating France. Who made the allegations? Hitler?'

Rachel ignored the joke, reminding herself all the time that this was a serious matter . . . the most serious, apart from murder. 'It's in the civilian police records of the time that you were accused of rape.'

'Now hang on . . .' Litton Boratski looked angry rather than guilty. 'That was all a mistake.'

'It was handed over to the military authorities, Mr Boratski. What happened?'

'The colonel will tell you . . . it was a mistake.'

'There couldn't have been much time for an investigation. You were off to France.'

'I told them what happened.'

'And they believed you?'

'It was the truth.'

'Tell me.'

'I wouldn't repeat things like that to a lady.'

Rachel, seething at this challenge to her professionalism, nevertheless had to play along with it. 'Will you tell my colleague here?'

'Guess so. Not much to tell.' He turned to Steve. Rachel moved her chair away and strained to hear what was being said.

'I had a girl . . . a local girl,' Boratski began softly, glancing at Rachel. 'Lots of the guys did. The old chapel was out of bounds but it was a good place for . . . you know.'

Steve nodded, a man of the world.

'I took this girl Muriel up there a few times . . . regular thing. We'd been seeing each other ever since I arrived in England. She was keen . . . all over me, you know, never objected. I met her one night as usual and a couple of days later word comes that I've been accused of rape. That was a hanging offence in those days. I just didn't understand it. We'd been . . . you know . . . for a couple of months. I couldn't think why Muriel would say a thing like that. She was a sweet girl. I was shocked. Luckily some of the other guys – Norm included, as a matter of fact – backed up my story.

166

We'd been out in a foursome a couple of nights before, me and Norm with Muriel and his girl . . . what was her name?'

'Marion,' said Rachel. Boratski looked at her awkwardly, not realising she'd overheard.

'Yeah, right . . . Marion. Anyway, the case was dropped . . . just like that. I don't know to this day why she accused me . . . we'd parted on good terms. I went over to France and I never saw her again. I can't understand why she would have lied.' Boratski looked genuinely puzzled. 'Nobody believed it, mind. They knew me better than that.'

'Did they, Mr Boratski?' Rachel stood up, stiff with suppressed anger. 'I'll be having a word with the woman involved, of course.'

Boratski looked up. 'Is she still around here? I sure would have liked to have seen her again if it wasn't for the things she said . . . the lies she told about me. She sure was a pretty girl.'

'We might want to talk to you again,' said Rachel, cool.

'Sure. And if you find out why Muriel said what she did you let me know . . . right?'

Rachel turned and left the room without a word.

'You were a bit hard on the old boy,' said Steve when they got outside.

'He's a bloody rapist, Steve. He was in a position of power and he abused it. They must have thought they were God Almighty with all those local girls throwing themselves at them.'

'Don't you think you should find out what really happened before making judgements? Or do you think all men are rapists, eh?'

Rachel walked ahead of him in silence. Normally Steve would have admired her legs from that vantage point, but somehow tonight he didn't feel inclined to.

Pam woke Wesley up gently, complaining that she could smell the oven chips burning.

'How's Sue?' he asked sleepily.

'There's good news. The housing association say there's a small maisonette up at Dukesbridge, but they can't get it till they're actually homeless. Let's hope it's not gone before the repossession. It's not ideal but it's a bloody sight better than bed and breakfast.'

'So they won't be coming to stay?'

'Well . . . er . . . only for a few days until it's all sorted out.'

'Great,' said Wesley, unconvinced.

He was getting the over-browned chips from the oven when the phone rang. Pam answered it. 'It's Neil . . . for you.' Her voice held a note of disapproval.

'Hi, Wes . . . been talking to Simon, the vicar. Can you get here now?' Neil sounded depressingly awake and enthusiastic. Wesley, who could hardly keep his eyes open, answered in the negative. He had a suspect to interview at half past six.

'Afterwards, then. Simon had a drink with us last night. He says we can have the church key any time.'

Neil had well and truly got his feet under the ecclesiastical table, thought Wesley.

'Meet you at the Bereton Arms when you've finished fitting up some unsuspecting innocent.'

Wesley put the phone down. His problem now was how to tell Pam he'd be late . . . and that his lateness wouldn't be entirely due to the administration of law and order.

Kevin Martin sat, his chin resting on his hand, studying the tape recorder as it whirred round. The duty solicitor, a dark-haired young woman, stifled a yawn and looked as though she'd rather be somewhere else. It was seven o'clock, and so far Kevin Martin had told them very little.

A young constable entered the room and Wesley announced the fact for the benefit of the tape. The constable thrust a note into Heffernan's hand. The inspector read it and looked up at Kevin, a triumphant grin on his face.

'Well, Kevin, I'm happy to tell you that you're well and truly nicked. It seems some diligent householder security-marked his valuables with a pen that only shows up under ultraviolet light. The lads downstairs shone their little machine over your things and lo and behold . . . a miracle. There it was, the gentleman's postcode. Anything to say, Kevin?'

The solicitor whispered something into her client's ear.

'No comment.' Kevin looked at Heffernan defiantly.

'Very well. We'll move on to something a bit more serious, then . . . murder.'

Kevin's defiance faded. He looked at the solicitor, genuinely worried.

'I never murdered no one,' he stammered.

'Your grandfather was murdered last Sunday night . . . about ten o'clock. Have you got a knife, Kevin?'

'No.'

'Not even a little one?'

'No.'

'What about a bayonet – wartime souvenir . . . or a sword?'

'No . . . I ain't got nothing like that.'

'What about the one we found in your flat? The one in the box with the jewellery?'

'That's just an ornament . . . for decoration.'

'Looked pretty lethal to me. Where did you get it?'

'Told you . . . I'm looking after it for a mate.'

'The mate you met on Sunday night?'

'Yeah . . . that's right.'

'Seen him since then?'

'No.'

Heffernan sat back, studying Kevin's face. 'An ornamental dagger just like that one was nicked from a holiday cottage on Tuesday night. But if this story about this mate in the pub's true you've had it longer than that. You could have got it at the pub then went to threaten your granddad with it . . . he was killed with a blade just like that.' He glanced at the solicitor, who was leaning forward, listening intently. 'Are you going to tell me the truth about these burglaries, Kevin, or am I going to have to charge you with murder?'

'Really, Inspector, I must object. You've no real evidence against my client.' The solicitor knew when she was on a losing streak but she had to make an effort for appearance's sake.

'He's got a motive and no alibi that he can prove and now we've found a weapon similar to that used to murder his grandfather.'

'What motive?' She was becoming curious.

'Money. He hoped to get some money out of the old man. All Yanks are rich, isn't that right, Kevin. Granddad was going to save the day. Trouble is the old man wouldn't co-operate. I'm sure we can make a case out of that, Miss . . . er . . .'

'Etheridge,' said the solicitor stiffly.

'And the thing is, Miss Etheridge, if your client was the busy little beaver who's been doing over all these holiday homes, he'd have a cast-iron alibi for Sunday night. One was done just outside Tradmouth . . . a neighbour heard the alarm go off at quarter past ten. Also, if he was our burglar he wouldn't have acquired that dagger till Tuesday night. You see my dilemma, Miss Etheridge. If he denies the burglaries then he's well and truly in the frame for Granddad's murder.'

Kevin Martin put his head in his hands. Miss Etheridge sat back, considering the best course of action.

Wesley, who had watched the proceedings with interest, spoke. 'Come on, Kevin, you've got a record for burglary.'

Kevin looked up. 'Okay. I did the cottages. It weren't like they were people's houses . . . only rich bastards who just use 'em at the weekends. You should see the stuff in 'em.'

'Okay, Kevin, save us the Marxist philosophy. You were busy doing over a cottage outside Tradmouth on the night of the murder.'

'That's right. Anyway, I wouldn't kill my own granddad . . . who'd do a thing like that?'

'It has been known,' sighed Wesley.

After the formal charges and Kevin's routine refusal to name his accomplices, Gerry Heffernan had one more question to ask.

'Did you ever meet your granddad, Kevin?'

Kevin shook his head. 'I tried but . . .'

'What happened?'

'It was on the Sunday, the night he was . . . you know. A mate gave me a lift over to Bereton in his van. We parked outside the hotel and I didn't know if I should go in or not. We sat outside in the carpark for about ten minutes . . . then I chickened out. We went . . . you know . . .'

'A-burgling?'

'Yeah.'

'So you sat outside for ten minutes. What time was this?'

'About half nine, quarter past . . . I don't really know.'

'Did you see anything . . . anyone going in and out?'

'Er . . . yeah. It was boring so we watched 'em.'

'Who did you see?'

'There was this old bird . . . got into a car – hatchback, dark-coloured.'

Sally Johnson, Heffernan thought.

'Then this old guy . . . tall . . . went towards the beach.'

'Towards the war memorial and that tank?'

'Yeah.'

The colonel paying his private respects.

'And there was this old couple . . . they walked out of the hotel separately, but once they thought nobody could see them they got all lovey-dovey and linked arms. We had a laugh about that.'

'Was he tall and white-haired and she quite small?'

Kevin nodded. Todd and Dorinda.

'Then this old guy came out. He was wearing a baseball cap and one of them baseball jackets with a name on.'

Wesley sat forward. 'Go on. What did he do?'

'Well, we were pissing ourselves. Old codgers shouldn't dress like that . . . looked daft. He lit a fag and walked out of the carpark up towards the village, I think.'

'Did you see the name on his jacket?'

'Yeah . . . began with B.'

'Buffalo Bisons?'

'Yeah . . . that sounds about right. And then there was the other person . . . came out after the old codger in the daft jacket.'

'After? You mean he was following him?'

Kevin thought for a moment. 'Yeah . . . looked like it.'

'Can you describe this person?' the inspector asked slowly.

Heffernan and Wesley sat on the edges of their seats. Even Miss Etheridge looked at Kevin expectantly.

'He was sort of hunched . . . in a dark coat. I didn't see his face. It was dark and he was all hunched over. Now that I think about it he was definitely following the other bloke . . . yeah.'

'This friend of yours, we'd like to talk to him so that he can confirm your story . . . put you in the clear for the murder.'

Kevin was in a quandary. But he reasoned that because his companion had been with him at 9.30 it didn't necessarily follow that he was still with him when he broke into a cottage at 10.15. He gave the name . . . a name very familiar to Gerry Heffernan: an old and valued customer of Tradmouth CID.

'Did you realise that the bloke in the fancy jacket was your granddad?'

Kevin looked genuinely dumbstruck. 'No, I never met him . . . I never knew. Was that him? You sure? Fucking hell . . . I never knew.'

'That means the person who followed him could well have been his killer.'

Kevin shook his head, unable to take it in. 'It was just a figure . . . not tall, not small.'

'Man or woman?'

'Man . . . well, it could have been a woman, I suppose. I couldn't tell. It was dark. But I remember one thing. Whoever it was wasn't young, I'm sure of that. And they wore a scarf . . . a long scarf round them covering half their face. That's all I remember.'

'And this person came out of the hotel?'

'I thought so . . . but I didn't actually see them come out – they could have been waiting in the bushes, I suppose. I don't know.'

Kevin flopped back into his seat and Wesley switched the tape off.

'You've done very well, Kevin . . . very well indeed,' Heffernan assured him. 'Now we'd like to offer you some hospitality. There's a nice warm cell waiting.'

Kevin, on his way out, escorted by a large constable, turned to Heffernan. 'I hope you get whoever did my granddad.'

'At least there's some family feeling there, Wes,' Heffernan said as Kevin was led away. 'Light-fingered Kevin may be, but there's no way he'd have done in his old granddad.'

'So who do you reckon did, sir?'

'This was waiting for me when I got to the station.' Heffernan fished in his pocket and handed Wesley a crumpled letter. Wesley read it.

'Fern Ferrars again.'

'Read what it says.'

'I have, sir. It makes no sense. "Old sins repeat. When you find the Armada boy you'll know who killed the soldier." She's a nutcase. We had one at the Met . . . always coming in the station and . . .'

'I don't know, Wes. I'm keeping an open mind. She did this before, you know. It was a case Stan Jenkins was working on. Stan never said much about it but he did tell me once over a pint that she'd been right about something . . . told him where to look for a body.'

Wesley still looked sceptical. 'Well, we've had a fair amount of boys in this case, most of them villains and none with any connection with the Armada that I know of. You don't think one of them's got Spanish ancestors, do you? Could that be it?'

172

'No idea. Your guess is as good as mine. Have you seen Rachel this afternoon?'

'No, I haven't. One thing I've been meaning to mention, sir . . . I've been reading through some accounts of Bereton during the war when the Americans were stationed here. One of them mentions a murder. A local man was shot by one of the Americans when he was out after rabbits. If Norman Openheim's murder's connected with the past . . .'

'No harm in looking. Have a word with Bob Naseby. There's records in that basement dating back to the Domesday Book, so I've heard. Coming for a pint?'

'I've arranged to meet Neil Watson at the church. He's looking for a grave.'

'He's gone to the right place, then. Off you go. I'll have a quick pint in the Tradmouth Arms then back home to a good book.'

The Tradmouth Arms was Heffernan's local, a few yards from his waterfront home. Wesley, knowing his boss led a lonely widower's existence, with his two children away at university and only his beloved boat for company, spoke on impulse. 'Why don't you come with me to the church, sir? Might be interesting.'

Heffernan's eyes lit up. 'Yeah. Thanks, Wes.'

Wesley found himself yawning as he drove towards Bereton. He parked by the church. The lights were on, illuminating the pictures in the stained glass so that they glowed, jewel bright, in the fading dusk.

'Does Pam know you're skiving?' Heffernan asked, mischief in his voice, knowing he was nudging Wesley's conscience.

'I told her I'd be late.'

'Wonderful things, wives. Mind you, don't tell her the truth . . . best that she thinks you're putting villains behind bars. Many's the time Kathy thought I was putting in a spot of overtime when I was having a pint with the lads or taking the *Rosie May* out on the river.'

'At least it's better than having another woman.'

Heffernan chuckled as they walked up the church path. 'I'm sure the vicar'd agree that archaeology's better than adultery. Evening, Vicar.'

The vicar was standing by the church door, looking as if he were preparing to shake hands with his departing congregation. 'Neil's just taking the books out of the cupboard . . . shouldn't be long,' he said. He sounded cautiously excited: the prospect of an important historical discovery in his church intrigued him.

'Hey, Wes, look at this I've found. There was a wooden box shoved to the back of the cupboard. This was inside.' Neil handed Wesley a sheet of parchment. He unfolded it carefully as it was obviously extremely old, then took it over to the table that accommodated church magazines and other books and leaflets for sale. He pushed them to one side and laid the parchment out flat.

By this time Neil was looking over his shoulder. Heffernan and the vicar were hovering in the background, awaiting the verdict.

'It's a will,' said Wesley, matter-of-factly. 'The last will and testament of Matthew Mallindale.'

'Come on, Wes, read it out,' urged Neil impatiently.

'I bequeath my soul to Almighty God and His Son Our Lord Jesus Christ and my body to be buried wherever I chance to die,' Wesley read slowly, deciphering the handwriting with difficulty. 'My sins are such that I should not lie in sanctified ground but I beg the Lord to have mercy upon me and beseech whoever doth find my poor body to bury it in some consecrated earth though I would not think myself fit to lie within the walls of a church.'

'Modest,' commented Heffernan.

'Very commendable humility,' affirmed the vicar. 'Go on, Wesley . . . what else does it say?'

'There's a list of his household goods. Some go to his wife . . . his second-best bed.'

'They can't have got on . . . why didn't he let her have his best one?'

'His best one went to his son, Matthew, and he got his cushions and tablecloth too.'

'Wow.' Neil was starting to lose interest. 'Come on, Wes, leave that. Let's shift this cupboard.'

Reluctantly Wesley put the parchment down and took his jacket off, ready to work. The cupboard was heavy, even without its contents which lay scattered on the nearby pews. The Victorians certainly knew how to build furniture of monumental proportions. Heffernan, fearful for his back, directed operations, while the vicar valiantly lent a hand. Between the three of them they managed to move the cupboard a couple of yards to the left.

Neil bent down and examined the floor. 'We've uncovered most of it. One more go . . . another few feet.'

Another effort and they stood, regaining their breath. It was there, revealed – a slab of stone set into the floor, six foot by two foot.

'Sacred to the memory of Roderigo Sanchez, sailor of the ship *San Miguel*. Aged 17. Our enemy but much wronged by his fellow man. Most unjustly murdered on the 1st day of September 1588. May the Lord avenge this wrong.'

'Bloody hell,' said Neil, forgetting where he was. 'What the devil's he doing here?'

'Looks like we've found the Armada boy, Wes,' Heffernan said softly.

Chapter Twelve

'And finally I beseech God to have mercy upon me and forgive the grievous sin that stains my soul with the blood of the innocent.'

Extract from the will of Matthew Mallindale,
dated 5 October 1588

Rachel Tracey had lain awake all night thinking of the visit she had to make ... thinking of the best, the most tactful, way of asking the necessary questions. She looked at her watch. Ten fifteen ... positively late by farming standards, where the day began at dawn. She looked around and saw that Wesley was reading a file, apparently engrossed in its contents. She stood up, papers in hand, and walked out of the room casually. Wesley didn't look up. Steve was on the phone and didn't give her a second glance.

The day was warm enough to venture out without a coat: the jacket of her suit would be adequate to protect her from the gentle spring elements. She had decided to walk. It wasn't far and questions might be asked if anyone missed a car. And she didn't want any questions asked ... not yet.

The inspector was absent: Rachel suspected that, it being Saturday morning, he had treated himself to a spot of sailing. Having a think, blowing out the cobwebs: those were his usual excuses. Not that Rachel blamed him: when she made inspector, she told herself, she might develop similar foibles ... and be allowed to get away with them so long as her results lived up to the super's expectations.

She had overheard a telephone conversation between Wesley and Heffernan earlier in the day. They were discussing some tomb or other . . . and some will that had been placed in a church safe. Wesley had finished the call with a cheery promise to see Heffernan later. She hoped the inspector wouldn't arrive back before her mission was completed.

She left the village hall and walked through Bereton, past the Restoricks' cottage, past the mini-market and the church. Two ladies of a certain age were walking down the churchyard path, their arms filled with flowers. They would be preparing for a wedding, Rachel thought, or maybe just decorating the church for the Sunday services.

There were cars parked in the lay-by near the chantry: the dig was still in full swing. That was another thing Rachel didn't understand; why expend all that energy digging up the remnants of the past when the needs of the present were so pressing?

Another ten yards or so and she came to a farm track: a battered wooden sign announced that it led to Seafield Farm. She hadn't realised it was so close to the chantry; that could be significant in itself, she thought. She walked up the track warily. Her smart patent shoes with their small heels were woefully inadequate for the terrain. She cursed herself: a farmer's daughter should have known better.

A tractor approached and stopped. Its driver, a swarthy man in his late thirties, quite attractive in an earthy sort of way, leaned down from his elevated position and asked Rachel if he could help her, his voice thick with innuendo.

'Can you tell me where I'll find a Mrs Muriel Napp?'

'That depends.' His eyes twinkled flirtatiously. 'You'll be from the health centre.' Rachel said nothing. 'You're better-looking than the last one we had. She had a face like the back of one of my sows.'

'If you can just tell me where I'll find Mrs Napp . . .'

'She's up at the house. You'd better watch it. Mum eats health visitors for breakfast.'

He winked and drove off down the track, churning up a mud puddle that splashed all over Rachel's tights. She looked down at her splattered legs: she was a mess.

The farmhouse was stone-built and symmetrical; every picture book's ideal of what a farmhouse should look like. Rachel crossed the hay-strewn cobbles of the farmyard and knocked at the door. She had to wait a good two minutes before the door was opened. She fixed her eyes on the centre of the door where she expected a face to appear. But there was nothing: for a split second she found herself staring into the empty hall until she looked downwards at the occupant of the wheelchair. 'Mrs Napp?'

The old lady nodded. 'You the new health visitor? Come along in, my luvver. Don't you go standing on the doorstep catching your death. You should have worn wellington boots . . . did nobody tell you?' Mrs Napp shook her white curly head as she contemplated the inefficiencies of the National Health Service.

Rachel produced her warrant card, suddenly realising she should have brought someone with her, not struck out on her own. But it was too late now. Mrs Napp's bodily frailty made her apprehensive about questioning her about the rape: there were some scars that never healed. It occurred to her that she should cut her losses and leave. Then Mrs Napp looked up at her, an unexpected toughness in her bright blue eyes. 'What is it? What do you want? I ain't robbed no banks . . . this chair'd never make a getaway car.' She chuckled at her joke and Rachel dutifully joined in. 'In you come and make us a cup of tea . . . and take them shoes off.'

Rachel obeyed. Muriel Napp – Carmichael as was – hardly fitted Rachel's mental picture of a scared rape victim. As her son had said, she'd have eaten a health visitor for breakfast and still had room for a policewoman. The frailty of the body belied the toughness of the mind.

Rachel made the tea in her stockinged feet. The old farmhouse kitchen had been adapted to suit a wheelchair user. Muriel valued her independence. Rachel found herself admiring the woman even before she got to know her.

As she sat down by the ancient Aga, Muriel sitting opposite her in her wheelchair, her head tilted expectantly, Rachel wondered how to begin.

'Go on, then, my luvver, spit it out. What is it you want to know?'

'It's about something that happened during the war. I found a file . . . a report that you were . . . er . . . assaulted by one of the . . .'

'I were never assaulted. That's wrong.'

Rachel paused. She had been trying to put it gently, but clearly semantics had got in the way. She'd have to be more blunt. 'There was a report that you were raped, Muriel. I know it's a painful memory and I don't want to upset you ...'

She looked across at Muriel who, to her amazement, was starting to laugh. 'Oh no, my luvver, you've got it all wrong. There's one good thing about being old ... you can speak plain. It were my dad reported that ... when he found out I was in the family way. He was that angry that he went off down the police station in Tradmouth and reported that my boyfriend had raped me. He wanted his revenge, you see. I never spoke to my dad after that ... Litton would have been hanged if he'd been found guilty, do you know that? It was just spite ... my dad wanting to punish him for what we'd done. I told him it took two for that sort of thing but he just dragged me over to the pump and washed my mouth out with soap.'

Rachel saw the determination and anger on Muriel's face, reawakened after fifty years. She had been expecting one tragedy, one set of agonising memories, but she was sitting there with Muriel Napp confronting another – very different but just as painful in its own way.

'So you weren't raped?'

'Oh no. Litton was a sergeant ... bit older than me. He was a very handsome man, and it was wartime. We didn't know if he'd be killed that next week or ... I still don't know what became of him; died in France most likely ... such a waste.' She sighed.

Rachel was in a dilemma. Should she inform Muriel that her wartime sweetheart was staying not a mile away? She told herself that she wasn't in the business of reuniting old lovers. She said nothing.

'Anyway,' Muriel continued, 'I knew Litton would face a trial when the Yank authorities heard ... the police had to pass the case over to them, you see. I wasn't having that. I went to see his commanding officer. Hard to get in, it was: there was something going on – they were getting ready for something, you could tell – but I was determined. I got in to see him and told him the truth. I made sure that the case was all dropped. My dad would have seen him hanged but ...'

'That was very brave of you. I hope Litton appreciated it.'

'I'll never know. They went over to France a few days later. I never saw him again. That's war, my luvver ... you count yourself lucky. We had to live for the moment . . . that's all we could do.'

'You said you were in the family way?'

Muriel's face clouded. 'Aye . . . I was sent away to my aunt's in Norfolk. No one had to know . . . that was the thing then.'

'What happened to the baby?'

This time Muriel's defiance cracked and her eyes filled with tears. 'Little boy, it was . . . taken away as soon as he was born. They said a nice couple adopted him. I still think of him . . . imagine what he's like, what he does, what he looks like. If he's like his dad he'll be good-looking.'

'I'm sure he is,' said Rachel gently, leaning across to put her hand on the old woman's wrinkled, brown-spotted arm.

'I've had three more children but I still think of him . . . funny, isn't it?'

'It's natural.'

'My late husband never knew . . . it's not something you admitted to in those days. And my children don't know they've got a half-brother somewhere.'

'And Litton never knew he had a son.'

'Best that way.' She looked up, regaining her strength. 'It doesn't do to dwell on what might have been.'

'You must find it hard to forgive your father for what he did.'

'He did what he thought was right. I hated him for years . . . never even invited him to my wedding. But now I'm too old to bear grudges, girl . . . you'll find that when you get to my age.'

'Did you know Norman Openheim . . . the man who was murdered?'

'He were courting young Marion Miles. She had a baby . . . folks swore it was Norman's but Albert Potter married her. That shut up the wagging tongues. She was lucky,' Muriel added philosophically. 'Litton and I went courting in the old chantry where poor Norman was found . . . along with half the rest of the US Army.' She laughed. 'The local lads kept away after the shooting, of course.'

'What shooting?'

'Well, it wasn't actually in the chantry . . . just outside. It was all out of bounds – all Bereton was – but it was overrun with rats and rabbits and the like, there being no people around. Lots of the locals came to Bereton to shoot the rabbits.'

180

'Why?'

Muriel gave Rachel a pitying look. 'There was rationing, my luvver. Food was scarce. If you could get a couple of rabbits for your pot you thought you were eating like the king himself.'

'So who got murdered?'

'A young man called Arthur Challinor home on leave. He went out shooting rabbits with a friend and an American soldier shot him. His friend got away to tell the tale.'

'Was the soldier charged with murder?'

'I don't know . . . shouldn't think so. He'd just say he shot a trespasser, wouldn't he?'

Rachel looked at her watch. 'I suppose so. I'll have to get back now. Thank you for talking to me.' She looked up. Something on the kitchen shelf caught her eye. 'Having trouble with rats, Mrs Napp?' Rachel had recognised the packet . . . the same brand as her father used on their farm.

'Aye. The buggers get into the barns . . . reckon they come in from the old chantry.'

'Could be.' Rachel stood up. 'Thank you again, Mrs Napp.' She hesitated, wondering if she should mention Litton Boratski's presence in Bereton, but decided against it. Leave Muriel with her memories and her illusions that Litton didn't contact her because he was dead. That was probably better than knowing that he hadn't chosen to.

She put her shoes on by the front door and squelched her way back to the village hall. She felt disappointed: she had been so sure that Norman's murder had been an act of revenge, but all she had found was a lingering affection in the women the US soldiers had seduced and abandoned. She found herself despairing of her own sex.

Wesley drove over to Tradmouth, parked his car in the police station yard, and realised he was hungry. The file he was looking for had stayed in the basement since 1944 . . . a few more minutes would make no difference. He treated himself to a pasty.

Strolling back along the cobbled quayside by the forest of clinking metal masts, he finished the pasty and wiped his greasy hands on a tissue. The brain, he told himself, always functions best on a full stomach.

'Hi, Wes.'

He turned to see Heffernan's face grinning up at him from the

181

deck of a small sailing vessel. 'Just rounded the headland . . . blew a few cobwebs out. Coming aboard?'

'I'd rather not, sir.' Wesley preferred the stability of dry land. 'I was just on my way to the station.'

'I'll come with you.' Heffernan checked the *Rosie May* was securely moored and leaped ashore with surprising agility for a man of his size. 'Good work last night, Wes. Now all we need to do is to find out who killed old Norman and then we can take a well-earned rest.'

Wesley smiled at his superior's optimistic view of police work. Unfortunately the criminals of the area wouldn't be so obliging; not with the tourist season coming up. Heffernan knew this too . . . but it was good to fantasise now and then. And they were no nearer catching Norman Openheim's killer. There was something – or someone – they had missed.

When they reached the station they found Bob Naseby holding court at the front desk with some lost Japanese tourists. With much bowing, the Japanese were duly directed towards the castle. As the swing-door shut behind them Heffernan found the melody of Puccini's 'One Fine Day' going through his head again. He wondered how Marion Potter was.

Wesley made no such association but made straight for the front desk. Bob Naseby's eyes lit up.

'Wesley . . . just the man I want to see. Can I put you down to bat third against D Division on the thirtieth?'

'Sorry, Bob . . . still tied up with this case over at Bereton.'

'But later in the season . . . you'll be all right for then?' Bob Naseby's massive brow furrowed with concern.

'Well, you know my wife's expecting . . . it'd be more than my life's worth to commit myself, believe me, Bob.'

Bob, deeply disappointed, looked at the henpecked husband with pity. 'Next season, eh?'

'Hopefully.' Wesley turned to see Heffernan behind him, grinning mischievously. He decided to ignore his boss and tackle the matter in hand. 'I wonder if you could do me a favour, Bob. I'm looking for a file . . . it'll be 1944. Is that a problem?'

Bob shook his head. 'We had young Rachel in looking for a file from 1944 the other day . . . you lot doing historical research, are you?'

Wesley and Heffernan looked at each other. Rachel hadn't

mentioned this: they each wondered why this was . . . and what she had discovered.

'What file was she looking for?'

'Rape case, it was . . . if that's the one you're after she's still got it.'

'It's another one, a murder . . . a man out shooting rabbits. Sorry I've not got more details, but it's just a long shot.'

'No problem . . . I'll send PC Jones down to the cellar.' Bob picked up the phone.

'Is that the probationer?'

'Aye. He were moaning about his mum having to get his uniform cleaned after getting Rachel's file. I told him it was an occupational hazard. I said, you wait till a drunk's sick all over you, then your mum'll have something to moan about.'

It was half an hour later that a dusty, cobweb-strewn PC Jones emerged from the cellar clutching a mildewed, dank-smelling file.

When Rachel returned to the village hall, she picked up the phone and rang Bob Naseby. She asked sweetly for another favour, then Bob gave her the bad news. The inspector and Sergeant Peterson were already in possession of the file she was enquiring about. They'd left five minutes ago. Rachel put the phone down . . . too hard. Resentment rose within her like a wave of nausea. It was her discovery: now her superiors would take the credit. She had taken a chance – leapt at it when it came along, pushed her personal life, her relationship with Dave, aside – all for nothing.

But she was a realist. She knew that showing bitterness, making enemies in the force, was the route to disaster. There was something else she could do . . . and she would do it now.

WPC Trish Walton was young and keen, anxious to please: she reminded Rachel of herself when she had first joined the force. Rachel summoned her over and explained that they were to pay a call on a possible witness . . . one who would need careful handling.

The fact that it was Saturday was auspicious. Rachel had stored the information that Annie Restorick cleaned at the Clearview Hotel on a Saturday in some deep compartment of her brain to be nurtured and used when the time was right. The time was right now: she would talk to Wayne without his guardian dragon.

She knocked on the door of Apple Cottage and heard a

shuffling noise from within coming nearer until the door opened and Wayne's head peeped out cautiously. 'What do you want? It's only me and Gran in. My mum said I wasn't to let anyone in.'

.   'That's all right, Wayne, I'm sure she didn't mean us. She meant bad men . . . people who'd hurt you. We're from the police: we're here to look after you.'

She smiled, watching Wayne as he performed slow mental somersaults, trying to reason out whether his mother's orders applied to friend as well as foe. He made up his mind. These two ladies would do him no harm. They were nice ladies . . . they smiled. He opened the door wide to let them in.

'Would you like me to make a cup of tea, Wayne?' asked Rachel gently. Wayne nodded keenly. 'Would your gran like one?'

He shook his head. 'Gran's asleep.'

Better and better, Rachel thought; they wouldn't be interrupted.

The kitchen, in Rachel's judgement, could have done with a good clean. No concession had been made to modern fads and fashions. The cupboards were laminate, *circa* 1965. An army of industrious ants marched purposefully across one corner of the stained lino floor.

'You should put some ant powder down, Wayne,' Rachel said, making conversation.

'I couldn't kill nothing,' Wayne replied with solemn conviction.

No, I don't think you could, Rachel thought to herself as she poured the tea into the chipped china mugs.

When they were settled, Rachel leaned forward. Trish Walton watched her intently. Watching CID at work was still a novelty . . . still like something off the telly.

'Wayne . . . look, we know you wouldn't harm anyone, but it would help us a lot if you told me what you saw up at the chapel last Sunday night. There's a very bad person around who killed the American gentleman and I want to catch that person so that they can't hurt anyone again. Do you understand, Wayne?'

He nodded.

'Were you at the chapel last Sunday?'

He nodded again, more nervously this time.

'Can you tell me what you saw?' Rachel asked in her sweetest, most unthreatening voice.

'He was dead . . . just lying there. He had his eyes open.' Wayne giggled. 'He looked surprised.'

'What did you do when you found him?'

'I asked him if he was all right.'

'And he didn't answer?'

Wayne shook his head.

'So what did you do then?'

'I wanted to run away.'

'And did you?'

Wayne nodded.

'Did you do anything before you ran away? Pick anything up . . . touch anything? Don't worry, Wayne, you won't get into trouble.'

'There were some fags. My mum won't let me buy them. I wanted to try them. I didn't like it . . . made me cough.'

'Did you take anything else?'

'It was just lying there . . . he didn't need it, not if he was dead.' Wayne suddenly looked bashful, a naughty child about to be found out.

'Will you show it to me?' Rachel smiled. This seemed to reassure Wayne. He left the room. They could hear his footsteps in the bedroom above. He reappeared holding something oblong and shiny. He showed it to Rachel proudly, not allowing her to touch it. The silver cigarette lighter bore Norman Openheim's initials and was engraved with the likeness of an animal . . . a buffalo, Rachel thought, during the brief glimpse she had of it before Wayne snatched it away and held it protectively to his chest.

'It's mine now . . . I didn't steal it. He was dead.'

'When your mum gets back will you let me write all this down? We need to if we're going to catch the person who killed him.'

'I didn't steal it,' Wayne said, protecting his precious treasure.

'Of course you didn't, Wayne. Don't worry about it. It's more important that we find out who killed Mr Openheim.'

'Was that his name?'

Rachel nodded. 'Did you see anything else, Wayne . . . was anyone else there?'

Wayne hesitated. 'No,' he said emphatically . . . too emphatically. Rachel knew he was lying.

'Where's Rachel?'

Steve looked up from his computer. 'Don't know, sir. She went out half an hour ago with WPC Walton . . . said she wouldn't be long.'

'Great.' Heffernan sighed with annoyance. 'Look in her desk, Wes . . . see if you can find this file.'

Wesley hesitated, unwilling to violate a colleague's privacy. But he knew there was no option. He tried the desk drawer. Locked.

'We'll wait till she comes back, then.' Heffernan lumbered into his office. 'She's got some explaining to do.'

A cheery good afternoon heralded the arrival of the Reverend Simon Bradshaw. Wesley went out to greet him.

'So glad I found you, Wesley. I went looking for Neil but someone told me he'd gone off to Exeter. I've found something that might be of interest to you. It was at the back of the church safe . . . behind the old registers. I was looking in the registers for details of the Spaniard's burial and I came across these things quite by chance. These are photocopies . . . I didn't want to let the originals out of the church. They're quite difficult to read, as you'll see.' He handed Wesley a sheaf of papers.

'Thanks. I'll have a look at them later. What exactly are they?'

'They seem to be an account of a sanctuary case: the Spanish sailor buried in the church gets a mention. It was presumably written by the vicar of the day . . . looks like a copy of his report to his bishop or the local magistrate.'

Wesley smiled. 'Paperwork . . . they suffered from it then, did they?'

'Looks like it. I'll let you get on. Let me know what you think, won't you.'

Wesley pushed the papers into his desk drawer. There were more pressing papers to study. He opened the musty file PC Jones had brought up from the depths and began to read.

Arthur Challinor, a sailor home on leave, and his friend Charles Mallindale went out shooting rabbits at 7 am on 5 May 1944. They went into a forbidden area near Bereton village, as rabbits were reputed to be plentiful amongst the deserted houses and fields. Near the old chantry they were challenged and shot at by a young GI, identity unknown. The case was handed over to the US authorities with the information that the GI had been dark-haired, very young and, according to Charles Mallindale, had lit a cigarette before the poachers were spotted, using a flashy silver lighter with an animal's head on it. How he got close enough to see, the report didn't say. The response from the US authorities was in the file. The serviceman had every right to shoot trespassers on land used for top-secret operations: they would get the man's version and deal with the matter internally. Another letter from the US authorities dated a few days later stated bluntly that investigations had been made and they were satisfied that there was no case to answer. That was that: case closed. As the police had not investigated the matter the only items in the file were Charles Mallindale's statement and the correspondence from a Major Shultz. Precious little detail, but Wesley had a feeling that at last they were getting closer to the truth. The young, dark-haired GI with the flashy silver lighter. There were hundreds – thousands – of American servicemen stationed in the area, but it was too much of a coincidence that this one fitted the description of the teenage Norman. He went to tell the inspector the news.

'I think it's about time we had another word with our American cousins . . . find out what really happened.'

'Of course, it might have nothing to do with Openheim's death.'

'I'll bet my bottom dollar it does . . . as our transatlantic friends would say.'

The phone rang. Heffernan picked it up. He mouthed at Wesley, 'Fern Ferrars.' Wesley dutifully smiled.

'Yes, Ms Ferrars . . . yes . . . yes, I've got that . . . thanks very much.' He put the receiver down with some relief.

'Know what she's told me now, Wes? She's said that now we've found the Armada boy we're to listen to what he has to say.'

'How did she know about that?'

'Search me. But he's been dead four hundred years . . . he won't be doing much talking.'

'Maybe she didn't mean it literally, sir.'

'I don't know what she means, Wes.' Heffernan heard a familiar voice from behind his partition. He stood up. 'Get her in here now. I want a word with DC Tracey.'

Wesley found Rachel looking very pleased with herself. A shadow of apprehension passed over her face, however, when he broke the news that the boss wanted to see her and he wasn't pleased.

She decided to take the initiative, marching into the inspector's lair with a confidence she did not feel. 'Sir, I've been making a few investigations and . . .'

187

'And you didn't think of sharing these investigations of yours with your colleagues?'

'I was going to, sir, but then I got this lead and . . .'

'The rape file?'

Rachel's mouth opened and closed. 'Yes, sir.'

'Come on, Rach, we work as a team. We don't go haring off doing our own thing without telling everyone else.'

'I took WPC Walton when I went to talk to Wayne Restorick, sir.'

Heffernan looked as if he were about to explode. 'Wayne Restorick? Was his mother there?'

'Not exactly.'

The inspector put his head in his hands. 'I would have credited you with more sense, Rach. Don't you know there has to be an appropriate adult present when we interview . . .'

'It wasn't an interview, sir . . . just a cup of tea and a chat.'

Heffernan rolled his eyes. 'And what did our Wayne have to say for himself during this cosy tea party?'

'He took Norman Openheim's lighter, sir. And I'm sure there's something else. I'm sure he saw the killer.'

'And what's this about a rape?'

'There was no rape. In 1944 Litton Boratski got on the wrong side of a local girl's parents. They reported that their daughter had been raped . . . as a sort of revenge, I suppose. The charges were dropped. The girl was pregnant. I just thought it might have had something to do with the murder . . . just a long shot.'

She told him about her visit to Seafield Farm.

'Another Madam Butterfly, eh?'

'Pardon, sir?'

'I like to see my officers using their initiative, but cover yourself, Rach. Do it by the book. Right? And let me know what you're up to.'

Rachel looked suitably chastened. She'd got away with it. Her only worry was that Annie Restorick might make waves when she found out about her visit.

This time Rachel went to Apple Cottage accompanied by the inspector himself. Annie Restorick answered the door and made for Rachel like a possessive mother tiger.

'What do you think you're doing sneaking round here talking to my Wayne ... making him say things he doesn't understand? I've seen it on telly how you lot fit people like him up, people who aren't clever and can't answer back ... anything to get an arrest, that's all you lot are interested in. Well, it won't work ... I'm getting my solicitor.' Annie, well versed in the jargon from nightly rendezvous with her favourite cop shows and exposés of miscarriages of justice, stood her ground, daring the officers to come any nearer.

'Okay, love ... calm down now. Your Wayne's not a suspect. We just think he might have seen something, that's all. Any chance of a cup of tea? I'm gasping.'

Annie opened the door resentfully, thinking better of her initial hostility. It wouldn't really do to get on the wrong side of the law.

Over the worst cup of tea Gerry Heffernan had tasted in a long time, he managed to persuade Annie that Wayne would come to no harm if he and DC Tracey took a statement – with Annie herself present, of course – to the effect that Wayne found Norman Openheim's body and took his lighter, thinking the dead man would have no more use for it. Charges would not be brought and Annie could stop the proceedings at any time if she thought it was in her son's best interests. He couldn't say fairer than that.

Annie had to agree. Wayne, a model witness, repeated what he had told Rachel. Annie was satisfied and the crisis was averted. Rachel knew she had had a narrow escape.

When the police had gone, muttering their gratitude, Wayne turned to his mother. 'I didn't tell them, Mum.'

'Tell them what? What didn't you tell them?' All Annie's satisfaction that she had kept control of the situation drained away.

'I didn't tell them my secret.'

'What secret? Wayne ...' She was nearly screaming at him with frustration. 'What secret? Tell me. ...'

Wayne, calm, grinning smugly, tapped the side of his nose. 'If I told you it wouldn't be a secret ... and I promised. You can't break a promise.'

'What did you promise? Who made you promise? Wayne, tell me ...' She took her son by the shoulders and shook him.

Chapter Thirteen

Sir, I would advise you of all matters concerning this case of sanctuary. Master Mallindale did come to me with true penitence in his heart and I, as prescribed by custom and the law of the church, did grant him sanctuary. I do assure you, sir, that this is in no way in defiance of your office. Despite his blaming his heinous crime on a young man truly innocent (albeit that he was a foreigner and a papist) I do judge Master Mallindale truly repentant and will continue to grant him sanctuary for as long as he observes all the conditions thereof.

Extract from the report sent by Rev. James Tracey to
Master Joseph Fawley, Justice of the Peace, September 1588

'Rather you than me, Sarge.'

Wesley looked up to find Steve looking at him, lolling back in his chair, a copy of the *Sun* open at page three on his desk.

'Those old papers . . . don't know what you see in 'em myself. I prefer something more juicy.' He indicated the young lady, sadly devoid of garments, who stared out, blank-eyed, from the newspaper.

'*Chacun à son goût*,' muttered Wesley, returning his attention to the Reverend Tracey's account of the events of 1588. He made a mental note to ask Rachel if he was any relation . . . but not now. She was busy.

The story that unfolded as Wesley turned the pages began with an account of how the brave villagers of Bereton had 'captured and executed divers Spaniards of the ship the *San Miguel* wrecked off the sands'. It seemed that nobody questioned the rights and wrongs of the case. They were Spanish, enemies of the Queen and the Protestant faith, therefore they were rounded up, taken to the ruined chantry chapel just outside the village and cudgelled to death, their hands bound behind their backs. Rough justice . . . if it could be called justice. The bloodlust of a mob does not display the most appealing side of human nature.

One Spaniard, however, a lad of sixteen or seventeen, was found injured near the beach and sheltered by a Master Wheeler, a well-known recusant often fined for not attending church and suspected by his neighbours, the Mallindales, of being Roman Catholic. In those days that meant that Wheeler's loyalty to Crown and country was assumed to be dodgy, to say the least. There was even talk of 'divers Roman priests' seen visiting the Wheelers' farm 'most secretly'.

Reading the account, Wesley could almost feel the claustro-phobic atmosphere of the village and its hatreds, suspicions and narrow horizons. The Reverend Tracey, probably the only educated man in the place, seemed to be the sole possessor of common sense and reason. In his account he claimed to have remonstrated with the villagers about their unchristian attitudes and their 'lack of brotherly love one with another'. Too right, thought Wesley. The Reverend also had a go at his flock for stealing from the wreck of the *San Miguel* and pocketing the possessions of their Spanish prisoners. He accused Master Mallindale of helping himself to 'a dagger of fine gold' belonging to one of the captured officers. The Reverend Tracey couldn't have been a popular man.

He read on, and came to the account of the murder of one Alice Vigers – the village beauty, by all accounts. Aged just sixteen, she was found raped and stabbed up near the old chantry. It occurred to Wesley that the chantry had seen more than its share of blood-shed . . . and other things. If the courting couples of wartime and the present day had known its history, would they have been so ready to frolic in the place after dark? Sex and death . . . Bereton chantry had seen it all.

The body of Alice Vigers lay in the undergrowth surrounding the chapel for several days before she was found during a search organised by the villagers. Matthew Mallindale, the good citizen, came forward to testify that he had seen a youth 'of Spanish appearance' up near the chantry with blood on his clothing and hands.

This was as far as Wesley got before he was interrupted by the inspector's return. He pushed the papers to one side.

'How did you get on with Wayne Restorick?'

'No problem. He found the body, pinched the lighter . . . that's it, really.'

'I thought there might be something else . . . something he wasn't telling us.' Rachel spoke quietly but decisively.

'What makes you think that?'

She shook her head. 'I don't know, sir . . . just a feeling.'

'Female intuition,' Steve mumbled, looking up from the forensic report he had hastily placed on top of his newspaper. Rachel gave him a cold stare.

'What do you reckon we should do, then, Rach?' said Heffernan. 'Bring him in?'

'That might be counterproductive, sir. If he's frightened he won't talk at all. And there's Annie to consider.'

The phone rang. Wesley picked it up. When he put the receiver down his face was solemn. 'Nigel Glanville died an hour ago . . . massive internal injuries.'

There were few seconds of silence. Heffernan spoke first. 'Aunty won't be too upset . . . I'd say it'd be a weight off her mind. Does she know yet?'

'They didn't say.'

'I wanted to go down to the Clearview, have a ferret around. We'll tell her the sad news . . . if the hospital haven't already been in touch.' He looked at the unusual set of papers on Wesley's desk, hardly standard police forms. 'What have you got there, Wes?'

'The vicar brought them over . . . photocopies of some papers he found in the church safe.'

'Have you read them?'

'Halfway through. I thought that in view of Ms Ferrars's insistence that the Armada boy has something to do with this case . . .'

Heffernan perched himself on the edge of a desk. 'Come on, then, Wes . . . read 'em out.'

Wesley reached for the papers, embarrassed. 'They're difficult to read, sir . . . and the language is pretty archaic.'

'Is there much of it?'

'Not that much.'

'Go on, then.' Summary

Wesley gave a quick résumé of the story so far, then, studying the text carefully, began to read. 'I shall set forth the events which led to this present case of sanctuary. Master Mallindale, having borne witness against the young Spaniard, caused the men of the village to search diligently for the lad. It was suspected that Master Wheeler did shelter him and the men did search the Wheelers' farm under the guidance of the constable. The lad was not found then but on the morrow was found stabbed to death upon the ground of the chantry chapel, resting upon the graves of his comrades.'

Heffernan's face was a picture of concentration as he tried to follow just who was murdering whom. 'Go on, Wes,' he prompted.

Wesley continued. 'The following morn, Master Vigers did come to me at the church. He was in much distress. His wife, he did say, had killed a man . . . the young Spaniard who did defile and kill her daughter, Alice. She had gone to the chantry in great distress to the place where her daughter had died and found the young man praying at the graves of his shipmates. When she had killed the boy she did run away towards the shore saying she would drown herself in her sorrow.'

'Hang on, Wes. So this Spanish lad is hidden by this Catholic farmer . . . he rapes and murders a local lass then her mum finds him and kills him in revenge?'

'That's about it, sir. There's not much more . . . shall I go on?'

Heffernan nodded eagerly. Wesley cleared his throat. 'A senight later I was sore amazed to find Master Mallindale in my church weeping before the altar. He did confess to me that he had defiled and murdered Alice Vigers for whom he had harboured a great lust these two years since she became a woman. He did kill her to stop her screams with the fine dagger he had stole from a Spanish officer and he had buried the weapon in the newly dug earth of the chantry where the Spaniards had their resting place.' Wesley looked up. 'Neil found a dagger buried above the graves . . . probably Spanish. It fits . . . that was the murder weapon.'

'Go on,' said Heffernan, impatient. 'What happened next?'

'He knew his neighbour, Master Wheeler, was hiding a young Spaniard so he did bear false witness against the lad. Mistress

Vigers, her grief bringing her close to madness, happened upon the lad as he prayed at the graves of his countrymen and she did stab the unfortunate lad to death, thinking he had cruelly murdered her only daughter. Master Mallindale, after his confession and fearing for his immortal soul, claimed sanctuary in the church and did swear to observe all the conditions of the same.'

Heffernan whistled under his breath. 'There's something familiar about this story, Wes.'

Wesley looked at his boss thoughtfully.

'Well, I've not heard it before,' said Steve Carstairs, who'd been listening intently. 'It's a new one on me.'

The inspector stood up. 'Right, Wes, let's get down to the Clearview and sort this thing out . . . get a few brownie points from the super.'

They gathered the American veterans in the hotel lounge . . . those who were there. Some had gone off sightseeing, but Heffernan said that this didn't matter: there were enough there for what he had in mind.

Sally Johnson sat in the corner, holding firmly on to her husband's hand. Their crisis seemed to be over. Todd Weringer and Dorinda Openheim sat, straight-backed, next to each other, her fingers hovering over his arm: the novelty of their relationship hadn't yet worn off. The colonel and Litton Boratski sat expectantly in their respective armchairs: only those with a clear conscience, Heffernan thought, could have looked so effortlessly relaxed in the face of police questioning. Three other veterans, sporting baseball caps and brightly clad bellies which overhung their trousers, sat back, staring at the policemen with bovine patience. The two coiffeured wives who sat with them looked more uneasy.

'Thank you all for being so patient,' Heffernan began humbly. 'I know it's been hard on you missing out on London, but Sergeant Peterson here lived there for years and couldn't wait to get out. The scenery's better down here, isn't it, Sergeant?'

Wesley smiled and nodded. Heffernan looked round, expecting an indulgent titter from his audience, but the faces around him bore expressions of unanimous solemnity.

He continued, 'I know you lot – ladies excepted, of course – were here in the war. I wonder if any of you remember an English sailor home on leave getting shot while he was out poaching rabbits in Bereton.'

The colonel spoke up loud and clear. 'Sure, I remember. They tried to pin it on one of our guys . . . had a Limey police inspector over. Some sonofabitch said it was one of our men. I told him it wasn't and to get his ass out of here . . . we had a war to win.'

'How could you be so sure it wasn't one of your men?'

'It sounded like Norm Openheim from the description. I remember it well . . . made me laugh.'

'Why?'

'All the guys, including Norm, were involved in an exercise on the morning the man was shot. They were crammed into tanks and landing craft . . . wading through seawater and crawling through barbed wire. When the guy said that sailor was shot we were right in the middle of the whole damned shooting match. Nobody would have been up at the village, I can promise you that, Inspector. All our personnel were present and accounted for.'

'And you told the English police this?'

'Sure . . . whether they chose to believe it or not was up to them. Or they could save themselves a job and blame it on the damned Yankees.'

Heffernan studied his feet. Closing the case by blaming it on an unknown member of the force that got all the best food, beer and girls must have been a great temptation. The officer who made that decision was probably long dead . . . no chance of him being faced with his negligence now.

'So this witness must have lied?'

'You said it, Inspector.'

'Would the locals have known that an American soldier couldn't have done it?'

The colonel shrugged his large shoulders. 'Possibly not. You've got to remember how things were back then . . . everything top secret. I guess the local gossips would have still pinned the thing on one of us . . . especially if the police weren't saying any different.'

Heffernan, unusually quiet and thoughtful, thanked the assembled American citizens and assured them that they were free to leave at any time.

The colonel stood up. 'How soon do you reckon you'll catch the guy who killed Norman?'

'I'd say an arrest is imminent . . . once I've been to see a certain lady.' He glanced at Dorinda Openheim, who was sitting sphinx-faced, giving nothing away.

Wesley Peterson was surprised at the speed with which his boss rushed from the hotel to the car. 'Where are we going, sir?'

'Madam Butterfly's . . . come on.'

Getting over to Queenswear involved driving back to Tradmouth and queuing up for the car ferry. Heffernan drummed his fingers on the dashboard impatiently as they waited for the raft-like craft to chug its way across the river. The radio was on. Classic FM. The love duet between Pinkerton and Butterfly began to ooze from the speakers.

'Lovely this, Wes.'

'Very appropriate, sir.'

They drove off the car ferry as the music reached its almost sexual climax and ended with a touching oriental motif.

'Wouldn't have been the same if Puccini had set it in Devon, would it?' Heffernan sighed. 'Cream teas instead of tea houses.'

They found Marion working in the garden, secateurs in her brown-spotted hand. She smiled shyly when she saw Wesley. 'Hello, Sergeant. Do you want to ask me some more questions about Norman? Have you caught anyone yet?'

Wesley introduced the inspector, who answered her question in the negative.

Surprisingly, Marion showed no resentment at the arrest of her grandson, Kevin. 'He's been nothing but trouble to our Carole . . . needs to be taught a good lesson,' was her comment on the matter.

They declined her offer of tea and talked to her as she continued to prune her roses.

'Did you know a man called Charles Mallindale during the war?'

'I'll say. He wouldn't leave me alone.'

'Was he in the forces?'

'He had a protected occupation. Can't remember what . . . engineer of some kind. He was in the Home Guard.'

'How did he react when you started going out with Norman?'

'He used to call at my house at all hours . . . obsessed, he was. Gave me the creeps. Stalking, they'd call it nowadays . . . it's nothing new.'

'How did you get rid of him?'

'I married my Albert. Norman had gone away and Albert asked me . . . I had to with our Carole on the way.'

'Didn't Charles offer to marry you?'

She nodded. 'I wouldn't have anything to do with him. There was something about him . . . something that frightened me. He got married later, though, a girl who wasn't from round here . . . had two children. Always odd, he was. Shame, because the rest of his family were quite nice.'

'Did you know an Arthur Challinor?'

'Oh yes. Him and Charles had been at school together. Nice chap, Arthur. In the navy, he was.'

'Do you remember when he was shot?'

'Oh yes. They said it was some Yank on patrol and a bit trigger-happy . . . some of them were, you know.'

'Would it surprise you to know that no American troops were in Bereton village that day? They were all up to their necks in muck and bullets doing some exercise or other.'

Marion shook her head. It was something that hadn't occurred to her. She, like everyone else, had accepted Charles Mallindale's version of events. The countryside was filled with thousands of trigger-happy soldiers from the land that invented the cowboy picture . . . everyone had assumed that Arthur Challinor had got on the wrong side of one of them.

'And did you know that the description of the killer that Mallindale gave matched Norman Openheim exactly . . . down to his silver cigarette lighter?'

Marion suddenly saw the truth. She dropped her secateurs and swung round.

'Charles Mallindale killed Arthur Challinor, didn't he, Marion? . . . And tried to frame your boyfriend out of spite, jealousy . . . whatever. He didn't reckon with the case being handed to the US authorities . . . the authorities who knew exactly where their troops had been at the time of Arthur Challinor's death. Did you know about this, Marion? Suspect anything?'

She shook her head. 'No . . . but it doesn't surprise me. There was always something . . . something I didn't like about Charlie. He only thought about himself and what he wanted.'

Heffernan looked at Wesley, who'd been listening carefully. 'Where is he now?'

The two policemen looked intently at the plump, grey-haired

woman standing contentedly in her garden. She was about to tell them where Norman Openheim's killer could be found.

'Bereton churchyard, I guess,' she said. 'He died five years back.'

'Where are we going now, sir?'

'Back to Bereton. June Mallindale must be his daughter. Marion told us he had two children.'

'You think she's inherited her dad's killer streak?'

'Who knows, Wes. Who knows.'

June Mallindale's house was a fine example of Georgian domestic architecture set on the outskirts of the village. Wesley studied it admiringly: it was the sort of house Pam aspired to . . . if she ever made headmistress and her husband Assistant Chief Constable. 'Nice place, sir.'

'Very nice. Either Ms Mallindale's books sell very well or her psychopathic dad did all right for himself.'

'They say a psychopathic personality helps in business.'

'And in crime. Let's have a word with the lady, shall we?'

June Mallindale answered the door. They heard a young voice behind her asking who it was.

'Nobody for you, David,' she called back. 'Haven't you got that homework to do?'

'But I'm not well.'

She smiled apologetically. 'I'm looking after my brother's son. His wife's in hospital and David claims he's not feeling well . . . that's why he's billeted on me for the day. Come in.'

She held the door open. Halfway up the stairs a fair-haired boy of about eleven was sitting, a bored expression on his face.

'Hello,' said Wesley. The boy looked up . . . at least someone was taking notice of him. 'David Mallindale?'

The boy nodded. 'Are you in Mrs Peterson's class?'

The boy nodded again, more eagerly this time.

'Mrs Peterson's my wife.'

David looked Wesley up and down suspiciously. It was hard at that age to imagine one's teacher having any life outside the school gates, let alone a husband.

Wesley continued. 'I've been having a look at some of the work you've been doing about the war.'

'Nineteen thirty-nine to forty-five,' David said helpfully.

'You wrote about someone getting shot while he was out shooting rabbits.'

Heffernan was watching June Mallindale's expression and saw a wariness in her eyes.

'Oh yeah . . . my granddad saw it. My gran told me.' The youngster still didn't know the reality of death. To him it was glossy, sanitised . . . something you saw on the telly.

Heffernan turned to June Mallindale. 'If we could have a word, please, love . . .'

Young David retreated up the handsome staircase. When June led them into the tastefully decorated drawing room, Wesley shut the door firmly behind him in case the boy was tempted to listen on the stairs . . . as he would have been at that age.

'We'd like to ask you a few questions about your late father.'

June nodded, her fair hair hanging across her bowed head, hiding her expression. Heffernan had a sudden urge to push the hair aside so that he could see her eyes when she answered . . . but he sat on the sofa, still, watching.

Then June Mallindale looked up; looked the inspector directly in the eyes. "My father killed a man. I suppose you know . . . I suppose that's why you're here.'

Wesley looked at his boss, who was staring at the woman in disbelief. He had hardly expected the confession to be so forth-coming. So much for family secrets.

'When he died five years ago he left an envelope . . . to be opened by me in the event of his death. It was a confession. He shot Arthur Challinor during the war and blamed an American soldier. He got away with it.'

'It must have been a shock to you, Miss Mallindale,' said Wesley gently.

'It's not something you go out and tell the world. I don't know why he had to tell me. I'd rather not have known.'

'Why did he kill Arthur Challinor? Did he say?'

She nodded. 'Arthur Challinor was well off. My father asked him for money to start a business. He knew the war wouldn't last for ever and . . .'

'Challinor said no?'

'Not at first. It looked like it was all going ahead, then Arthur backed out . . . said he had plans of his own for his hotel after the war. They went out poaching together one day when Arthur was on leave. They were shooting rabbits. There was rationing . . . everyone round here did it. My father came back alone. Arthur had been shot. According to my father he was shot by an American on patrol . . . he gave the description of this GI who'd been seeing a girl my father fancied.' She went over to the fine marble mantelpiece and picked up a box. She unlocked it and drew out a sheet of typewritten paper. 'Here . . . here's his confession. I keep it up there to remind me . . . remind me that I'm the daughter of a murderer. I've never married. That's probably why.'

'Your brother hasn't had your scruples. He's got children.'

'My brother doesn't know about this . . . or my mother; she's still alive in a nursing home near Maleton. They still believe the story my father told the police at the time. I could hardly enlighten them, could I?'

'So where did your father get the money?' Heffernan looked around the elegant drawing room; there was no shortage of funds here.

'My mother was an only child who'd just inherited a substantial fortune . . . she's also a stupid, unimaginative woman who couldn't see what was going on under her nose, didn't know what was happening in her own family. He could be very charming when he wanted to be.' She stared into space, chewing her thumb knuckle. 'It was me he told . . . me he confided in . . .'

'Why was that?' asked Wesley, quietly.

'I was . . . I was special . . .'

'What do you mean?' Wesley half knew, half dreaded the answer.

'As soon as I was twelve . . . he . . . we shared secrets . . . things nobody else knew.'

Heffernan sat on the edge of the sofa, holding his breath, wishing Rachel was there. In his opinion cases like this needed the female touch. 'He abused you?' he asked with studied gentleness. He was the father of a daughter himself – albeit a grown-up one – and he found cases that involved the exploitation of a vulnerable child particularly hard to deal with. He had no wish to hear any details of June Mallindale's suffering; such details sickened him.

June nodded meekly. 'He liked to have control . . . power . . . over people. He didn't care about their feelings. My brother never knew . . . he was sent away to boarding school and grew up oblivious to everything that went on.'

'And your mother?'

'I don't know whether she knew or not . . . nothing was said.'

Heffernan knew that sometimes this was how such families functioned – nothing was mentioned, no questions were asked: outward appearances were maintained. In this way the mother could pretend that all was well. The shroud of normality would be drawn across the rotten, stinking mess beneath.

Wesley changed the subject. 'The vicar's given me some papers from 1588 that were in the vestry safe. They refer to a case of sanctuary. Have you seen them?'

She nodded.

'You didn't mention this in your book . . . or the Spanish boy's grave in the church. You see, it seemed strange to me that you left it out. You'd obviously researched the book thoroughly and with the evidence there in the church . . .'

'It was four years ago . . . after my father had died. The last vicar showed me the papers, told me about the grave. I saw the similarities and it . . . it wasn't something I could write about.'

'And you were frightened that people might notice that one member of the Mallindale family had murdered and blamed someone else – a foreigner, someone outside the community, someone people resented. If it had happened once . . .'

She nodded again.

Heffernan asked the next question apologetically: he would have to get out of this habit of sympathising with his suspects. 'Did you kill Norman Openheim?'

She looked up, indignant. 'No. Why should I?'

'If he found out who had accused him and put two and two together, threatened to tell the truth . . .'

'I don't think he even knew he'd been accused . . . did he?'

The answer to her question was probably not.

Wesley's mind was racing ahead. There was something he had to ask. 'Does Arthur Challinor still have relations around here?'

'Yes. He owned the hotel on the sands . . . the Clearview. One of his daughters runs it now.'

'Dorothy Slater?'

'That's right.'

Wesley thought hard. Rat had come to Bereton to see his grand-mother. Wesley certainly hadn't met her, although she might have been interviewed when Norman's body had been found . . . or had she? He resolved to find out. 'Mrs Slater's mother . . . she'd be Arthur Challinor's widow?'

June Mallindale nodded again. 'Judith Challinor . . . yes.'

'Do you know her?'

'I know her by sight. My father avoided the family – for obvious reasons – and I never had much to do with them, the hotel not being in the village.'

Wesley stood up. Heffernan, who had no intention of leaving at that point, looked at him enquiringly.

'Thank you for talking to us so frankly, Miss Mallindale. We may need to talk to you again.' Wesley spoke with hurried formality, anxious to be away.

June Mallindale smiled sadly, wondering whether she had been right to reveal her father's secrets; but unexpectedly she felt a little easier – a burden had been shared.

Gerry Heffernan looked puzzled as his sergeant marched ahead of him towards the village hall. 'Hang on, Wes . . . where are we going?'

'To arrest Norman Openheim's killer, sir,' stated Wesley, as if the answer were obvious.

Annie Restorick was paid for two hours' cleaning per day during the week and on Saturdays. When she received the phone call from Mrs Slater to say one of the other cleaners had rung in sick and could Annie pop up to the Clearview for the second time that day to help out, she thought of the extra cash and reached for her coat.

Wayne would be all right: he had his orders not to answer the door to strange men. And Mother was asleep so she wouldn't be any trouble . . . and Wayne was capable of getting her to the toilet if necessary.

Annie found Mrs Slater in a talkative mood. As she donned her overall she was offered a cup of tea, newly brewed. She was never one to refuse tea. Mrs Slater asked how Wayne was these days.

'He's well enough,' Annie replied, glad of the opportunity to chat. 'But he does have these fancies. He told the police that he found that Yank . . . you know, the one who was staying here. He said he found him dead and the police seemed to believe him. I take everything he says with a pinch of salt. Then he goes and says he's got some secret and he's promised not to tell. Piffle . . . he just says things like that to sound important. He's not easy, Mrs Slater . . . not now he's growing up. We all have our cross to bear, don't we?'

Mrs Slater nodded, her face impassive. Annie Restorick looked up in time to catch a fleeting glimpse of a figure behind the frosted glass of the office door. But then she could have been mistaken. What with the worry of Wayne and her mother to look after single-handed, the strain was affecting her . . . was it making her see things as well? Probably.

The tea was finished and Mrs Slater's manner suddenly became more businesslike. The Americans' rooms needed doing, she told Annie, and they were very particular . . . very particular indeed.

Annie was halfway through her labours when Gerry Heffernan and Wesley Peterson arrived. Mrs Slater showed them into her office. Her face had registered surprise and a little unease when they told her that they wished to speak to her rather than her American guests.

'I'm sorry to hear about your nephew, Mrs Slater,' Wesley began. 'The Met have informed his family in London, I believe. Your sister didn't come down when he was taken into hospital?' The last remark was a question rather than a statement of fact.

'I don't blame her after all he'd put her through. Still, it's over now.' She sighed. Rat's demise had been a relief, although convention forbade her to say it.

'How did your mother take the news? They'd been close, hadn't they?'

'That was a long time ago when he was a child. She never knew he was here . . . it was best. She's an old woman.'

'She doesn't know he's dead?'

Mrs Slater shook her head. She had dealt with the subject of the black sheep of the family with her usual calm efficiency . . . and ignored it.

Wesley's next question was unexpected. 'Have you got a bayonet?' He asked it casually, as if asking for the sugar bowl.

Mrs Slater's eyes widened, but her calm exterior was unruffled. 'A bayonet?'

'Yes. Have you got one around the place . . . wartime souvenir?'

'Er . . . I think there was one amongst my father's things. They were in an old trunk in the attic. He was killed in the war.'

'Do you know how he died, Mrs Slater?'

She didn't reply.

'Can we see the bayonet, please, Mrs Slater?'

She looked as if she were about to refuse, then she opened the drawer in her desk and produced a key. They followed her upstairs in silence.

The attic wasn't the dusty, neglected roof space of Wesley's imagination, but a series of fairly well-ordered rooms containing furniture and equipment not currently needed by the hotel. In the furthest of the rooms, well lit by a dusty skylight, the family's unwanted possessions were stored. A large trunk, the old-fashioned kind that children took to boarding school, stood against the far wall. Mrs Slater knelt by it and opened it slowly, as though she were afraid some Jack-in-the-box would leap out at her. She gave the trunk a perfunctory search and turned to the two policemen.

'It's not here. It's a very long time since I've seen it . . . probably since before I was married. I suppose someone must have got rid of it.'

'Would your mother know what happened to it?'

'I really couldn't say.'

'Where were you when Mr Openheim was killed? I know you've told one of my officers, but just remind me,' said Heffernan.

'I was in my office . . . dealing with some bookings. I've told . . .'

'And your mother. Where was she?'

'She was in her flat. Why?'

'Can we talk to her? It might help us clear up a few things.'

'I don't want her bothered . . . she's an old lady.'

'We're very good with old ladies, aren't we, Sergeant?'

Wesley said nothing but tried to look sympathetic. Mrs Slater thought for a moment. They could see her weighing up the situation in her mind.

'Very well . . . but one of your officers told me that it wasn't necessary to interview her.'

'Really?' The inspector resolved to have a word with whoever that officer was. 'By the way, Mrs Slater, did you know that your

204

father was supposedly shot by an American serviceman who fitted the description of Norman Openheim?' He watched her carefully, noting her reaction.

The woman's mouth fell open and she stared at Heffernan. 'No . . .' she mouthed. Then her self-possession began to seep back. 'It can't be . . . I don't believe you.'

'It's true, Mrs Slater.' Wesley took over. 'You knew about it, didn't you? Your mother told you. It's not something she'd keep to herself. It's not as if he'd died disgraced like a deserter . . . he was murdered. How did you feel when the Americans booked in here? One of them had murdered your father. Did you wonder if it might have been one of your guests? Then when you saw Norman Openheim flashing that lighter around . . .'

'There must have been a lot of silver lighters around then . . .'

'But this one was distinctive. And with a bit of imagination he could have fitted the description of your father's killer fifty years back. That's why you killed him, Mrs Slater. You could have lived with it if he'd been killed in France, but when you saw he'd got away with it . . .'

'No.' She shook her head. 'It wasn't like that.'

'You can tell us what it was like down at the station,' said Heffernan. 'In the meantime we'd like a word with your mother.'

'She's not well,' Mrs Slater said with some vehemence.

'We won't alarm her . . . just a quick word. Where's her flat?'

'Sir . . .' Wesley tried not to show his alarm. His boss couldn't burst in on a sick old lady. He should at least get a WPC to go with him. Heffernan ignored him and marched down the stairs after Mrs Slater.

The stair carpet in the family quarters was threadbare: all resources had been concentrated on the hotel and the comfort of the guests.

They reached a plain wooden door. Mrs Slater raised her hand to knock. It was, Wesley noticed, a surprisingly gnarled hand: she was a wartime baby, no longer a young woman. She knocked very softly. There was no sound from within the room.

'Try again, please, Mrs Slater.'

She knocked again, louder this time. 'She must be asleep. I'll not disturb her.' She turned to face them, defiant.

'I don't want to disturb her either, love . . . but I do want to have a look at her room.'

'No. I've not got the key. It's a self-contained flat. She values her privacy.'

'Even when she's ill and her daughter's under the same roof? Have you got rats in the hotel, Mrs Slater?'

She glared at him, horrified. 'Rats?'

'Yeah . . . nasty furry things with four legs and a tail. Have you got any?'

'No, of course not . . . why?' Her voice was starting to sound hysterical.

'Just asking. Don't worry, we're not the environmental health . . . but we can get in touch with them if you like. Are we going to see your mother or not?'

'No.' Definite.

'Mrs Slater . . .' A woman's voice called up the stairs tentatively. The accent was local, the voice familiar. 'Mrs Slater, are you up there? I've finished in the Yanks' rooms . . . do you want me to start in the lounge?'

The voice's owner appeared: Annie Restorick in her nylon overall of office, carrying her spray polish and duster like an orb and sceptre. 'It's no use knocking at Mrs Challinor's door . . . she's not in. I saw her going out five minutes since.'

Wesley and Heffernan exchanged looks. 'How did she seem?' Heffernan asked casually.

Annie shrugged. 'Fine. Why?'

Wesley noticed that Mrs Slater's hand had gone to her mouth as if suppressing a scream.

'Has she been ill?'

Annie shrugged again. 'Nobody's mentioned it to me. You should ask Mrs Slater.'

Mrs Slater's eyes searched the pattern on the carpet as if looking for inspiration. After a few moments' consideration she looked Heffernan in the eye. 'It's not physical, Inspector. She just gets a little . . . confused.'

'Don't we all. Where is she now?'

It was Annie who answered with helpful gusto. 'I thought I saw her earlier . . . near your office, Mrs Slater, after we'd been talking about . . .'

'About what?' Wesley was beginning to feel uneasy.

'Oh, only about our Wayne . . . some nonsense.'

'What was it?'

Annie looked embarrassed at repeating her son's flights of fancy. 'He said he'd got a secret . . . something he saw when he found the Yank's body. It's only his imagination . . . he likes to feel important. He . . .'

Wesley interrupted. 'Was there any way Mrs Challinor could have overheard?'

'I saw someone behind the glass . . . it's that frosted stuff in the door. But it could have been anyone. I . . .'

By now Heffernan's brain had latched on to the implication of Wesley's questions.

'I think we'd better get to Mrs Restorick's cottage, sir . . . just check if the lad's all right.'

Heffernan looked at his sergeant. The words had been spoken calmly so as not to send Annie into a panic.

'Do you mind if I make a phone call, Mrs Slater?' asked Wesley casually. The proprietress said he could use the phone in her office.

Wesley dialled the number of the incident room. It would be quicker this way: they were only a hundred yards from Apple Cottage. It was Rachel who answered. He explained the situation.

'Who am I looking out for, Sarge?' There was excitement in Rachel's voice as she contemplated action after a morning filled with paperwork.

'A little old lady.'

'A what?'

'A little old lady . . . by the name of Judith Challinor.'

Chapter Fourteen

I now set down the most sorrowful part of my account. All Bereton did know the young Spaniard to be guilty of the cruel violation and murder of Alice Vigers, and Margaret Vigers, mother to the said Alice, did chance upon him up at the old chantry. I cannot say why she carried the knife upon her person. I can but surmise that in her grief at the loss of her only child, she did intend to kill herself on the spot where Alice died. Such is the nature of human evil that it doth spread to all about it.

I can be certain, sir, of no facts in this matter . . . all is surmise . . . but Margaret Vigers did stab the Spanish lad in the back as he prayed by the graves of his comrades, and then did flee to the sands, covered in the blood of her victim, where she did kneel on the shore and turn the knife upon herself.

It was when he discovered the awful consequences of his evil lusts that Master Mallindale did repent of his sins and seek sanctuary in my church. I did bury the Spanish boy in the south aisle of the church and I caused a memorial to be carved so that all my flock should repent of their unchristian ways and embrace the words of our Saviour regarding the forgiveness of our enemies. For the boy was truly innocent and the guilty one will pay for his vile crimes with a lifetime of penance and sorrow.

Extract from the report sent by Rev. James Tracey to
Master Joseph Fawley, Justice of the Peace, September 1588

Judith Challinor was no little old lady. She was a tall woman, well built but not fat; she held herself well. With her white hair fashioned into a neat French pleat she looked much younger than her seventy-five years. She was an elegant woman, sprightly and fit; strong, even, for her age. Physically she had been fortunate, and as to that other failing of old age, the mind, she still retained her faculties, was still as agile and reasoned in her thought as she had been fifty years ago . . . whatever her daughter might think.

It had happened nearly fifty years ago: her life had been changed by a young American, flash and arrogant like so many of his kind. He had killed her husband and her unborn son.

She had thought that her revenge had not been witnessed. It had been so easy. She had recognised him . . . Marion's boyfriend. She had known it had been him who had pulled the trigger from Charlie Mallindale's description. She knew he had possessed a silver lighter just like the one Charlie had described.

He had got away with it . . . got away with the murder of Judith's husband and the murder of her very being. When they had invaded Normandy she had prayed so hard for his death: not a quick death – a bullet in the head – but a slow, painful death skewered on the end of a German bayonet so that he would suffer as she had suffered. For nearly fifty years she had been sure her prayers had been answered. She knew that Marion had never heard from him again . . . it was the subject of common gossip. Then she had seen him that night in the hotel bar, showing off the lighter. They had been laughing, joking and drinking as though nothing they had done in that place had brought harm to anyone.

Judith thought of the day in 1944 when she was ordered to leave the hotel: their home, hers and Arthur's. Arthur was away fighting; she had coped with the move alone and lost the child she was carrying. Six months pregnant – she remembered the pain of her labour and the tiny, dead thing that had been pulled out of her . . . a son. They had had two daughters but Arthur had longed so much for this son. Not content with killing her child they – or one of them – had murdered its father too: her beloved Arthur, smiling, gentle Arthur.

When she had followed that man – that evil, unthinking man – to the chapel and watched him standing there, deep in thought, she hoped as she stuck Arthur's bayonet between his ribs that he was thinking of the day he had shot her husband. The bayonet had gone in so easily. Then, when he was dead, she had seen the dead rat, kicked it towards the body and stabbed at that as well as it lay on the ground – a symbol of her suffering.

She had washed her bloodstained clothes carefully, soaking them in salt water as her mother had taught her, and she had washed and cleaned Arthur's bayonet. She felt inside the plastic carrier bag her daughter had brought home from the supermarket in Tradmouth. The bayonet was still there, safe, comforting. She wouldn't risk discovery now, not after everything she'd been through . . . not after fifty years of enduring the numbing longing for vengeance.

She walked up the path to Apple Cottage and knocked on the door. She knew where Annie was – she had heard the hum of the vacuum cleaner in the hotel lounge when she had crept out. She knocked again – a brisk, cheerful knock, the knock of a friend.

She heard a noise from within the cottage – a shuffling, like a large, slow animal. The door opened an inch or two . . . then wider. Wayne stood there staring at her. His eyes, blank at first, flashed into life as he recognised her. His mum had said he wasn't to let strange men into the house. Mrs Challinor didn't count. He opened the door wider and asked, as he had heard his mother ask visitors, if she would like to come in . . . would like a cup of tea. Wayne could manage tea.

He reached for the carrier bag. He must remember his manners . . . his mother was always reminding him. 'Let me take your bag, Mrs Challinor.'

She looked at him strangely and held on to the bag. Wayne was confused. Was it the bag he should take first or her coat? Manners. Mrs Challinor owned the hotel . . . he must remember his manners. But she wasn't helping him. She was standing staring at him, clutching the plastic carrier bag to her as if it were a baby.

Then she spoke . . . softly, almost in a whisper. 'Wayne . . . have you been telling people our secret?'

Wayne shook his head vigorously. 'No . . . I've not told no one. It's a secret. You don't tell secrets, do you?'

'Are you sure, Wayne? Can I trust you?'

'Yeah . . .' he said uncertainly. 'It's a secret.'

She began to fumble in the carrier bag. 'You forgot about our secret, Wayne . . . you've been talking to people about our secret . . .'

Wayne stared at her. He had told his mum about the secret but he hadn't told her what it was. He was confused. Had he told his mum? He couldn't remember. The front door was still open. He must close it, keep the warmth in . . . his mum was always telling him. He started towards the open door and was startled to see that nice policewoman running up the path. He looked round at Mrs Challinor, unsure what to do. His mother hadn't told him the correct procedure to be followed when two visitors arrived at once. The policewoman was reaching out to him, screaming something at him. But Wayne was too puzzled to move. He stood, staring at Rachel, not registering what she was saying.

Then he felt himself being grabbed. The man in the leather jacket who had followed the policewoman up the path was pulling him out of the house and down the front step.

Wayne turned, appealing to Mrs Challinor for help. All he saw was a flash of bright metal as the policewoman disarmed her in the narrow hallway.

'You all right, Wayne?' The man in the leather jacket spoke quickly, roughly. Wayne couldn't answer. He didn't know whether he was all right or not.

The nice policewoman – he'd thought she was nice – was leading Mrs Challinor out, her arms handcuffed behind her back. She said something like 'Get the weapon, Steve'. The man left his side and, after a few moments, stood in the open doorway of Apple Cottage holding a plastic bag containing a thing which looked like a cross between a knife and a sword. It was like the thing he had seen Mrs Challinor stab the American gentleman with.

Wayne was too eaten up with curiosity not to ask what it was.

'It's a bayonet. You had a narrow escape there, son,' the man called Steve answered. 'You sure you're all right?'

Wayne nodded, still confused. He didn't have the courage to ask the question that was most troubling him. Why was Mrs Challinor from the hotel carrying a bayonet in a carrier bag?

Judith Challinor was taken to Tradmouth for questioning. Heffernan, seeing that it was going to be a long night, told Wesley that he had better go home for an hour to grab something to eat and to remind his wife what he looked like. The inspector sat alone in his office with a cellophane-wrapped sandwich: since Kathy had died he had no one to report back to at home. Let Wesley make the most of it; life was short.

Pam looked nervous when she greeted Wesley in the hall. She smiled and kissed his cheek but he knew there was something amiss . . . and it didn't take a CID officer to guess what it was. She took his hand and led him into the living room, all the time smiling nervously, her free hand on her swollen abdomen.

Jim was sitting on the sofa beside his wife while their baby crawled happily up to the table and hauled himself up, dislodging several of Pam's school books as he did so and sending them toppling on to the carpet.

Jim stood up, embarrassed. 'Hello, Wesley . . . er . . . I hope you don't mind about this . . .'

'The bastards have been this morning and taken the keys,' said Pam. 'The furniture's in storage. It's only for a week . . . I said you wouldn't mind.'

Wesley looked round at the encroaching chaos caused by a small child and two extra adults. Cases, bags and baby equipment were strewn across the floor. A cereal-encrusted highchair was already installed next to the dining table.

Wesley took Pam's hand and led her out into the hall where they couldn't be heard. 'It's too much for you, Pam . . . with the baby on the way . . .'

'You mean it's too much for you? I'm fine . . . never felt better.'

Wesley looked down, uneasy. Nobody wanted to be thought of as mean-spirited but he felt he had to be honest about his feelings. It was his home, but if what Pam had said was true . . . if it was only for a week . . . He returned to the living room.

'Where will you go?' he asked Jim, trying to sound casual.

'We've been allocated a maisonette in Dukesbridge but it isn't available for another week. I'm really sorry about this, Wesley. I know it's an imposition and we'll find somewhere else if . . .'

The week's limit had set Wesley's mind at rest. 'Don't worry about it, Jim. Glad to help out.'

'That's what I said,' Pam chipped in as she rescued another exercise book from the baby's exploring hands. 'We've all got to help out in a crisis. You should read what happened in the war when everyone was evacuated . . . we've been doing it at school. At least it's not as bad as that,' she continued cheerfully. 'They didn't know what was going to happen to them.'

'Too right,' said Wesley with feeling. 'Far worse things happened in the war.' He put his arm around Pam's shoulders and gave her a kiss.

Wesley switched on the tape recorder and said the required words. The police surgeon had examined Mrs Challinor and pronounced her fit to be questioned. Heffernan had been careful to do everything by the book . . . the hatchet-faced solicitor sent for by Dorothy Slater would give him no choice.

The inspector asked the questions quietly and gently, suppressing his own personality, listening carefully to the mumbled answers.

Norman's lighter . . . that was what had condemned him. Judith Challinor had walked through the bar with her daughter when he was showing it off to one of his friends and saying loudly and cheerfully how it had seen him through the war. No remorse . . . no mention of how he had lit a cigarette with it before he killed her husband. She had watched him, followed him when he went out for a walk alone. She had taken the bayonet from the trunk in the attic and hidden it beneath her coat. It was only right that he should die that way . . . justice.

She had seen a dead rat at the chapel . . . it had probably been poisoned by some farmer and crawled there to die. She had kicked it next to the body and stabbed at it. It was a symbol, she said. When she had returned to her hotel after the war, widowed with two small daughters, the place had been battered by shelling and overrun with rats. The things were everywhere. The killer of her husband had brought them to her home: rats, eating the very fabric of the place, gnawing at her broken heart. The rat had been an appropriate embellishment to Norman Openheim's execution. That was how she referred to it . . . his execution.

As for Wayne, he had been watching, had witnessed it all. She had made him promise to keep her secret, saying she had rid the world of a very bad man . . . a murderer who had killed her husband and baby. He had promised to keep silent but he couldn't be trusted. That was why Wayne had to die.

The subject of executions gave Gerry Heffernan his cue. 'Do you know one of the reasons why we don't hang people any more, Judith?' She shook her head. Heffernan continued, 'Sometimes they'd find out years later that they'd hanged the wrong person . . . and the guilty one had got away with it.'

Judith Challinor looked down and said nothing.

'I can understand your feelings, Judith, but Norman Openheim had nothing to do with your husband's death. Another man confessed to his murder . . . blamed Openheim because he'd taken a girl he fancied – blamed him out of spite.'

Judith Challinor's eyes widened. She stood up and the plastic chair toppled backward with a crash. 'You're lying.' Hysteria was rising in her voice. 'You're lying . . . you must be.'

The solicitor, a middle-aged female, took Judith's hand and suggested calmly that she sit down. Judith shook her off.

'I really think you should terminate the interview now, Inspector. My client is distressed and . . .'

Heffernan ignored her. 'I'm not lying, Judith. Charles Mallindale confessed to shooting your husband because he refused to lend him money. He wrote it all down before he died. I've got a copy here.' He waved a photocopy of Mallindale's confession in front of her. She snatched at it, tearing it into pieces before she collapsed, sobbing, on to her knees.

Wesley terminated the interview and told the WPC sitting near the door to take Mrs Challinor back down to the cells and get the police surgeon to have another look at her.

The investigation into how Judith Challinor, a woman of seventy-five, had hanged herself with her tights in a cell in Tradmouth police station made the front pages of the local papers and the middle pages of the national broadsheets.

Detective Inspector Heffernan had given evidence at the inquest and the inquiry that followed; so had Detective Sergeant Peterson. The police were cleared of blame but, it was said, lessons could be learned from the case.

Gerry Heffernan had been subdued since. He took the *Rosie May* out on the river alone at every opportunity, and his usual wisecracks were few and far between. The tragedy of Judith Challinor had affected him more than he was willing to admit.

Wesley knew he had to say something. He felt for the man, felt his doubts and his guilt . . . was even starting to ask himself the eternal question: if they had done things differently could the tragedy have been avoided? He came to the conclusion that the answer was probably no. He went into Heffernan's office and closed the door behind him. 'Can I have a word, sir?'

'Sure, Wes. Sit yourself down.' He sounded distracted, his thoughts far away.

'It's not your fault, sir.'

Heffernan sat forward. 'I didn't have to tell her about Charles Mallindale, did I? If I hadn't she'd be alive today.'

'She would have found out some time . . . when the case came to court.'

The inspector shook his head. 'I suppose you're right.'

214

'If anyone in the force is to blame it's that inspector in charge of the case in 1944. If he hadn't been so ready to take the easy way out and blame the Americans . . . The calibre of the bullets would have been different . . . he just took Mallindale's word for everything. Never even bothered to check.'

'If he hadn't been so bone idle and incompetent, you mean?'

'Exactly.'

For the first time in a fortnight Wesley saw Heffernan's familiar grin again.

'I think what really gets to me, Wes, is that Charles Mallindale got away with it all . . . killed his mate, abused his daughter, screwed up Judith Challinor's life, caused Norman Openheim's death . . . and he got clean away with it. Do you believe in hell, Wes?'

'I was brought up to . . . come from a very God-fearing family.' He smiled.

'Well, I just hope they're right.'

Wesley thought of the account of Matthew Mallindale's sanctuary back in 1588, the anguish and regret that Charles's ancestor had gone through. 'The fact that he experienced the urge to leave a confession for June means he must have felt something.'

'Fat lot of good it did Judith Challinor,' was Heffernan's only comment. But he knew Wesley could be right. He changed the subject. 'Is Pam okay? How long is it now?'

'Three weeks . . . but the midwife at the hospital says it could be any time.'

Heffernan sat back, his chair tilting precariously. 'They change your life for ever, kids.'

The phone rang. Heffernan signalled Wesley to pick it up. He covered the mouthpiece and whispered, 'It's for you, sir. Fern Ferrars.'

'I'm not here,' mouthed the inspector before sitting back and staring into space.

'Sorry, Ms Ferrars, he's not available right now. Can I take a message?'

He put the phone down.

'What did she say?' Heffernan tried his best not to sound interested.

'She just said to ask if she was right about the Armada boy. Was she?'

'Hate to admit it, Wes, but I think I owe her a phone call . . . she was spot on.'

Epilogue

The little group gathered around the large open grave in Bereton churchyard. The bright May sunshine glinted on the sexton's shovel as the vicar recited the words of the burial service.

The boxes containing the bones of the seventeen Spanish sailors dug up in the excavation of Bereton chantry were lowered reverently into the English earth. They had undergone examination at the university laboratory and they had now come to their final resting place amongst the villagers who had been their enemies.

Wesley looked around the assembled faces; suitably solemn, but none bearing the marks of tears. Nobody cried for you after four hundred years.

No sooner had he had this thought than the tiny bundle in Pam's arms let forth a whimper which, in spite of Pam's rocking and crooning, gradually built up into a full-blown howl. Pam left the circle and strolled off towards the church porch to give him a discreet feed. Hunger had a terrible urgency when you were only ten days old and young Michael Peterson was a better baby than most . . . or so Pam assured his bleary-eyed father.

Wesley stayed put, studying his fellow mourners. Dr Parsons was there, her head draped in a black silky shawl, showing proper respect for the bodies she had handled and studied. Neil and his colleagues had taken time off from the continuing excavation of the chantry college buildings. Gerry Heffernan had been keen to come when Wesley had told him about the service. He stood with his head bowed. He hadn't mentioned the case recently but Wesley knew that he was thinking of Judith Challinor.

Ed Johnson had come along with Sally. His old comrades had

long since returned to Buffalo and their everyday lives. They stood, hand in hand, looking into the grave. They had told Wesley before the service that they were settling in Devon: Sally would be coming home to see out her days in the land of her birth.

A solitary woman stood, apart from the rest, dressed in unadorned black. Only her shining gilt hair relieved the gloom of her appearance. Wesley had been wrong about the tears. There were some rolling down June Mallindale's face.

The vicar finished and the final amen was said with feeling. As the sexton began his work, Wesley strolled towards the porch to see how his family were faring: he was still a new enough father for the novelty not to have worn off, and he had even found himself changing nappies . . . something, his mother had told him, his father would never have done.

June Mallindale was walking to the church in front of him as young Michael emerged from the porch in his mother's arms only to be surrounded by his public. Gerry Heffernan was being particularly attentive, as was Dr Parsons: it was always those one least expected who went glassy-eyed in the presence of a baby.

Wesley decided to leave Pam to deal with Michael's admirers. He walked into the cool of the church and stood watching as June Mallindale knelt on the hard stone floor of the south aisle. She wasn't aware of his presence as she placed a small posy of flowers on the Spanish boy's grave. She stood and turned, starting a little when she realised she wasn't alone. She looked embarrassed; anxious to be gone.

'Nice gesture,' said Wesley softly.

June didn't answer. She just gave a nervous smile and made for the door, her face stained with tears.

Wesley waited until she was outside before he went to the grave of Roderigo Sanchez and stooped to pick up the flowers. There was a card.

'For the innocent,' it said. 'Please forgive us. The sins of the fathers have been visited upon the children.'

Wesley put the flowers back carefully and went outside to look for his wife and child.

Author's Note

The account of the wreck of the *San Miguel* is entirely fictitious. There was no such ship in the Spanish fleet. However, there have been accounts of Spanish sailors from wrecked Armada ships elsewhere being murdered by locals as they came ashore.

The wartime events described in this book, however, are loosely based on fact. The area of Devon known as the South Hams was evacuated at the end of 1943 so that the D-day landings could be rehearsed there by US troops. About three thousand people, their animals and belongings had to find alternative accommodation. Valuable herds of farm animals were dispersed and the churches were emptied of valuables and sandbagged. There were, however, tales of locals creeping back to the evacuated area to catch rabbits and GIs courting local girls in the deserted villages.

There is a memorial on Slapton Sands in South Devon to the American troops who died during Exercise Tiger, a practice for the D-day landings held in April 1944. Nearly eight hundred men (more than the number who died during the actual invasion of Normandy) were killed on the exercise, one of the great tragedies of World War II.

When the evacuated villagers returned to their homes many found them shelled and overrun by rats. Gradually the area returned to normal as the houses and churches were repaired and the farmers cleared their land for the autumn sowing. There is another memorial on Slapton Sands erected by the Americans 'as a lasting tribute to the people of the South Hams'.